rose guild

iAGO'S

PENUMBRA

REDFeather™
MIND | BODY | SPIRIT

For Jimmy
Val to my Vee

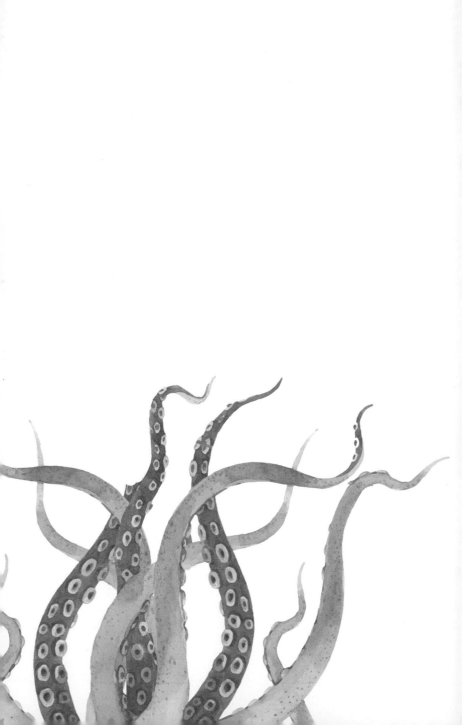

• • •

"One of the most unusual books I have read in recent years. To begin with, most of the characters are dead right from the start, thus allowing an exploration of life after death, the Otherworld, and all points between. In what is part love story; part metaphysical exploration of loss, desire, and wisdom; part occult novel, the author has created an original and at times deeply unsettling account of what it means to be human, what it means to lose humanity, and what it means to discover something beyond the physical, time-bound world in which we live. Rose Guildenstern is an exciting new voice that we will most certainly be hearing from again."

John Matthews, *Taliesin the Last Celtic Shaman*

• • •

"*Iago's Penumbra* is a rare piece of dark magic leaving you spellbound until the last luscious page."

Sasha Graham, *Dark Wood Tarot*

• • •

"I don't think it would be possible to expect anything quite so entirely creative, clever, and consuming, full of surprises, romance, drama and, of course, magic. . . . No doubt Will himself would be proud."

Emily Carding, *So Potent Art: The Magic of Shakespeare*

FOREWORD

Even if you don't consider yourself overly familiar with the works of Shakespeare, you probably hear or even speak his words more often than you realize, such is the extent to which he has become a part of popular culture around the world. In his poetic and dramatic works, people have found a voice for something unspoken within themselves. His complex characters, which tread the line between light and darkness, have survived and thrived over the centuries in the imagination of all who have connected with the works. As for those of us fortunate enough to step into the shoes of his characters, to do so is to step into an energetic current forged by all those who have trod the word-spun path before us. A "potent art" indeed.

The roots of theatre and magic have been intertwined from their birth (at least in the West) in ancient Greece. My own life path has echoed this pattern, in a microcosmic reflection of the greater macrocosmic truth. I trained as an actor in the North of England in a drama school called Bretton Hall, which was set in the grounds of a nature reserve. As I learnt my craft as an actor I also took my first real steps on my magical path, communing with the spirits of the land, forging friendships with Oak, Ash, and Yew. Thorn would come later, as I raised my child in the primal moorland landscape of Cornwall and focused on parenthood, art, tarot, and writing. An MFA in Staging Shakespeare at the University of Exeter, urged by something deep within me, brought me back to the bard, and while I rediscovered my passion for embodying his words more than ever before, I also started to work on the thesis, which would eventually become *So Potent Art: The Magic of Shakespeare* (Llewellyn, 2021).

So Potent Art looks at the occult, esoteric, spiritual, and supernatural content of Shakespeare's plays and poems and encourages the reader to dig deeper into the works and into their own being. It asks the question "What if Shakespeare himself was knowledgeable in the magical arts and wove them into his writing?" I was delighted to see that question addressed in this wonderful novel, as well as the significance of connections such as the Queen's astrologer, John Dee, and the philosopher Francis Bacon.

It's actually through the tarot that I first got to know Rose Guildenstern, and though we've never met in person, over our ten years of online connection we have discovered much in common, including our love of Shakespeare. This overlap of classic literature and the esoteric is a rich ore of imaginative material that Rose mines with a skillful pick, building a unique vision on the foundations of those who have gone before. Shakespeare himself, of course, did much the same, drawing upon existing works and creating them anew, weaving his own compelling magic into them. In turn, over the centuries, countless numbers have been inspired by his works to create their own, and *Iago's Penumbra* is a worthy addition to that list.

Iago's Penumbra is not, however, a retelling of any Shakespeare play, though it draws on many of them. For those familiar with certain underlying alchemical structures in the plays, however, something of that magic may be found in these pages. It does look at many of the same themes—life, love, death, and forgiveness—and takes a fascinating plunge into the possibilities of what lies before, after, and between. I was honoured to be asked to write this foreword, even though I did not know what to expect. I don't think it would be possible to expect anything quite so entirely creative, clever, and consuming, full of surprises, romance, drama, and, of course, magic.

So now, dear reader, open your mind and prepare for a visionary journey into "the undiscover'd country" from which you will most definitely return feeling valiantly victorious! No doubt Will himself would be proud.

—Emily Carding, Hastings, UK, April 2022

Anything we cannot quite see is the Penumbra—
the shrouded, the pernicious, the nebulous, the subtle, the
uncomfortable, the shunned and despised.
An eclipse.
The fringe.
That bothersome truth implied beneath and throughout
all our sensible order.
The Penumbra is that part of ourselves that we hate,
that part of our past we regret, that part of our future we fear,
that part of our world we cannot abide.
We think that death is the ultimate Penumbra, but it's only
a threshold that we all will one day cross from the Penumbra
created by light to the Penumbra created by darkness.
Both sun and moon cast an eclipse.
Love is the Penumbra between life and death, that shadowy,
mysterious, addictive connection that makes it all worth doing and
yet brings greater harm, pain, and misery than anything else.
The Penumbra is the Thing we may not wish to be but have a
lurking suspicion is really the point of it all.

HERE

ONE

"Hang there like fruit, my soul, Till the tree die."
—*Cymbeline, attributed to William Shakespeare*

My death was a catharsis, not a calamity. More an edge than an ending. Fuzzy, sure, but also refining. Like being thrown into one of those Monet paintings with all the water lilies. Only as my head dipped beneath the surface of the fragmented pond, the world flipped, and I swam upward into the mottled waters rather than down. The light beneath, the darkness above, squirming pigments shifting everywhere, squelching and oozing, until the colors ran together and, at last, I lost track of my own color in the exquisite beauty of it all.

I've been told people don't really get that Monet's art is all about shattering the light—can't appreciate chaotic impressions too far removed from how humans generally make sense of reality. In order for anyone to read on, they must find my story personal, relatable somehow.

But how can the living relate to the dead?

Allow me to draw back from the nameless truth of disembodiment, then, and instead begin my story a little smaller—a bit more singular. To when I was merely a teenage girl whose cells had turned against her.

Before I died, everyone was so afraid for me. Frightened of the darkness I would face before they did. The minister assured me that I'd soon meet the "Light of the World," and my dad told me that I'd lived such a "bright life" for someone so young (this, of course, as his eyes were blinded by tears). My mom didn't say much—she never could tell me all those small, light lies that other mothers tell their daughters to help them face the brokenness of this world.

They were all speaking for themselves, of course, not for me. I've always felt more at home in the shadows. Maybe I've known the darkness too well—but I will let you be the judge of that.

Cancer killed my body, but it was the Light that annihilated me. And surrendering to the Darkness is what saved me.

I'm no longer strictly human—never really liked my humanity for the most part even when I was alive—but I will begin this tale with what is left of my human memories. At least, the few I can recall. They're choppy, unclear, sort of like watching an HD movie streamed on dial-up internet with buffering issues. You probably won't like them very much, probably won't like me very much either, for that matter—my brother simply loathed me. But out of these frail memories I hope to share a story worth far more than its meager parts.

Come with me into the ghost of my past to better understand what I dreaded to admit. . . even to myself.

I remember being in a hospital room, dying of cancer, hopped up on morphine and sundry other drugs. My mom and dad were there by my bed, as well as my jackass of an older brother, Tom, who is probably the only person for whom I wish hell existed. There was a searing pain and the biggest, smelliest hot flash of my life.

Then, all of a sudden, the pain stopped.

All of it.

I don't just mean the physical pain of dying—which, if you're scared of it, I'm here to tell you is worse than you can imagine.

I mean the pain of *being* alive.

You don't realize you're in constant pain: the closest you see to the pain of existence is an infant's blinded cries of protest when it has the life literally squeezed into it.

All my vivid—and most painful—recollections resolve around Tom. I'm not sure how old I was in my first memory with him, but I know I couldn't walk yet. I woke up in my brother's arms, and he promptly dropped me. On my head.

Thus began the short, tragical history of my hospital-filled life.

When we first found out I had cancer, Tom complained ad nauseam about the time we spent in the hospital. He whinged so much that my parents finally bought him one of those huge iPads with its own cellphone service so he could stream movies whenever he wanted. I think it actually meant a lot to him, though to hear him you'd never know it. But I could tell it helped assuage just the tiniest bit the tremendous resentment he felt toward me for taking so much attention away from him during my illness. I mean, come on: nothing upstages like the death of a kid. From the day I was born premature to the night I died of cancer, most of the time all I ever did was take our parents away from him. I'm not sure what life was like for him before he was cursed with my existence, but I know my arrival made it much worse. We all owed him. So he wouldn't let me touch his iPad, even to watch my favorite movie the morning I died.

My mom's and my favorite movie was *The Princess Bride*, which early on Tom declared he hated as he hated all things sacred to me, but every Saturday morning after my diagnosis, while Tom and my dad went off on their various sporting wastes-of-manhood together, my mom and I would toast everything bagels in our pajamas and afterward pile them high with cream cheese and smoked salmon. My mom added sliced raw red onions that made my eyes water and her breath reek in a way that I absolutely love-hated, and then we'd cover the entire mess with copious amounts of lemon pepper and dig in. We'd snuggle onto the old turquoise couch that had sat in the same place as long as I could remember—the one she told me once in the hospital she'd never throw away because it smelled so much like me—cuddle up under a fluffy comforter together and watch Wesley tell Buttercup that life *is* pain. My mom would start laughing, and then she'd look at me and start crying, and then she'd trace my cheek with her hand, and I'd start crying, and then we'd both start laughing until one of us got a raging case of the hiccups and nearly choked on our everything bagels.

The Princess Bride is the best cancer therapy I've ever known.

Out of everyone from my life, I miss my mom most. She understood all my misty and twisty places, the darkness that made my father so awkward around me and my brother want me gone. She taught me that laughter and tears come from the same place, and to dig in deep and experience each without reservation.

The morning I died was a particularly painful one, and I was really struggling with the tears side of breathing. Tom watched some martial arts movie he'd seen over and over on his iPad, huddled in the corner of my hospital room just waiting for me to kick off already, when I asked if I could watch *The Princess Bride* one. . . last. . . time. He looked at me, the manipulative bitch who stole his childhood, and said, "Movies are for the living."

He was right, of course. Movies are for the living. The dead don't sit in darkened theaters staring at a giant screen and eating popcorn or stay up into the wee hours of the morning finishing the final pages of a novel. The dead don't tell each other stories in hushed voices around the campfire. We have no need to use our words or images to order the light into buttresses of meaning to dam the impending darkness of chaos in the hope that life is anything more than pain and suffering with an expiration date, for the chaos has already taken us, stripped away the civilizing forces of light and life so that only the monster remains.

We know firsthand how the story ends.

From day one, my brother recognized the monster within me, that I harbored eVil with a capital Vee in every atom and particle of my being. Most people believe that babies are born a blank slate *a lá* John Locke, but that's just another story the adults tell themselves so they can sleep at night. Human bodies arose from water-saturated stardust, and to the stars our dust shall all eventually disperse, but the collective tale of humanity is a cosmic horror story that began long before anybody alive today.

And I've always had a sneaking suspicion it was my unwelcome job to tell it.

Although our parents christened me "Silvia," and my father called me "Silly" for as long as I can remember, they originally intended my nickname to be "Sil" or even "Lily."

Nameful wishing.

L can be such a lovely letter, full of Light and Longing. I could never have been a light-hearted Lily.

Lily is the sort of girl who's born laughing and sacrifices her life to save Harry Potter. My dad, on the other hand, said I came out with a scrunched-up frown, refusing to cry. While everyone else in my family had the most beautiful brown eyes, like maple syrup on Sunday-morning pancakes, mine were almost black, as though my pupils had kidnapped my defunct irises and hidden them in an everlasting Monday.

My brother let it slip once that I made the other babies cry in daycare. I'm not sure if there's any truth to this, of course—he was always making extreme statements where I was concerned. But I do think he was a little scared of me. Horrible nightmares tormented him when I was little, though no one ever spoke to me about them. He'd wake up, screaming in the middle of the night, and my mother would sit by his bedside stroking his forehead until he fell back asleep. If I tried to toddle into the room, she'd silently shake her head with a worried expression and gently close the door in my face.

Even the books I read bothered my brother. I suppose any older sibling might have been irritated that I was reading by age three and had already finished *Grimm's Fairy Tales* and *One Thousand and One Arabian Nights* by my sixth birthday, but it was when I started religiously reading Poe, Shelley, and Lovecraft that he started sleeping with the light on.

You all think light is good, but I'm here to tell you that you have it ass-backward.

Light is where all the problems begin for the living.

So many of your religions worship the light: you think darkness is evil and the light will save you. Monsters hide in the darkness to get you, and your crooks use cover of darkness to perpetrate their wicked acts.

It's the ultimate lie you tell yourselves to live with the unending pain of individuation.

Light separates the darkness, and life results, and "God saw that the light was good."

At least that's what it says in Genesis, but everyone seems to conveniently forget God's next insidious act was to "separate the light from the darkness."

I don't get why so many of you want to worship that dude.

Tom had a little leather-covered Bible on his nightstand that he read from time to time. My dad was an atheist and my mom an agnostic, so I don't know where he got it. He threw it at me once, but other than that he never let me near it.

At this point, you're probably wondering why Tom reviled me so, about this supposed evil that I brought into the world just by being. In truth, it wasn't until much later in this tale—almost the end, to be frank—that I began to understand it myself, but the signs were there throughout my brief life:

In my eyes brimming with darkness.

When I spoke my first words: "Watch out."

When I scribbled my first poem in the third grade that made Poe look like an optimist.

Perhaps my affinity with what disturbs irreversibly rigor-mortised within me the night Tom locked me in the bedroom closet. I was eleven, he was fifteen, and our parents were out on a much-needed date. They had let us (translation: my brother) pick out a new movie to stream, and we each had our favorite food for dinner: fish sticks for me and pizza for he-who-shall-not-be-named.

Fast forward to when, as I contentedly read *Sophie's World* in the corner while my brother watched the war movie he'd chosen, he ordered me to bring him his pizza from the kitchen. I've always had the tendency to lose track of myself, especially when immersed in reading the history of philosophy, and so as I dropped his pizza, face down, on the kitchen floor, it didn't matter that it was an accident, or that I had been bringing it to him in the living room so he could continue watching his movie uninterrupted, for when I spied the murderous wrath in his eyes, I bounded up the stairs and into my bedroom closet to hide, wondering if he had finally decided to end me.

I heard Tom's familiar menacing laugh outside the door, and then a shuffling and strange scraping sound, followed by a crash and profuse cussing.

Then black silence.

Complete and utter darkness is rarely experienced in the modern human world. From electric lights to media screens to even starlight, humans are constantly being lulled into stupored complacency by ubiquitous light.

I grappled with the door, trapped. After grabbing a couple of warmer jackets from above me, I formed one into a pillow and one into a blanket and proceeded to nestle down for the wait. I felt my senses sharpen with each passing moment, as the absence of light made me notice a host of sounds, smells, and feelings I'd never perceived before. The down jacket under my scalp was soft and warm but also seemed to jab me as though to remind me that nothing is truly safe. I noticed that wooden doors actually have a distinct odor—sort of like what would come of wax crayons gang-banging a number two pencil. I swear the house was breathing all around me, great deep groans of inevitable settling decay. With so much irritation, violence, and expiring around me—and my persecutor pitilessly outside—my pitch-black cell began to feel like my refuge from the vindictive day, and I embraced my darkness, grateful for its womb-like safety.

That's when a loud banging on my closet door whacked the camping flashlight off the top shelf, causing it to click on and then continue its descent toward my cave-blind eyes, separating my forehead soundly between said eyes and knocking me unconscious and into yet another hospital visit.

Falling light is overrated.

What you call light is really fallen light. Lucifer incarnate. Only when light annihilates itself can you see anything. Your philosophies take the corpse of light and resurrect it.

The truth is each of you is a rebel darkness seeking to absorb the light.

You fallen smudges, enmeshed in the living world of matter, can only experience light's drug through the opposition of darkness, and so you demonize the dominance of darkness as you seek your next hit of the ecstasy of light.

Speaking of ecstasy, my older brother eventually started using. His behavior was so erratic—usually mean, sporadically depressed, but every now and then eerily affectionate—and he had this annoying habit of sucking on ring pops all the time. He used to steal my pain meds after I was diagnosed, which I didn't mind because I preferred the pain to the zombie-like haze they immersed me in anyway. The combination of his dirty fingernails and sticky ring-pop fingerprints left telltale smudges on my prescription bottles.

That's why I call you smudges.

When I see one of you, you look like a sad schmear on a master's painting. As though some little shit vandalized Vermeer's *Girl with a Pearl Earring* right across her celebrated cheek.

It's not that you're ugly, per se. Each smudge is quite lovely and unique, like the photographic negative of a dingy snowflake. I find myself watching you to preoccupation, and I've learned so much about Being because of you.

You're born a smudgy black hole and from that moment onward commence to fill your void with every piece of light you can cram inside in the desperate attempt to return to the beautiful oneness you feel you've lost.

Come to think of it, consider your synonyms for "beautiful"— stunning, dazzling, radiant, resplendent. The worship of the light is built into the way you organize and describe good and bad themselves. It's no wonder you're so mixed up about what happens after you die: You haven't figured out what it means to live.

Of course, I didn't die yesterday. There's no time Here, so it's difficult to explain with the words of the living, but if it bothers you to be schooled about the secrets of life and death by a dead seventeen-year-old girl, don't get stuck on the age of my deceased body.

I am not, and never really was, my body. Neither are you, for that matter. But that didn't stop me from falling in love with a smudge anyway.

Hard and dirty.

So back to my body's end (or my own unending, depending upon your vantage point):

The pain stopped.

TWO

"The prince of darkness is a gentleman!"
—*King Lear, attributed to William Shakespeare*

After the pain stopped, the first thing I remember is not being able to open my eyes.

Or move my body.

Or breathe.

In fact, I couldn't do anything, in the conventional sense of the word.

Everything seemed sluggish, and torpid, and muffled—like being underwater, without the crushing need to suck wind.

As those feelings passed, I dissolved into a peculiar unsubstantiality. It was a gradual process, sort of a shedding of great blobs of goo drip-drip-dripping the bulk away. With each globule released, buoyancy ballooned within me, followed by an ethereal weightlessness. I was without mass, and it was glorious.

I kept trying to open my eyes to no avail, only to eventually realize I had no eyes. Seeing, as the living classify it, was impossible. But my potential for perception was now limitless.

Best to confront that oddity of "now," right now. Here, there is no now as you living understand it. There is also no past, no future, no goals, and no lack. Here we are not limited by the relativity of a space-time continuum, for separation only exists as an organizer rather than a reality.

"Here" is purely a euphemism, a generic placeholder we few souls who can communicate with the living use to avoid adding substance to an insubstantial truth.

Here, we have the capacity to perceive without constraint. With no body to stop us, our only limitations are our own beliefs, decisions, or denials.

My own altered perception activated bit by bit. I was still "me," minus my body. Although my body had been me, it was equally not-me. An expansive endlessness surrounded me yet also whirled within me in ever smaller inside smaller fractals. At long last, I allowed my perception to progress beyond the compactness I had grown used to inhabiting during my meager seventeen years of life, and I extended myself outward.

And outward.

And outward.

Out of the not-blue, I had the oddest experience: I was someone else, and he was a dandy in a black Armani suit.

He was me, and I was he—or we were both? or neither?

We were the same, and then we were separate—the same, yet not.

Argh, how to explain this in living terms?

We were one and two equally.

The further outward I reached, the more I realized I was and yet had never been—or had never allowed myself to be. . .

My god, how your time words get in the way of explaining this. And your inadequate words for perception. I'm going to use your common vernacular for these concepts, even though there isn't any actual time or eyesight involved, just to streamline this process.

Next, I was a Doberman pinscher. At least, I think I was—I didn't really know dog species in life, but I looked like what I think a Doberman looks like.

The more I extended my seeing, the more I was and yet was not. It was freeing. It was exhilarating.

It was terrifying.

At the moment I was a serial killer intent on my next victim, I snapped inward back to my own small self.

Somehow, now there were still two of me. Wait. . . me and not-me.

I found myself regarding the dark gentlemen in the expensive suit again.

"Hello," he said, grinning like the Cheshire Cat.

"Uh, hi."

"Do you still wish to be called Silvia, or do you prefer a different descriptor?"

"Um. . . eh?"

Always the height of oral eloquence, that's me.

He sighed (and yes I realize he wasn't breathing, but I swear that's what it looked like) in an I've-done-this-a-million-times-before sort of way, and said, "Your name when living was Silvia, but you are free to choose your own designation if you prefer. May I suggest Sylvie? I've always liked that name. I've been called many things during my sojourns in physicality, but I prefer to be called the prince of darkness when Here."

He looked at me expectantly.

I felt like I was stark naked on a stage in front of a host of critics, and I'd forgotten my next line.

Great, I'd died only to face my own worst nightmare.

I had nothing.

After an interminable silence, he said, "Silvia it is, then."

He regarded me, looked me up and down as though deep in thought, and then murmured, "Yes, I think this just about does it—you can change whatever you wish, by all means."

All of a sudden, we were surrounded.

Where there had been no ground before, we "stood" (remember, no actual, physical legs or feet Here—only the perception of them) at a crossroads. Dazed, I saw a golden sun peeking over the horizon in the distance.

Frozen in time, I couldn't tell if the sun was rising or setting. I'd never realized how much alike sunrise and sunset appear without the context of the passage of time.

Trees were everywhere, and a few little picturesque cottages dotted the landscape. It sort of looked like a photograph from my mother's kitchen calendar. June, if I recall.

Was that a hobbit hole to my right?

"Does this make you more. . . " the prince of darkness asked, ". . . comfortable? Or would you prefer to add something?"

There weren't any animals, which was odd. Then a flock of geese flew overhead in characteristic "V" formation just above me. A grey squirrel zipped from one tree to another. A dog barked.

I watched the landscape begin to change, as though it was my attention itself that transformed it. Distant trees converged upon a V-shaped slash of shrubs dappled in sickly greens and blemished purples, growing ever thicker and closer. The trees cast shadows that tangled together at the base of the V, looking exactly as I'd imagined a moor to look when I read *Wuthering Heights* in the sixth grade.

That is, if the moor was covered with rotting heather and choked by dusk.

It was the "blasted heath" straight out of Shakespeare's *Macbeth* or Lovecraft's *The Colour Out of Space*. I half-expected three witches to appear at any moment, joined by a nameless horror escaped from some Miskatonic attic.

The prince laughed. "You really have a dark side, don't you?" He reached what can only be called a not-hand toward me, and for the first time I felt what passes for touch without a body to sense it, like the cool wind on my shoulder within a dream. "It doesn't have to be this way, you know. Change yourself and the world changes with you."

I focused all my energy on restoring the prior bucolic paradise, and succeeded. The only thing missing to re-create the daydreams of my childhood was a stuffed bear living under the name of Sanders. . . and then he appeared to my left, Winnie-the-Pooh himself.

"Hullo," the tubby bit of fluff said to me. "I'm not lost for I know where I am. Is this lost for you?"

Then he peered at me with the most disturbing, unblinking sort of stare.

I knew what Rabbit must have felt.

"Yes," interjected the prince of darkness, "it can be quite disconcerting, dying. But consider the flip side: Now you can stop looking for your own small lie in life and enjoy becoming the truth again."

"Life's not a gift, it's a curse: A horror story that lulls us and leads us and deceives us into seeking the next hit of anesthetizing light to escape the stark truth of the dark," I countered dourly.

The prince pondered me blankly, and I noticed his not-eyes for the first time: dark with no iris or sclera to speak of, as though his pupil turned inside out and devoured his eyeball. At last, he grinned. "You really aren't what I expected," he remarked with a quirked brow, "which I confess a remarkably rare occurrence."

"It's Vee, actually," I volunteered.

"What's that?"

"My name. I prefer to be called Vee, with one syllable, rather than SilVEEa. If you don't mind."

"Wonderful! Fantastic! Magnificent!" he said as though I'd invented the lightbulb. "Suits you seamlessly. Speaking of suits. . . what do you think of mine. Too much?"

"Um. . . personally, I prefer something brighter. More Joker than Batman."

Vigorously, he was swathed in a violently violet Varvatos. The silk vamped with such vehement vibrancy that Pooh visibly winced, and vamoosed.

Wearied of the very vandalized letter V, I verbalized, "Valiant, but also vain."

Then I noticed the Vs piling up in the scene around me: in the geese formation, yes, but also in the V-shaped mark on the hobbit's front door, the clouds shaped in a puffy V, the Doberman with a brown V on his forehead, the closest tree had little Vs carved into its trunk like love notes. . . now that I looked at it, even its leaves seemed to have a crinkly V shape.

What the vell?

"All these Vs are a bit vexing," I said.

"Oh, that's all you. You're fixating."

"I'm what?"

"Fixating. It's common as one accepts one's demise, although obsessing over the letter V is a new one. You're seeing something everywhere you think you need, in order to keep from losing your past identity. As soon as you are honest with yourself about the lie of what you lack, it will cease."

"So, this is hell."

"It often is. You'd be surprised how many prefer to create their own hell Here rather than heaven or nirvana, or even a David Bowie concert. It's all relative, but without the tedious holiday meals and ugly sweaters."

"Are you saying it's all up to me?"

"Oh, hardly—wouldn't that be nice—not."

"I'm sorry, I really don't understand what you're talking about."

The self-proclaimed prince of darkness viewed me vigilantly before answering, and I realized we had been moving whilst we visited. "You can form your own Here into anything you want, as can others—allowing for your own denials and deceits, which even Here can still prevent you from free creation. When you enter another's Here, or choose to operate in the joint Here occupied by All, however, things start getting limited. There are some basic rules for functionality, certainly, and some worlds operate in an entirely different fashion than most, but that pretty much sums it up."

"Are we in my Here or your Here or the joint Here right now?"

He flinched. "My summation was inadequate. You are in all three simultaneously, my dear. There is only Here."

During our dialogue, we'd meandered toward a dark building that stood out in harsh contrast to the quaint vista (damn, another V). A somber monument contrived of nothing but what seemed odd angles opposing one another, it both beckoned to and taunted me.

Sensible even after death, I balked.

"What's that?" I asked, afraid of the answer.

With a bit of pride in his tone, he explained, "That is our court system Here, Known Abomination and Reincarnation into Material Accountability or KARMA, as we prefer to call it. The court is only used for the truly criminal who start harboring the light and lie of separation. Eventually, they are sentenced by KARMA to be compressed out of eternity, what the still-living call being born. . . "

A blurred figure, hunched over and translucent—like a dynamic greyscale window—strode toward us. Furtive, it glanced up and we made eye contact: a youngish male with a striking pair of noir-ish sapphire eyes deep set in his see-through face. He swiveled sideways as though in shock, and continued on his way.

He had a red V emblazoned on his chest.

The V tantalized me, like he was the earth drawing down my moon.

The prince of darkness and I were enjoying an impeccable climate, but this diaphanous fellow was garbed in a drenched trench coat, struggling against some invisible cloudburst as I watched him.

Why, when everything else seemed so rich and vivid, was he transparent—sort of like a monochrome ghost?

He reached in front of himself, grasped what appeared to be an unseen handle, moved his arm as though pulling open a pantomimed door, and disappeared into no-air.

The prince of darkness had been speaking this entire time, but I hadn't heard a word he'd said.

". . .the still-living judge accuracy by its massiveness—the density of people who agree with it, the weight of evidence proving it, the gravity of historicity behind it. They collect significances through consensus as the dead seek to shed them."

I interrupted his lecture, "Where did that boy go?"

Discomfited, the prince hemmed, ". . .what boy?" Then he hawed, "Oh, so you can see him, can you?"

I honored the purple prince with my most pointed glare.

He capitulated.

"Most cannot see them Here. In fact, I've only known a handful in all my eternities who could see them."

"Who is 'them,' exactly?"

"The exiled, of course—the living."

THREE

"Why, stand-under and under-stand is all one.
—*Two Gentlemen of Verona, attributed to William Shakespeare*

"You'll find most everyone who remains Here has lost track of life. Many loathe the very idea of the living," the prince continued, "it reminds them of their corruptible mortality. There are even a few who insist they've never lived before."

"Why does he look like that—colorless and blurry? Where's he going? Why can I see him?"

"Hmm. . . there's no easy answer to your questions. I can't tell you why you see something a certain way, I can only tell you what I see. Seeing may be believing, but that doesn't make it true. And just as all Heres are concurrent, so the Theres of the living also exist. . . . I suppose he's going about his daily life, whatever largely inconsequential but singularly important matter that is, and you can see him because you are cursed."

"I'm. . . cursed?"

"You can say doomed, if you prefer. Star-crossed. Noticing the living is at cross-purposes with your own unfolding."

I moved over to the empty space to inspect where the boy had vanished.

"Can I choose to see them, or is it only by chance?"

"When you've decided you cannot do something—you can't."

I looked more closely at the space, and could just see the barest hint of a ghostly rectangle.

"I wouldn't recommend it."

I reached toward the outline with my not-hand, and pushed. Then

I stepped over the threshold.

The stark, colorless interior of. . . a barn?. . . assaulted my not-senses. The strong, sweet odor of damp hay and the musty smell of old wood was overwhelming at first. Even though the building clearly hadn't sheltered animals for a long time, the lingering musky scent of livestock still clung to the walls like a much-loved memory.

Straight away I knew this was There. Everything looked as though it was bathed in moonlight, with that strange spectrum of insipid greyish hues. A deafening crash of thunder heralded a rainstorm outside, and as it occurred to me I was hearing without ears and smelling without a nose, I also understood from the dreamlike pallor of the setting that this place was physical, and therefore seemed curiously fragile to me.

Feeling like Alice in Wonderland—only I'd fallen up the rabbit hole instead of down—I found myself missing the prince of darkness, my own Cheshire Cat. For all his circular reasoning and nebulous explanations, he was a gentleman and, I think, my friend.

That's when I heard the weeping.

I followed the hushed moans, past decaying rough-hewn timbers and abandoned animal stalls, to their source. In front of a meticulous handmade cross, hung above a makeshift altar of half-burned candles and scattered books, knelt the sapphire-eyed youth, still soaked.

He was praying.

I'm not sure how I could hear his whispers. I suppose it had something to do with not using physical ears to listen.

He looked to be about my age, although he might have been a few years older. On the tallish side, he had the awkward thinness of late adolescence and a certain indefinable theatrical air—as though he had to solve all the problems in existence right now or else the whole world would collapse in some dire disaster—that I had often struggled with myself during life. Of course, I had been dying of cancer.

What was his matter?

I tuned into the murmurs to try to understand his turmoil.

". . .I don't know what to do, Father. I've waited and waited for some sign of Your will, but if You've answered me, I haven't understood it. How can I continue to live with this?"

His voice, tortured as it was, was pure velvet on falling snow. It enveloped me in luxurious tingles that radiated first outward and then inward, filling nooks I had no idea were empty, and would have taken my breath away if I'd had any to lose. I eavesdropped further, spellbound.

"Is my uncle right? Am I being tempted by demonic forces, Lord? Or is Peter's theory true—that I'm like Jacob, wrestling with the angels?"

What the literal hell?

I still didn't know if there even were demons, or for that matter how the prince of darkness fit into this infernal equation. If there were angels and demons, what did it say about me that the prince of darkness was my tour guide to the hereafter?

"I've ignored. Pretended. I've tried walking away. Why do you refuse to take this cup from me?" He prayed with his eyes wide open. An eccentric quirk, almost like his blue eyes couldn't stand to be separated from their color source in the sky. "I know one of them is with me at this moment, but I don't know what to do. Please help me to understand your will."

His sobs slowed, and ceased. I kneeled next to him and tried to reach out to comfort him, but the shape of my not-hand only made a hand-shaped part of his shoulder disappear, like he was a shadow and I'd blocked his fleeting light source.

Then he turned and looked at me.

His eyes mesmerized me. Such a brilliant blue in his grisaille face. I was shocked he could see me, but then what did I know? I was so new to being dead. Since I had never seen a ghost or known anyone to see a ghost while alive, I was still fairly certain it was rare.

He stared at me for a few beats, then sighed. "What do you want?"

Worst nightmare, take two.

"I don't want anything."

"Oh, come on, your kind always wants something."

My kind? "You seem sad."

His eyes crinkled in the most adorable fashion as he responded, "Well, that's not like the others."

"Why were you crying?"

He paused as though deciding how much to reveal, and then said, "I see ghosts."

No shit, Sherlock. "Have you always been able to see... uh... us?"

"I think so. . . . But I didn't realize it wasn't normal until grade school. Before then, my parents just thought I had imaginary friends."

Huh. "Why does it bother you so much? I mean, if you've seen ghosts your entire life, why do you care now?"

Again, he hesitated before answering, weighing his words as though each was a gift made of the purest gold, quite the reverse of my own bull-in-the-china-closet tendencies. "I'd say I want a normal life, but that doesn't really exist, does it? I could mention how you're all quite disturbing to look at, with your cadaverous pallors and auras of foreboding. . . . You're the first ghost with whom I've ever had a proper conversation, actually. Most just moan, or howl, or keep repeating the same phrases over and over. . . . By the way, how can we talk like this?"

Good question. "I'm not sure—I'll need to ask the prince of darkness about that."

He blanched, taking a step backward. "My uncle's convinced I'm being enticed by evil spirits. If the prince of darkness is your master, does that make you a demon?"

I laughed out loud. "My master, I mean really. The prince isn't my master, more of a dandified docent at best. And I don't think he's the devil at all—he doesn't feel evil, just pretentious. I suspect he's really quite a nice fellow—I'll introduce you sometime."

By the horrified look on his face, I knew I'd gone way too far.

Hastily, I proposed, "Maybe the reason we can speak together is I'm not technically a ghost. I mean, from my understanding of ghosts, they're the spirits of dead people trapped on Earth who, for whatever reason, can't move on. I'm not like that. I actually died just recently, embarked upon my own afterlife, and after a pithy repartee with the prince, saw you and followed you back."

Horror turned to bewilderment. "Followed me? How could you have followed me? I wasn't in heaven, or hell, or wherever you come from."

"It doesn't really work that way. Apparently, rather than a bunch of separate wheres, existence is one big paper folded multiple times upon itself. Most people merely lack the capability to see all the different layers. I happen to be blighted with the ability to see between them."

"I'm also blighted to see what others cannot."

We stared at each other in silence, each taking in the other's foreign similarity. I felt a tingling burning hijack my not-cheeks. Apparently, even ghosts blush.

"I'm... uh... pleased to meet you, Mr. Also-blighted."

Something ineffable changed in his eyes, as though the sky plunged itself into the deepest ocean.

Lucky ocean.

Desperate to steer the conversation back to shallower waters, I said: "Let's look at this another way. Rather than viewing your supernatural sensitivity as wicked, could it actually be a gift from... um... God? I mean, weren't there lots of holy characters in the Bible who could talk to angels and stuff?"

"That's what my best friend, Peter, says. But my uncle's the expert."

"What makes someone an expert about demons?"

"He's a Baptist minister."

"Oh... well, that explains a lot."

His scowl was precious. "My uncle is the best person I've ever known. I've grown up coming to his house in Milan every summer since my dad left. I didn't tell him about the. . . visitors. . . until I moved in with him this summer before I start my freshman year at Eastern Michigan University in the fall. Needless to say, he was appalled."

As delicately as possible, I prompted, "So. . . it was your uncle's reaction that really made this a problem for you?"

He was silent at first, but finally admitted, "No doubt."

"What does your uncle think you should do?"

"Besides pray? I think it scares him, and he doesn't know what to do. I know he loves me, but I don't think he's sure what I see is even real. If I'm actually seeing spirits, then it must be evil from his stand-point, since souls don't remain on Earth but either go to heaven or hell after they die. So, any supernatural experiences that don't involve God or angels must be demonic. . . " He brushed his long bangs out of his eyes, reminding me of a young Brad Pitt, only taller. ". . . but I also think he suspects I might be going crazy and hallucinating or something, despite the fact he's never actually said that to me. Which I completely understand."

If his words were golden, mine were copperish—far too many of them pouring out of me and somewhat hard-wired to disturb. Maybe I could learn to measure my own words with greater care—from someone like him. "You know, I think understanding's overrated. If you understand someone else, you run the risk of standing under his opinion rather than listening to your own. It's important you listen to your uncle, sure, but it's not your job to support what he believes. You need to decide for yourself what's true." I added my final caveat. "Most of us are far too understanding, pretending ourselves to be outstand-ing, yet sorely starved for the upstanding."

He looked at me with a rather wry expression. "Were you a phi-losophy major when you were alive or something?"

"I never graduated high school—I spent the last year of my life dying of cancer. My dad always called me his 'little philosopher' though. From what I've read, it's common for terminally ill kids like me to read too much and wax a smidgen profound. There's a lot of time to think when you're stuck in a hospital bed with nothing else to do. . . and I wrote stacks of short stories. Mostly horror."

I thought he would be uncomfortable with the turn our conversation took, but if anything, he seemed more at ease discussing my death. Was he somewhat morbid, or just accustomed to dealing with peculiarities that others couldn't?

A bit of both, and an intangible something else, I surmised.

"What's it like. . . being dead?"

"I'm pretty new at it, but so far it has been. . . inspiring. . . confusing, and. . . a little alarming. The jury's still out on what I think of it, but I side with Peter Pan: It's an awfully big adventure."

Finally, he smiled, and it was like seeing my first sunrise. Warmth suffused me, beginning with my not-toes and not-fingertips I hadn't even realized were not-warm, and progressively bathing my entire being in effulgence. I felt all the platitudes I'd disparaged and swooned over while a melancholic teenager ascend within my not-bosom, and take flight.

I reached toward him at the same time he reached toward me, my not-hands blocking the light from his smudge-hands as the shadow reflected the light back to me, illuminating upon me what looked like the freaking aurora borealis.

If I'm really honest with myself, it wasn't just the refraction of colors that tantalized me. There was something. . . else. . . about this boy. I'd read of the very French idea of déjà vu, of course—that feeling that we have been somewhere or done something or met someone exactly like this before—but that failed to name what was happening right now between us. I'd never been in this barn reaching for these long-fingered hands of this clairvoyant heartthrob before, or anything remotely like it.

And yet, somehow, I recognized him. I'd known him, or someone very much like him, not just once but many times before. The bent places deep inside me so despised by the others smoothed into curves rather than jagged precipices in his presence.

Eyes wide with wonder, he stretched one lithe finger toward my not-hands, tentatively tracing the unsubstantial outlines of my tiny fists as he whispered, "Take her, and cut her out of little stars, and she will make the face of heaven so fine that all the world will be in love with night."

"That passage's about Romeo, not Juliet. And let's not get ahead of ourselves, Mr. Speaks with Spirits. I'm dead. You're alive. And you hardly know me. What are you, some sort of Don Juan to the Ghouls?"

"If I'm Don Juan, it's more in line with Byron's interpretation—it's you who's seducing me with your ghostly Aurora-like ways."

Okay, how was this dude so well read? What self-respecting teenager reads Shakespeare and Lord Byron—I mean, other than hospital-bed-ridden me? And how the hell did he know I adored Shakespeare? I couldn't stop myself from asking, "Valedictorian much? Sphinx in your family history? You seem impossibly mythical."

"This coming from an apparition."

I laughed despite my skepticism. "My conversations with others were generally one long awkward silence peppered by uncomfortable truths. I'm not very good at small talk."

"I've never really liked small talk either. So let's engage in something else." He looked directly at me even though I supposed he could see straight through me, like he was mentally squaring his shoulders. "I'm in a relationship, with a girl named Julie. She's smart and feisty and beautiful and has no idea I communicate with the dead."

"Sounds perfect," I said, bemused by my sudden loathing of perfection.

"Yes, she is. Perfectly human. Far too perfect for someone as faceted as me. We're from a nice little town filled with pleasant people with little problems who have made her believe she's much smaller than she'll ever be. I've tried to love her into realizing that she's far more than the shade of her skin or the gender she was born with—tried to get her to escape them all in Merced and attend Eastern Michigan with me—but she's so busy proving she isn't little that she can't leave."

"Are you in love with her?"

He looked up into the roof supports, sighed, and at last shrugged, hooking his thumbs through his belt loops. "I love my uncle and aunt and mother. And Peter, of course. I thought I loved Julie that way, for a time—tried to love her and be what I know she deserves—but I always knew I was waiting for someone else—something more. . . visceral. Until now."

He leaned into me as though magnetized, his two blue suns puncturing the polarity of my bloodless moons, lips inches from not-lips.

The little V hiding between my not-legs stirred as though called to attention. Wait just a haunted minute—with no body to feel or hormones to course through it, how was it possible I even had a little V to rouse anymore?

Squirming to silence the V of molten chocolate oozing around my core, I asked, "Are you saying you might love. . . me?"

"I might. Perhaps already have. Surely can. And right now I've never wanted anything or anyone more in my entire life."

In answer to the longing in his eyes, with no-thoughts or hesitations, I shifted my spectral body forward to surround and permeate his corporeal one. A sound akin to a deep-throated purr emanated from somewhere deep within his chest at our mingling; it occurred to me that if I smiled any broader, the prince of darkness would be out of a job.

He moaned just a little with what can only be called contentment.

It wasn't kissing. It wasn't touching. It certainly wasn't sex by any stretch of the imagination. But it was singularly ours, and it was some kind of wonderful.

So this is what my mother meant when, what seemed forever ago, she told me: "Love comes when we least expect it, Vee. It may take many different shapes and forms throughout the course of our lives, but it's never what we think it should be. If it's convenient, it isn't love."

But why now, when my time was over?

Just my luck that the French playwright Jean Anouilh turned out to be right. Life really is the enemy of love.

Yet as I glimpsed myself in his sky eyes, I didn't care.

Somehow, despite me being dead and him being alive, we were the same. I understood him. He saw me.

We might stand out, but who cares?

The poets and playwrights messed up big time describing this one—that moment of tottering over (or under?) this precipice we call falling in love. Perhaps it's because they were still alive when they tried to capture those dimensional words on plane paper, or maybe they simply wanted to keep one profound secret for themselves, alone.

Because that's the whole point, isn't it? Contending with the singularity.

You don't "fall" in love, you *let go*: of your separateness, of your individuality, of standing on your own—of any standing at all, really. Seeking love is the most generic of human experiences, perhaps second only to avoiding that which we fear. We gather ourselves together, and by becoming just like everyone and everything else, the most hackneyed stereotype conceivable, we at last feel uniquely special.

All I wanted in this moment was to be as common as spit, just once. Wondered what it would be like to share spit, actually. The epitomized trope. I didn't want to understand, didn't care about losing myself. I stood with a body that no longer was, entranced by the interplay of light and shadow, of life and death, of him and me.

I'm not sure what he saw in my dead eyes. Perhaps the same refraction of his own abyss.

Not-quite-a-ghost stood with a-bit-more-than-human, and for the first time existence felt a little less alone. . .

Together.

THERE

FOUR

"At first I did adore a twinkling star, but now I worship a celestial sun."
—*Two Gentlemen of Verona, attributed to William Shakespeare*

Julie read it over and over, hating herself for not being able to stop.

Dear Julie,

Val had never started an email with "Dear" before, that should have been her first clue.

> *I want to thank you for being such a wonderful part of my high school years. We've shared so many amazing firsts, and I will treasure each one as we go our separate ways in college.*

"Go our separate ways?" She thought they were going to grow old together.

> *I know we said we would always be together, but this summer has changed me. I've realized that even with all the good times we had, I never allowed you to get to know the real me.*

She scoffed at just how intimate they'd been.

> *You helped me grow up, and for that I am thankful. But I have fallen in love with someone else, someone who may not share my past, but who's meant to be my future.*

Julie's eyes filled with stubborn tears. . . again.

> *I'm sorry if this hurts you, but I know you will understand with time apart and when you find the one who's meant for you.*
>
> *Fondly,*
> *Val*

Miserable, she closed her pink laptop.

A stranger had penned that email, not her (ex?) boyfriend—so stilted, so final, so distant. She'd always admired Val's distinctive eloquence, his precocious gift to put thoughts and feelings into almost lyrical words and sentences. It seemed impossible this crude break-up letter could end her reason for living.

Outside her bedroom window, the hulls were just beginning to split open in her father's orchard, ready for harvest. Julie staggered to the opulent bay window, gulping in great deep breaths of the delicious nutty almond tree scent wafting toward her from her family's farm. Normally next week would have been her favorite part of summer: she loved watching the machines shake the trees until the fruit tumbled to the ground to be collected by her father's workers. Although August days sweltered in Merced, the cool California nights were invigorating in their defiance of the day's heat—but then, she'd always found the darkness refreshing, somehow. A preference she'd once shared with Val.

At the thought of him, her breaths turned short and shallow; she struggled to keep breathing at all. Just then the delicate fairy lights that she and Val and Peter had strung up under her window together three summers ago—what Peter said would "light up her lonely nights"—twinkled to life beneath her, interwoven throughout the trellis and the landing like a glittering teardrop web of the lost hope she felt welling up inside.

How could she let go of the one person who made taking her next breath possible?

Restless even in her despondency, she wandered toward her rosewood armoire to pick out her evening attire. Not that it mattered. Nothing mattered anymore. Her best friend Peter didn't care what she wore, her parents didn't see her anyway, and her Val wouldn't be there to see her ever again, it seemed.

She tore open the top drawer to grab whatever she found first, disregarding all the expensive possessions her mother and father had given her during her eighteen years as their adored little heiress. The rising thickness in her throat threatened to choke her—if only, just once, she could have had a mom and a dad. Julie had only ever been allowed to call her parents "mother" and "father."

She was trapped in a hollow world of stuff with no meaning.

Her parents didn't love *her*, they loved the part she played in their lives: the dutiful, beautiful daughter who brought home good grades and lavish compliments from others. She was the crown jewel at the summit of their success.

But they had no idea who their daughter truly was, and Julie doubted that they'd ever even wanted to know. Their gifts reflected the perfect image that her mother and father required, not the little girl who'd grown up. . . regardless. They had no idea that Julie despised rosewood, and that the antique armoire, which cost more than Julie's car, reminded her every day that she was an outsider—like a changeling left by the dark faeries at birth, abandoned to wither away in an alien family to which she never truly belonged. Her mother, who "could have been a Rhodes scholar," had given up her "considerable prospects" to marry Julie's father after a "whirlwind courtship" (translation: he'd gotten her knocked up). This same saccharin-ficial mother washed Julie's mouth out with a bar of Ivory soap when she dared call her father a "bully," and locked Julie in her bedroom for three weeks straight last summer when she had the audacity to show up in a micromini at church.

Her father showered extravagant favors upon the daughter to whom he rarely spoke except to lecture, calling Julie "weak-willed" and "spoiled" when she struggled with growing up the rare Black girl in a segregated rich white and poor Hispanic community. He insisted she was an "ungrateful brat" and that she "better start appreciating" her "fairy tale life" as he ignored his wife's ever-more stringent punishments, relieved to be relieved of having to deal with the segment of parenting he found most repugnant.

The first time Julie introduced Val to her parents in the ninth grade, they fell in love with him and—as they never could their daughter—were even willing to overlook the unfortunate circumstance of his white skin for his Prince Charming ways. But Val saw right through them—in fact, he often said that Julie's problem wasn't just her parents, but that the whole damn family was haunted by ghosts they refused to acknowledge.

Val was always writing something—by hand, on paper. It was his defining peculiarity. He eschewed computers the way others eschewed cursive, only using them when absolutely necessary. Their first Christmas together, Val gave Julie a hand-written copy of his own retelling of Cinderella, wherein Cinderella's stepmother made Cinderella ritually cut off ever greater portions of her toes and heels to force her feet to fit into ever-smaller-and-smaller glass slippers until Cinderella at last had only bloody stumps at the end of her legs, which her father and mother insisted looked "so much more attractive than common vulgar feet." The tale ended with her marrying a prosthetics cobbler rather than a prince, their wedding vows closing with Ophelia's famous line: "We know what we are but know not what we may be."

If Julie had to hear one more of her parents' fairy tales about how "blessed" she was to be "at the top of the food chain" with all the "prejudiced and entitled idiots in this world," she would run away stark raving barefoot, blood be damned.

For her birthday that year, Val gave Julie one single second hand shoe that was two sizes too big; Peter gave her a novelty Bigfoot keychain.

Val and Peter were Julie's true family.

Her breath caught in her throat—*only Peter. . . now.*

But, if she were completely honest with herself (which almost no one ever really is), a tiny part of Julie feared this statement was horribly false.

For some time now, Julie had had the feeling she was never alone—even in her most private moments. She was being watched.

Influenced.

An unnamed dread had begun to insinuate itself deep within her isolated core, causing her to even occasionally glance over her shoulder, positive there was someone stalking her. Verging upon paranoia, there had even been distinct moments of fear when she worried her own sanity had begun to forsake her. What Julie didn't know was that this unfamiliar apprehension was enhanced by the glimmer of a wraithlike old woman who frequented the despised armoire, constantly mumbling the refrain, "It's not fair. It's not fair. It's not fair."

Despairing, Julie toppled onto the brocade duvet at the foot of her silk-canopied bed that her mother had found at an estate sale during one of many excursions to Europe. As she clutched the duvet around her, Julie had no idea she shared it with the specter of a jealous little boy who hated her intensely for growing up as he never did.

She had no idea under the floorboards of the home that had been in her family for generations, dwelt a murderer who walked the halls at night with a plod, plod, plodding echo, inhabiting every creak and sigh of its ostensibly cheerful walls and foundations, bent on avoiding damnation.

She had no idea she was surrounded by an aphonic world of shrill, restless tones, all just an inch or two out of kilter from her own corporeal resonance, that like clandestine mosquitoes sucked off her lavish squandering of vibration with a vengeance. Intensity filled these synchronized ballads of abandonment and agony—for agony is exactly what these spirits lived and re-lived in every moment of their endless Nowhere. Agony, and a relentless hunger for more than their lot in the brief snatches of the lost discordant narrative each could barely revive.

The worst, of course, was the spirit that lived in the pendant, the very brass pendant in the shape of a shell Val had affectionately given to Julie their last Christmas together. Bequeathed to him by his maternal grandmother years ago, it was engraved on the cover with a scrolled heart containing what Val and Julie had decided was Aphrodite, the Greek goddess of love, next to an exquisitely detailed swan. Like a buried treasure, it opened to reveal a tarnished silver watch face that looked to be so old it only had an hour hand. A tiny moon encased within a semicircle floated at the top that Val said had probably once tracked the phases of the moon, and around its outermost rim were twelve strange symbols he surmised represented the signs of the zodiac.

The clock didn't work, but that didn't matter to Julie. It was a gift from Val, and she cherished it because he had given it to her. She'd bought a 14-carat gold chain that let it dangle between her breasts, next to her heart, having no idea that over time the entity inside it was steadily infiltrating her chest cavity and seeping into her.

Tainting her.

Corrupting her.

She had no idea her emotions, her reactions, even her thoughts were not entirely her own.

They also belonged to a powerful spirit, neither living nor dead, that called itself Iago.

FIVE

"...the devil hath power, T' assume a pleasing shape."
—Hamlet, attributed to William Shakespeare

Iago was not its true name. Iago is the villain from Othello who falsely convinces the title character to destroy his entire life in the pursuit of uncovering his wife's apocryphal infidelity.

Shakespeare's Iago was a nice guy compared to this Iago.

This Iago had not always been ensconced within a lady's trinket.

Neither Here nor There, this Iago preferred to dwell upon the edges of Nowhere.

Although Iago had wandered the globe for millennia before the onset of this particular human civilization in Sumer—once an unwilling bondservant to those ancient Evils doomsday mythos now calls the Great Old Ones—humanity caught its attention when it became enraptured with Henry Plantagenet, King of England, for his ruthless temper and captivating older wife, Eleanor of Aquitaine. It passed from Henry to Eleanor, and from Eleanor to their son, Richard the Lionheart. With Richard, it reveled in revolting against its prior companion, King Henry, and thrilled in the carnage of the Third Crusade.

It continued roving throughout the Plantagenet line, instigating the passionate flirtation between John of Gaunt and the voluptuous Katherine Swynford that forever transformed the British monarchy. Fastening itself to the Tudors through John and Katherine's granddaughter, Margaret Beaufort, Iago's lust intensified as it convinced Henry VIII to mercilessly discard five of his six queens.

It had known Queen Elizabeth I familiarly, and thought her a self-righteous prude. It disdained the charlatan who called himself

Shakespeare even more. This Iago had followed King Charles II to his restored throne in 1660, and ricocheted back and forth between swaying the Earl of Rochester and the Duke of Buckingham against Barbara Palmer, the king's notorious mistress, until at last being trapped by the celebrated astrologer and erstwhile magician, William Lilly, in this damned lady's timepiece.

Designed by royal clockmakers to the French court at Versailles, the watch pendant had been commissioned by King Charles as a Twelfth Night gift for Barbara in perfunctory compensation for his waning appetite toward her, as well as to excuse his pursuit of his latest conquest, Frances Stuart.

Barbara, who often sought the advice of astrologers, wore the kingly present during a visit to Lilly, reckless in her need of the astrologer's services because she was—yet again—with child, but none too sure if it was King Charles's brat or not.

For all her beauty, Barbara was little known for her constancy, especially in lovers. It was one of Iago's favorite things about the strumpet.

But the King must never know, of course. At least, not positively. Not publicly.

As she stood before Lilly's casting table—covered with parchment, quills, and ink, as well as his very expensive clockwork armillary sphere used to track the intricacies of the planetary motions—she worried the watch pendant about her neck, opening it and snapping it shut again in agitation, impatient for Lilly's calculations to be complete.

The vixen was giving Iago a headache. Which was impressive, since it had no head.

Lilly looked up at her with pregnant prognostication.

"Well? Well? Damn your blood, what does it say?" Barbara demanded, never one to mince words.

"The stars, my lady, foretell this child to be the King's own issue."

She dropped into her chair like a fat toad, feeling the babe move within her quickening belly as though in agreement.

"Oh, la—thank the heavens! I am beholden to you, sir, and am well-endowed to reward you for your comfort."

In a fit of temper at Barbara's fatuous willingness to be duped by this impostor, Iago made a grave error: It pricked Barbara's hand on the watch pendant.

She cried out, jumping to her feet and suckling her bleeding finger, astounded.

Lilly, ever the academic, lifted the offending jewelry from her bodice and studied it. He released the silly bit of ostentation and proceeded to walk around Barbara, muttering low words under his breath until, impudent in its exasperation and having no idea the man was other than the fraud he seemed, Iago reached out with Barbara's foot and kicked him in the shins with her high-heeled shoe.

"Oh no! Oh, sir! I do not. . . I mean I cannot. . . I am not much myself today."

"There's a fiendish presence about you," Lilly said, thoughtfully. "It must be expelled, lest it destroy you. But I think this piece of feminine frippery just may pose the answer we need to contain it. May I?"

Eyes the size of planets, Barbara raised her watch pendant over her head and proffered it to him.

Crossing to a large bookcase filled with several obscure tomes, Lilly removed a newer text with veneration. "This is a copy of the private journals of Doctor John Dee, advisor to Her Majesty Queen Elizabeth. It reveals his most secret Enochian book of magic. Our answer lies within these pages to dispel this demon, but before I proceed, I must have your promise that you will never speak of this, for I will deny these proceedings most heartily."

Barbara nodded, shuddering as she self-consciously arranged herself on the edge of her chair, still fidgeting.

Iago watched, helpless, as the astrologer picked up a piece of chalk, drew a circle on the floor of his tenement, inscribed the circle with enigmatic magical symbols, and placed the watch pendant at the center of it all.

It tried to impel Barbara to speak, to get up and stop the astrologer's drudging, but the woman's new awareness of its presence within her emasculated Iago's efforts, rendering it powerless.

Lighting a black candle as he murmured dark words too quiet for Barbara to understand, without warning Lilly grasped the back of Barbara's chair and tipped it over—propelling her into the circle and then blowing out the candle. He clapped his hands with finality and closed his eyes, a smug look spreading over his shrewd face.

Rushing wind consumed Iago, as though it was trapped in the orifice of a rapacious tornado, followed by a terrific wrenching which dragged it juddering and shrieking all the way from Barbara's warm body of flesh and into this cool prison of time.

Barbara Palmer promptly put the watch pendant in a locked box and threw away the key.

Until the perturbing watch pendant, Iago had never made the mortal mistake of merging essences with a crude physical form, thus it could never accurately be termed male or female. It remembered no true name with which to identify itself, for it never owned one body alone, but instead attached itself like a discarnate parasite to the nearest opportunity for the next inebriating glut of emotions.

You might well wonder how it could do this? How was Iago able to journey through time, hitchhiking onto the physical bodies that belonged to other spirits or transferring back and forth between them, and then exploiting them so effortlessly?

Through the simplest means imaginable, an act most consider, whether innocent or ardent, the most basic human expression of affection.

A kiss.

Henry II had an unusual predilection for kissing his hunting dogs, which Iago used as its first foray into human possession. The King made a habit of regularly kissing his Queen (although this happened much less often after he imprisoned her for treason), and she forthwith transferred Iago to her son, Richard, whereupon it gleefully continued to wreak its newfound hominid havoc during successive generations of royalty.

Lovers, friends, family—men, women, children—none were safe from the burden of Iago if its interest was piqued.

We have Iago to thank for much of the warring, whoring, and most deploring chapters of the Middle Ages, Renaissance, and Reformation in the Western world. But for its incarceration within the pendant by Lilly, the Industrial Revolution would probably have yet to be.

For the first time in its existence, it was melded to matter and forced to occupy a fixed space and time.

Like a bitter genie in its lamp, Iago dwindled within its timely cage for over three hundred years.

And.

The.

Years.

Were.

Never.

Ending.

The space was diminutive, and worse, insignificant.

In its own private hell, within the truncating inanimate contraption, the defining dark, time without movement, Iago festered.

Much like the human hosts to which it had grown accustomed, it told itself stories to pass the time. Narratives to explain its plight. Justifications to defend its past actions. Myths to buttress its aims.

Although Iago wasn't sure it even had the capacity to generate feelings of its own, it remembered the emotions it had experienced by proxy, and those addictive remnants of sensation fixated it to almost fanatical proportions.

It formulated a plan.

When Val's great-great-grandfather, Frank Hill, smashed open the locked box, no one was more surprised than he to discover a delicate, if oxidized, lady's pocket watch buried within its coffer. He cleaned it up and gave it as a wedding gift to Val's great-great-grand-mother, Lola, who in turn gave it to her eldest daughter on the day of her wedding.

Iago bided its time, quietly probing the lives of Val's ancestors, preparing for the proper moment to act.

When Val, the sole grandchild, inherited the feminine heirloom, he put it in the top drawer of his bedroom bureau and forgot about it. It wasn't until he re-discovered it by chance and presented it to Julie, who wore the token faithfully, that Iago twisted its centuries of acquired insight into human vice, exploiting the charming guise of the watch pendant as it never could a kiss.

Iago's time had come.

SIX

"And this our life, exempt from public haunt,
finds tongues in trees, books in the running brooks, sermons in stones,
and good in everything. I would not change it."
—*As You Like It, attributed to William Shakespeare*

Outside the remote cabin, cicadas chirruped, and a lone mourning dove crooned its haunting lullaby. Inside the cabin, an austere mantle of silence so thick it might suffocate a lesser soul enfolded Peter as he grasped the carving knife firmly, centering himself as he began to whittle the rare white alder. He'd discovered the wooden treasure while exploring a small birch thicket down by Merced River last Sunday. The poor branch had been almost entirely eclipsed, drowned among stripes of white rotting underbrush and stifled by patches of grey decomposing leaves. When Peter reached down to pick it up, he found the branch remarkably undefiled by its hostile environment. Running his fingers along the uncommon snowy white hump at one end, the smooth head of the branch seemed to call to him to release it from the fine wood grain, stretching toward the heavens like a whale arising from the abyss.

Perhaps if he could free this forsaken corpse of wood, he could at last awaken Julie's lost smile.

Julie stopped smiling when Val left for college. These past two months of summer, usually the trio's happiest time of year, passed Julie and Peter by as though they both stood still. Julie's moods wavered between restless to out-and-out cynical, leaving Peter to not only miss his best friend, but worry about his best friend's girl even more. It was as though the head had been cut off their body, and now they just flopped around aimlessly, waiting for the end.

Peter refocused on the branch. Within every piece of wood existed the chance for a second life: A rebirth that, if carefully coaxed from its recesses by the truly devoted, liberated the wood's essence to become a work of art. Through the story of wood Peter recognized both the tree and the forest within himself and those he loved.

When he chose to go to work as apprentice foreman on the Steadman's farm straight out of high school rather than pursuing a four-year degree like his best friend, it was his love of the woods that wooed him. He preferred the Sierra Nevadas he knew so well rather than explore the possibility of new woods to romance.

Julie insisted physical labor looked good on him, as his normally pale skin soon tanned to a burnished brown—only a few shades lighter than her own natural hue—and his once-wiry muscles broadened and deepened to the look of chiseled mahogany. The increase in attention from random females made Peter uncomfortable.

But to feel the rich brown earth and verdant green stalks between his fingers all day long and fall exhausted but fulfilled onto his twin bed every evening, moist with his own sweat, satisfied Peter in a way book learning never did. Working the land was the truest occupation he knew.

He preferred the company of his fellow working class to the condescending overseers who owned the land yet never tended it, barking out orders as though employees were mongrels rather than men. Even though Peter's family appeared close-knit and comfortable, more and more it was the darker hues of human experience that lured Peter. Folk who sacrificed for love rather than donating it.

Dusk was his favorite time on the farm, as he and his mates gathered their tools to begin the long trek homeward, dark skin set ablaze by the florid amber and crimson rays of the fading sun, like so many phoenixes arising from the embers of the day and away from the great white fantasy.

Val always said there was a reason God gave Peter green eyes, as he had more in common with the woods than with humanity. Like the forests he loved, Peter planted his roots deep and gave far more than he ever received.

Val and Julie were the only ones who understood Peter, his one reprieve from his otherwise interminable solitude. He was most alone when surrounded by the others, whether sitting at the dinner table with his family or in church packed with people calling hallelujah so loudly that he couldn't hear God at all.

Peter never closed his eyes during prayer the way everyone else did. It seemed counter intuitive to him. His choice irritated other church members, especially Julie, who didn't understand his stubborn refusal to abide by such easy traditions.

As he did every Sunday since Val left, Peter returned alone after church to his tiny workshop behind his parent's home, where he carved with only the music of the cicadas to accompany his secluded endeavors late into the evening. He uncovered one lone fluke from the dormant branch in his hands and thanked the lord for this blessing of woodcarving, asking for an equal measure of grace to endure the isolation married with it.

A knock at the door interrupted the white alder's emergence.

"Peter, are you in there?" Julie's voice whimpered through the closed door.

Bounding upward, Peter fumbled with the latch. Julie stood on the threshold with puffy eyes and unwashed hair, wearing the mottled purple of a bruise and looking for all the world like a blighted weeping willow.

Peter only just checked himself from enveloping her in his arms. "What's wrong?"

"Do you have a moment?"

He motioned toward his workbench, "Always."

She didn't so much sit, as wilt, fiddling with the necklace Val had given her.

That's when Peter knew it was bad. Really, really bad.

"Val broke up with me," she said with dull eyes.

He stopped breathing. "That's not possible."

She snorted. "Well, maybe someone should tell him."

Time distorted inward upon itself, incompatible with space. Life could not continue without the Val-Julie continuum, because Peter's ability to relate depended on it.

"He's lost his mind. I'll call him now," he said, hitting speed dial on his cell.

"Don't you dare!" She slapped the phone from his hand. "He'll never forgive you if you get involved."

The cell crashed to the floor amongst the wood shavings, its screen cracking into three distinct pieces.

Stunned, Peter bent to gather the fragments. "Breaking my phone is a little extreme, don't you think? I'm involved. I've always been involved," he grimaced as he tapped the damaged screen. "Val's confused, and I need to fix this."

"I-I'm sorry," she stammered remorsefully. "I'll buy you a new one. A better one. I don't recognize myself. . . anymore. . . ." Her voice drifted off, ending in a hollow whisper.

"We need to talk some sense into Val."

Julie's eyes flitted uneasily about the room, at last settling upon the partially carved piece of wood, askew on his worktable next to the knives, chisel, and sandpaper lovingly ordered in a precise row. "Beautiful," she marveled as she picked up the wood medium, small fingers tracing the smooth dorsal fin and single sleek fluke he had already sculpted.

"It's not nearly finished."

"It's beautiful. . . like you," she said. "Are you going to sell it?"

"Not this one. It's for someone special."

Her smile was weak and water-logged, but a smile, nonetheless. "Who is she? Do I know her?"

Julie had been through so much, first with their whitewashed high school, then with Val going away to college, and now this. "She doesn't see herself clearly, but I'm going to change that."

"She's one lucky lady."

Heartbeat quickening, he said, "She deserves to be."

"So do you. You're too good, you know."

Longing filled him, so intense it ached. "Goodness is just a nice way of saying unexceptional. I'd rather be great than good. . . " His voice quieted so she barely heard him add, ". . .like Val."

Clenching her teeth, Julie muttered, "Greatness doesn't come home."

They stared at each other, unable to reach across the chasm that was Val.

Dropping the pendant like a hot coal, Julie jumped up. "I'm going to get him back."

Peter began pacing the room, wondering just how much she knew. "Did he say anything else?"

Her heartsick eyes turned strangely vicious. "He's met someone."

Peter's mouth fell open, incredulous. Julie still didn't know. How could Val do this to her? Another woman, what a pathetic excuse for making the worst mistake of his life. Maybe he ended things just so he wouldn't have to tell her?

Her bitter eyes turned soft and pleading. "Will you come with me? Will you come to Michigan and help me get him back?" She clasped his arm, stopping him.

She smelled of vanilla and almonds; her proximity intoxicated him. Without hesitation, he answered, "Of course I'll go with you. Let's go get him back."

Her necklace pierced his chest as she threw herself against him in a painfully platonic hug. For the first time in his life, he closed his eyes as he started to pray.

SEVEN

"So many horrid ghosts."
—Henry V, attributed to William Shakespeare

The communion table remained crooked, and Duke Hill was not a long-suffering man.

A kind man, a compassionate man, a gracious man, perhaps even a noble man—but patient, not so much.

Which brings us back to the communion table. The communion table that refused to stay straight.

Duke initially noticed the incline during morning worship. When it was time for sharing the Lord's Supper, he positioned himself just to the right of the table as he did every first Sunday of the month, while the church elder delivered his prepared communion meditation to the congregation. Four deacons, bowing their heads in humility, stood ready to apportion the unleavened bread, representing Christ's broken body, and the grape juice, representing Christ's shed blood, to their fellow believers.

While Elder Stephen exhorted "Jesus died for the forgiveness of our sins" and "repetition is only boring if we fail to pay attention to what we are doing," Duke observed the grape juice, sitting in the hundreds of diminutive plastic cups on the communion table, was lopsided, the ritual blood of Christ teetering just inches from be-smirching His liturgical broken body.

After the service, Duke spent the remainder of the day trying to level out the table, to no avail. Once one side was fixed, the other insisted on going awry, as though the devil himself was having a giggle at his expense.

When Val entered the sanctuary to call him to supper, all semblance of levelheadedness had long departed Duke's usual equanimity. He huffed and puffed. His nostrils flared. He nearly bit off his tongue, so intent was he as he tried to solve his irreconcilable dilemma.

Val watched his uncle—flat on his back under the communion table, growling under his breath—and suppressed an amused grin. His uncle was so endearing when he was trying to control his anger. "Is everything okay?"

Sitting up too rapidly, Duke banged his head on the underside of the table. Rubbing the throbbing knot forming on his sore forehead, he said, "Besides my own vanity? Everything's fine."

And then Val felt it more than heard it: the subtlest change in atmosphere, as though the air around him shifted the slightest sliver to the left. The hairs at the base of his neck started to prickle.

Duke continued, "I suspect this is my own cross to bear, but if you could help me carry it a little, I'd be much obliged."

Val joined his uncle under the communion table, desperate to appear as though an unnerving hum that only he could hear hadn't begun pulsating the air around them.

"It's definitely uneven," Val offered, tiny beads of sweat forming along his upper lip, "but Aunt Blanche says it's time to eat. Can we maybe take a break and attack this fresh in the morning?"

As Duke beamed at Val in response, he could see the sincere compassion in his uncle's eyes. If only he could talk to Duke about his ghosts as easily as they worked together to balance a communion table.

Duke chuckled. "Sounds good. I admit I'm feeling mighty carnivorous."

That's when the humming warped into singing. A faint, childlike voice chanted, "The clock strikes three. . . "

Another tenuous voice joined in, ". . .beast is coming for thee."

"You okay, boy?" Duke asked as the dreaded far-away troubled look crept into Val's eyes.

"The clock strikes four. . . "—a tinny crooning only Val could perceive continued—"there's pounding at the door." Val jerked upward as he heard lunatic cackling followed by what sounded like the slamming of a heavy, wooden door.

Val shook his head once, twice, then slowly looked at his uncle with miserable eyes.

But the visitors would not be ignored. A chorus of tiny voices latched onto the eerie refrain, desperate for Val's attention. "The clock strikes five. . . " echoes around the hollow sanctum, "we struggle to survive."

The room chilled swiftly.

Without being aware he did so, Duke zipped up his jacket.

"The clock strikes six . . . ," hushed voices continued, "they cross the river Styx."

Shadows began to coalesce on the ceiling and in corners with no source of illumination to cast them.

"The clock strikes seven. . . "—a single, piercing shriek swelled from behind the altar at the front of the church as rippling water rhythmically began slap-slap-slapping against the baptismal walls—"want to go to heaven."

Val sensed the strongest presence before he saw it—an overpowering wave of malevolence so titanic it strained beyond the room itself and stretched out not only to the tiny graveyard at the outskirts of the property, but into the exposed cracks within Val and Duke as well.

Duke dismissed the mounting foreboding in his gut as his own misgivings about his nephew's increasing agitation grew. Val, however, knew from experience with spirits that these rifts, these vulnerabilities, these repressed openings inside the living—wherein a corporeal being does not inhabit or possess itself fully—attract disembodied spirits like a starving wolf's feeding frenzy at the end of a lingering bitter winter.

"The clock strikes eight," a deeper, ominous voice from on high silenced the children's susurrations, "the arbiter is late."

Like a regressive rainbow in every hue of green, an imposing monstrosity of prismatic crystal and non-Euclidian mirror edges burst from the baptismal, churning colors converging as it lifted high into the rafters and lurched toward the tilted communion table. It looked as though all the stars in the universe had been stolen and shrouded within a gelatinous tentacled nightmare.

"The clock strikes nine," boomed the viscous reverberation, "thou shalt not god malign."

That's when the shaking began.

Like in a massive earthquake, the church rattled on its foundations. The chandeliers swayed. Val watched the cross above the altar gyrate as though taking part in a ghoulish dance. The entire building vibrated in time to the terrifying tempo.

Duke cleared his throat as he scrutinized Val, oblivious to the supernatural bedlam around him but aware that Val was not himself. "What do you say we join Blanche for supper?"

Val glanced from the advancing specter to the crooked communion table, realizing the fiend seemed relentlessly drawn to something about it—or to Uncle Duke.

The Lilliputian shades in every corner of the room hunched together, holding each other away from the garish blob of jelly hovering above the communion table. Desiccated Play-Doh wings composed of gunky pearly scales surged upward from the blob's back. The undulating spirit bloated and recoiled as though trying to become flesh, but failing utterly.

A guttural roar ripped through the room like too-close thunder.

The surging phantasmagoric mass encroached upon his unsuspecting uncle. "The clock strikes ten. . . " It reached legion diamond-like protuberances around him. "To claim this world—*again*."

Three serendipitous phenomena materialized:

Val knocked Duke away from the communion table, hollering like a faith healer as he struck the table. Holy grape juice sprayed in every direction.

This, Duke did see.

An ectoplasmic door appeared to the left of them as if in response to Val's outcry, whence Vee stepped over the entrance with a forest of Vs in every shade of green depicted on her not-vest.

This, Duke did not see.

Third, Vee both surveyed the situation and surmised what she needed to do.

This, even Val missed.

As Duke was hit full in the face with a mouthful of Christ's blood, Vee seized the livid apparition with her not-hands and stretched it flat like a massive piece of taffy. She proceeded to fold it many times upon itself, as though preparing to cut a child's six-pointed paper snowflake, halving it over and over until it resembled a miniature splinter of seething unicorn candy.

Vee enclosed the protesting candy in an odd little lavender-colored box and placed it in her right vest not-pocket.

A dazed look clouded Val's bewildered eyes. "When did you learn how to do. . . whatever it is you just did?"

A cheeky V detached itself from Vee's not-vest, zoomed over to Val, and licked him on the cheek as Vee said, "It's different Here than it is There. Outside of time, everything happens in the eternal Now. Past, present, and future are only physical constructs. You know, one day is as a thousand years, and a thousand years as one day."

As Duke sputtered and coughed up consecrated grape juice, Vee cocked her head to the side and asked Val, "So this is your uncle? He's adorable. And so very. . . mortal."

Val's eyes filled with warmth as he said, "You're both quite precious to me. Thanks for the eleventh-hour save. How did you know I needed you?"

"A part of me is a part of you, but then again I enjoyed solving your protuberant puzzle. I'm going to give this angry brute to the prince of darkness as a thank-you gift—this paltry beast may be a fun diversion for him. Little dictators of Nowhere always unravel when they realize they've been wasting their eternity playing frivolous dominance games."

"Why do you call it a beast—wasn't it human once?" Val asked, amazed anew at Vee's transition on the other side in the relatively short span of their budding relationship. Barely a month had passed for him, but with each visit Vee seemed so much *more* than the time before, as though decades or even centuries had transpired for her. These unsettling shifts only deepened his attraction somehow, with an added hint of danger he found as alluring as it was inhuman—as though a subterranean Circe skulked behind her vying Vs.

She giggled in a decidedly un-ghost-like fashion that ended in a snort. "Nothing human about this beast. Dwelling halfway and between—in a perpetual state of dusk, I'd say." Vee patted her not-pocket. "Thus, the umbral container fashioned of twilight. I doubt it's ever inhabited a physical body. Quite gender fluid, although it might fancy itself male just because of the lopsided notion that men rule the earth. Definitely compensating for something." Rolling her stygian eyes, she continued, "Gender's voluntary rather than compulsory outside of a physical body. More to the point of your question, I attended a party recently with e.e. cummings—an absolutely capital chap, contrary to what's written about him—and he's correct: The mystery of the flesh unravels when we take the sun in our mouths and set our teeth in the silver of the moon. Something about which this beast is clueless." Her sheer not-lips parted as her features softened. "Of course, you should have seen the cat fight between e.e. and Kant on that subject."

Even though he knew he couldn't physically touch her, Val instinctively moved closer to Vee. "You're my hero."

Vee's effervescence heightened to a rosy flush. "Love you. Oh, and don't worry about all the little ghosties. Now that the Big Nasty is no longer captivating them, they're already starting their release to the other side."

"Love you more."

Blowing him a kiss, she said, "See you in the barn later?"

"Wouldn't miss it."

Departing through her door that wasn't There, she glanced one last time behind her and asked, "By the way, did you realize this room's lopsided?"

HERE

EIGHT

"To die, to sleep—to sleep—perchance to dream:
ay there's the rub, for in that sleep of death what dreams may come
when we have shuffled off this mortal coil, must give us pause."
—Hamlet, attributed to William Shakespeare

Everybody's haunted by something.

The dead are haunted by dreams.

Dreams are different Here. Spirits don't have bodies that need dreaming to survive the weight of physicality. We don't have hearts that ache for the oneness we've lost. On this side we still dream, or we call it dreaming, but our dreams are explorations of form without substance and darkness without light, the choices we either refuse to make or are actively making but refuse to understand.

They don't overtake us as we lie asleep, waiting to pounce when at our most vulnerable. For the dead are always awake.

Imagine every dream you've dreamed, the dreams you couldn't dream, the dreams you wish you'd dreamt, and the dreams you prayed you'd never dream—with you, simultaneous, all the time.

Spirit dreams are the source of the mortal concepts of parallel universes and concurrent timelines.

Everything is equally real, Here.

Dreams.

Fantasies.

Nightmares.

We have no buffer of flesh and mass to protect us from what we imagine.

The only time the living touch Here is while dreaming. You

smudges couldn't continue to live in the light without your nightly infusion of darkness.

But the dead are always dreaming.

When we dream, we touch both Memory and Possibility, far more hideous than the realities of the living.

Here, I dream of Val without ceasing.

My dreams haunt me like an elusive eidolon of what was, what is, and what might have been.

There, Val experiences me leaving him with his uncle in the church sanctuary after effortlessly saving them both from the Big Bad.

I know I will continue to haunt him There, as he haunts me Here, for every love story is a ghost story—in the end. We're haunted by the ghost of what our love could be, what it should be, what it was.

What it never can be.

Now that death has freed me from my capricious brother, my feeble body, and my monkey mind, I'm also free of the impediments built into that whole massive mess of physicality. Here, I'm only limited by the dreams that haunt me, but There—as long as my dreams remain apart—if I can conceive of it, I can do it.

Except for corporeal action. I can't move a paper clip or touch Val.

My capture of the gummy-beast might have seemed miraculous to him, but "miracle" is but a word that's placeholder for phenomena one can't apprehend.

The prince of darkness often calls me "foolish" for what he says is "my morbid fascination" with Val and my ever-increasing Vs, but I say Shakespeare's fool is the wisest character of us all.

I've always had a thing for Shakespeare. Especially his sonnets. He wrote his plays to earn a living, but he wrote his sonnets to live in earnest.

When I found the prince of darkness, he was lounging next to a vivid facsimile of the famous Neptune pool from Hearst Castle, slumming it in a velvet smoking jacket, shorts, and what looked like diamond-studded slippers. I presented him with the angry lavender box.

He clicked his not-tongue. "So, it begins," he said as he gently placed the pulsing box inside his left jacket pocket.

He's so infuriating at not-times. "Cryptic much?"

He leaned over and swished away a coffin-shaped V lingering at my not-brow. "You've more of the crypt about you than I ever will."

"It keeps the phantoms at bay," I said as I squished a particularly vexing V between my not-hands like the pesky vermin it was.

"Your Vs are not the phantoms. Vee is," he said as the V that I just tried to squish rebelliously grew and took shape before our not-eyes, becoming Viola from Shakespeare's play *Twelfth Night*.

You're probably wondering how I knew she was Viola? Since I died, that tiresome dependence on the senses, reading, and understanding that so consumed me while alive became obsolete. Here, I look at a thing, and if I'm honest with myself—ay, there's the rub—I know.

She was dressed as her alter ego, the page boy Cesario, and I wondered to look at her how anyone could think her anything but what she was: a noble lady disguised as a young man to shield herself, alone in a foreign land, employed by the Duke Orsino, whom she secretly loved.

What foolish things we do for love, and how easily we're tricked by our preconceptions.

That's when I looked down and realized that my own appearance had changed as well. I was dressed as Feste—bedecked in jester's belled cap and pointed shoes—the famous fool from *Twelfth Night*.

Perhaps at last I judged myself wise enough to play the fool?

The V that had been stuck fast to my not-chest since I first met Val loosened itself and flickered away as a moth toward the light. At first it seemed but a frail fragment of tissue paper floating on an undetected breeze, but it soon broadened and deepened in size, shape, and color until it reformed into the handsome lover Valentine from *The Two Gentlemen of Verona*, dressed just as the character might have been in a production at the Globe Theatre of Shakespeare's London, with fancy ruff, padded doublet, and slashed breeches.

Besides his Elizabethan costume, he looked suspiciously like my own Val.

My god, he's yummy.

The familiar churning started in my not-belly, that slow-burning flame that's always kindled when Val and I are together. How is it that, despite not having a body to feel the physical sensations of desire, this visceral wanting of him so wholly consumes me? It's as though his spirit merged with my spirit, and the parts of him that have become parts of me tremor endlessly to be rejoined to their source.

"Poor lady, she were better love a dream," Viola said to this Valentine, quiet humor in her violet eyes.

Valentine raised his eyebrows at Viola and then winked at me with Val's lopsided grin. "Love hath chased sleep from my enthralled eyes. Forgive me that I do not dream on thee."

Sometimes I hate these conversations with fictional characters. They utter the uncomfortable truths we all avoid, unhampered by our notions of reality.

And they talk funny, too.

I saw the irascible look in the prince's eyes just before he morphed his smoking jacket into a long brown monk's cowl with knotted rope belt at his suddenly plump waist. Great, he'd joined this counsel of Vs as the trickster Duke Vincentio from *Measure for Measure*, who masqueraded as the fat Friar Lodowick, of course.

What was it with disguises today?

With a smile that reminded me of a little boy full of too much Halloween candy, the friar-prince said, "Thy death, which is no more. Thou art not thyself. For thou exist'st on many a thousand grains that issue out of dust. Happy thou art not; For what thou has not, still thou strives to get, and what thou hast, forget'st."

I stamped my not-foot. "My world's not so contracted. Permanence is a cosmic joke, yet the jest is lost on the living. We're all splintered for love."

"Disguise, I see thou art a wickedness," the Lady Viola added.

I was about to agree with her, when it occurred to me that I wasn't sure if she was chastising the friar-prince—or me?

Valentine chose this inconvenient moment to chime in, "And why not death rather than living torment? To die is to be banished from myself; and Silvia is myself: banished from her is self from self: a deadly banishment!"

I granted him my most disapproving glare. "You may look like my Val, but you're nothing like him. Death did not banish us from each other, it brought us together. Love's the end of our story."

Valentine cocked his not-head to the right with an arrogant laugh. "Love is your master, for he masters you."

Okay, I really did not like this Valentine. It's as if all my doubts were scribbled on a page, crumpled up, and smoothed out to become this noxious prat.

And, of course, here came Viola's two cents. "How easy it is for the proper false in women's waxen hearts to set their forms!"

Wait just a minute. If Vincentio posed as the prince, and Valentine symbolized my qualms about Val, who was Viola?

Dead dreams suck corpse butts. "What lies beneath your mask, Viola?"

With a long pause and the slightest narrowing of her not-eyes, she answered me, "It is too hard a knot for me to untie."

What a knotty trio they made: the fat friar-prince, the fractious Valentine, and the fetching Viola.

Triangles have always bothered me. Three lines perpetually intercepting, in a never-ending struggle for dominance. Each the boundary of the other.

Perhaps I could solve this vector of Vs if I could find that elusive third line and craft them into triangles.

But how?

"Upon the very naked name of love," Valentine said with an

evocative smile.

I hate him.

But then the friar-prince one-upped him entirely. "Believe not that the dribbling dart of love can pierce a complete bosom. Thou art death's fool."

Without warning, the entire dream scene transformed around us. We stood in a pit in front of a raised rectangular platform below a thatched roof supported by two wooden columns in front.

Three stories of roundish open-air seating surrounded us. A million little V-shaped stars glowed in the sky above us.

Aside from the plague of Vs, it looked like a facsimile of Shakespeare's Globe Theatre.

Hushed, we watched as five people swathed in black robes moved with purpose on the dim stage before us. Their faces veiled in darkness, their shrouded figures came to rest in a five-pointed circle around a single lit candle located on the wooden planks of the stage.

A pentagram.

They looked upward as one.

The night sky, a revolting shade of brown, began to bubble vehemently, stars flung left and right like miniature marshmallows churning in an empyrean hot chocolate.

A joint incantation commenced on the stage, at first in unison, but then diverging into separate parts as deliberate and melodic as a Gregorian chant.

The fiery marshmallows stilled their chaos to form a loathsome circle in the cocoa sky.

Something unnamable pierced through the center of the sky circle and began to emerge from the void, clawing and crawling its demonic way out.

The person at the apex of the pentagram stooped toward the center and blew out the candle.

Abruptly, my perspective shifted. No longer Vee, but instead a rather pretty man with a dapper mustache and quite sure of myself at the apex of it all. Before my altered eyes, tendrils of smoke advanced from the extinguished candle to combine and intensify, forming a whirling vortex that surged from the circle's middle to a point about 10 feet above the stage, before rushing heavenward with a raging whoosh.

The scenery shifted, and I was Vee once again, standing with the prince who was back in his signature suit, by the not-Neptune pool.

Viola and Valentine had vanished, but a new triangle of Vs orbited my head.

The prince crossed his not-arms and started tapping his not-foot. "The goal is less, not more."

I was trapped by these vaporous Vs. What did these dreams mean? Why couldn't I evade my damned Vs? Despairing, I asked, "How do I vanquish these vices?"

"There's a reason so many stories include a good love triangle."

What's love got to do with a triangle?

A particularly captivating V the color of bittersweet chocolate drifted to my not-ear and whispered in dulcet tones, "What about Julie?"

Val's ex? She had nothing to do with me. That was over.

Or was it?

The prince's smirk spoke volumes. "Now is the winter of our discontent."

The opening line of *Richard III*, my favorite play.

Brat.

"For once, could you stop the secrecy?"

The prince squared his rather broad not-shoulders, grasped my own lesser ones, and looked firmly into my not-eyes. "Unequivocal it is, then. You've broken a triangle that needs mending in your hereafter love, wantonly dissolving three disguises carefully built one upon the other. In fact, you've a history of disturbance and devastation with regard to all disguises but your own."

The unwelcome memory of five cloaked figures, shifting beneath a distressed brown sky, assailed me. What had been done that blasphemous night?

And why did it feel so freakishly familiar?

That old accustomed flush tingled across my not-cheeks. "I don't really know myself at all, do I?"

The prince faded away, and in his place stood my beloved Val, sans his body. And somehow, I knew that Val was deep asleep in his bedroom at Hill Manor, dreaming of me.

Just like the prince, Val's newly not-hands held my not-shoulders, but the touch lightened from chastising to cherishing, cradling me. His dreamy not-eyes registered surprise at first, then the bottomless craving to unite with that part of himself that is me darkened them to midnight blue. Instinctively, we reached for each other, not-lips tenderly meeting for the first time.

My helpless response terrified me. The power of our bond ignited me. I felt as though he smothered me and at the same time breathed into me the spark I'd sought my entire existence, a fractured agony mixed with a perilous ecstasy so beyond this shell I called "Vee", I must explode across everything until I became it.

And just as we began to move in rhythm together in this dream within a dream, I heard the intimate whisper of the prince's voice in my not-head: "Perhaps we are all god in disguise to each other, after all."

THERE

NINE

"Good without evil is like light without darkness which in turn is like righteousness without hope."
—*All's Well That Ends Well, attributed to William Shakespeare*

Iago hated Peter.

It judged him through Julie's eyes, revolted by the boy's so-called virtue, his nauseating attentiveness to its girlish host.

It bristled at the pathetic way the boy collapsed onto the lavish art deco sofa in their room at The Queen's Residence Bed and Breakfast, watching in disgust as he kneaded the back of his neck and heaved a weighty sigh. Convincing Peter's parents to let them fly across the country to see Val had been easy—Peter was perhaps the most trustworthy eighteen-year-old in existence, and since he earned an adult's income and paid rent, they seldom questioned his decisions. Persuading Julie's parents had been stickier. But for Iago's silver-tongued intervention, and Julie's willingness to use her own savings to pay for the plane ticket, she would probably still be sitting at home pining for her long-lost boyfriend.

Julie's insistence they keep their trek to Milan, Michigan, a secret from Val obviously discouraged Peter, yet the dolt's emasculated idea of turning their trip into a mini vacation by splurging on this outlandish pretext for a place to sleep made Iago want to rip Julie's face off and throw it at him.

Why didn't he just have his way with her already? Iago would relish piggybacking a good fuck.

Iago's own history brimmed with missteps in response to a pretty face. The worst fumbling, of course, was when that slut Barbara

Palmer, with her sultry blue-black eyes and glossy chestnut hair, lulled its normally first-rate instincts into a lazy ennui, prompting its critical oversight—well, that and its own misjudgment of Lilly's learning in the black arts of the Old Ones. It regretted letting down its defenses on that fateful night long enough to allow Lilly to mastermind its doom.

Never again.

Some might call Julie handsome, but all Iago saw in her lengthy corkscrew curls and dewy topaz eyes was Jezebel zombified.

Julie, and anyone with lady parts for that matter, was the enemy.

The quaintness of the Queen's Residence grated on Iago, twisting its characteristic crabbiness into pure spite. It had been trapped in this horrifying little town named "Ypsilanti"—or "Ypsi," as the locals insisted—with these nitwits for two days now, about twenty minutes north of where Julie's ex-boyfriend had spent the summer with his uncle in Milan. They'd settled in this gods-forsaken dump because it was home to Eastern Michigan University, the college Julie's wayward ex would be attending in a few short weeks. Unfortunately, Ypsi was also the birthplace of a repugnant establishment called Domino's Pizza, and the two adolescents had already made Iago suffer through three meals of overcooked tomatoes and spoiled calf's milk slapped on cardboard crust since their arrival.

Iago itched to slap Peter and Julie with punishments far more appalling than anesthetizing junk food. How could these youngsters squander so much time in this tedious inn, frenchified with flowers and lousy with antiques, now that they were so close to their objective?

Julie luxuriated in the immense king-sized sleigh bed while Peter, after failing to sleep restfully on a couch far shorter than he, cozied up with a pillow and blanket on the floor. Although Julie had suggested they stay in the cheapest place possible, Iago knew she secretly reveled in the upscale luxury to which she was so accustomed.

Woman, thy name is hypocrite.

"Are you sure you don't want the bed?" Julie asked for the hundredth time. "I'm sure I can fit on the sofa."

"Wouldn't hear of it."

Iago realized it needed to exert further pressure if these infants were ever to accomplish anything other than stare at each other with deer-in-the-headlights eyes.

"We need to coordinate our plan of attack," it vocalized through Julie's lips.

"I've been trying to figure that out since we boarded the plane. I think our best bet is just to go talk to him, no more of this sneaking-around stuff."

Chagrined, Iago barely suppressed a growl.

At Iago's impatient prodding, Julie leapt off the bed and strode toward the bathroom. After a hasty look-see, she grabbed the nail scissors off the marble vanity, seized a long hank of hair, and started hacking away at it.

Peter vaulted across the room toward her, capturing her hand. "What in god's name are you doing?"

"Disguising myself."

He gawked at her. "Do you really think Val won't recognize you with cropped hair?"

She firmly removed her ringlet from his hand and continued her carnage. "This isn't for Val. It's for everyone else."

"I don't understand."

"You are going to pay a surprise visit to Val's house. Say it's one last hurrah before he starts his college life. Scope out what he's feeling about me, about us. Investigate his Achilles' heel, the chink in his armor—if he has any—and start picking at it."

"And you. . . you're going to cut your hair?"

"I am going to erase Julie. Become Nobody. I'll cut my hair, dress incognito, spy around town, and find this mysterious girl who's seduced Val."

With a furrowed brow, Peter crossed his arms. "There are so many holes in this misguided idea that I don't even know where to begin.

You, of all people, can't become a nobody. Even if you ruin your hair, you'll still attract attention. You can't help it. And why would you need to conceal yourself anyway? It's not like anyone knows you from Eve in Ypsi."

She halted her slashing, "You're right."

Peter exhaled the breath he hadn't even realized he'd been holding. "I'm glad you see reason. Now, I th—"

"Oh, you're wrong about most of it. The scheme's nearly seamless. But even if I lurk about, I'm no wallflower. Camouflage isn't enough, I'll have to give myself a new identity. Hmm. . . " Her eyes wandered the room, at last fixating on the gilded oval mirror right in front of her inconveniently fair face. "Of course, how obvious! The boy Bastion it is, then."

Peter blenched. "I'm sorry—boy? Did you say 'boy'?"

"Why not, it's the perfect cover."

"You could shave your head and still no one could ever mistake you for a boy."

"Don't be silly. I'm tall for a woman. I can easily hide my small breasts under a big shirt. I already have thick eyebrows and a strong jawline. Without makeup, and perhaps with a baseball cap, I can totally impersonate a guy. Besides, I've always felt like I have more in common with you and Val than any of my girlfriends."

"Suppose you can pass yourself off as male—" Peter crossed himself as though speaking blasphemy, "—which I doubt, there is no way anyone would accept a boy named Bastian in this present century. It doesn't matter if it's from your favorite novel, it's still impossible. Like this plan."

Looking down and studying the nail scissors, Julie said, "*The Neverending Story* is the best book ever written. And this plan is my last bastion of hope for Val and me. I like the symmetry." She snipped another tress defiantly. "You don't have to help, you know."

Unsure of this headstrong stranger mauling herself before him, he said, "I'll go see Val. Although I won't lie to him outright, I won't reveal you're here either. I'll find out whatever I can and try to convince him what a mess he's made of things. You can play dress-up and do as you wish. . ." he exhaled upward, as though she was a balloon he had to keep afloat. "But please don't do anything rash. Promise me."

"I promise." Iago realized Julie may have crossed a line for Peter, and so it nudged her to add plaintively, "Please be patient with me. Don't give up on me. I need you."

Iago watched Peter finally break before its puppet mastery. In hushed tones, the boy said, "Of course I won't give up on you. We'll figure this out together. But honestly, you can't call yourself Bastian, you precious she-bastian."

"Sebastian—that's it! Oh, Peter, that's the perfect *nom de guerre*."

"Well, it's not perfect. Julie is perfect. But, at least it's better. . . "

"We passed a campground on the way in. What if we rent a cabin for me there, and you can stay with Val while I look for the other woman?"

Iago watched the lovelorn crack in the boy grow as Peter held out his hand to the shorn soon-to-be boy.

Against its better judgment, Iago was intrigued by its neophyte host. Though burdened by all the societal handicaps of the weaker sex, this was the first female Iago had ever infiltrated who seemed willing to act beyond her prescribed role. Iago may have prompted her to action, but it had been she who conceived of an impromptu plan so outside her genital box.

The babies joined hands and walked down to the pub in the basement of the Queen's Residence to share a snack, deep in what no doubt seemed to them a stimulating, world-changing conversation. Ignoring their prattling and mentally high-fiving itself, Iago basked in the insipid hope that defines youth.

Iago had no intention of satisfying their optimism by actually finding the upstart whore who tempted Julie's errant boyfriend to stray, although it would continue to foster the delusion in Julie as they explored the town. It was not interested in the reconciliation of two stupid children.

During its tenure within the nobility of Europe, Iago had decrypted how to manipulate the disposable flesh body for its own devices. Despite avid declarations to the contrary, human governments by and large view the masses as expendable assets meant to be used and generally lied to, never esteemed. Iago felt no remorse for a human's experience as marionette, for as soon as a human body reasserted itself in protest, Iago would simply begin to force-feed the flesh bad food, bad opinions, and bad entertainment, making it feel insecure and never enough in comparison to the other bodies surrounding it, persuading the human to believe itself unworthy. Iago had found human nature to be, by and large, quite weak-willed and pliable to the machinations engineered by the Ancient Ones.

Long before the first human walked upon this marbled orb, when Iago was perhaps its own version of a youngster, the being-that-would-one-day-call-itself-Iago became schooled in social theory at the lashes and shackles of its original overlords, the Old Ones. The daily torture and nightly torment inscribed these truths upon the then-child-like spirit: Even though every group may begin with the goal of freedom from oppression of some sort, eventually that group, as it survives, becomes more and more consumed with lasting and must therefore increasingly control and restrict the freedoms of its group's members in order to persist.

What begins as numberless divine sparks will inevitably distill themselves through their alliances. The puppet master merely need pluck the appropriate strings of an individual body to make it fall into rank and file. And now, Iago steered Julie's body to find its prey within her own capitalistic society.

For Iago was obsessed with the restless spirits of this trifling town. Ypsi was founded in 1823, but before its establishment the land had been a Native American burial ground for several tribes. This collection of Indigenous and immigrant ghosts, in various stages of spiritual deterioration, retained the essence of form deprived of hope, the spark of function deprived of divinity, the enigma of time deprived of space, the penumbra of light deprived of darkness.

Only in the shadowy Penumbra, that illegitimate and oft-ignored step-child of Light and Darkness conjoined, can the biting thorns of Light and buried tubers of Darkness be confronted.

And more importantly, exploited.

Exactly the Between Iago needed to ensnare its own eternal mastery, once and for all.

But it must be judicious, it must be assiduous, it must be sure. Most of these ghosts were commonplace debased spirits, drifting through their disenfranchised dis-eternities, by virtue of their very misery failing Iago's purposes. It required a whole or nearly whole unspoiled being.

Off to find a Penumbra amongst all this delusional hope.

TEN

"Friendship is constant in all other things,
Save in the office and affairs of love."
—*Much Ado About Nothing, attributed to William Shakespeare*

Val had become downright chummy with the ghosts on his uncle's land.

There was the one he liked to call the Banker, with the ridiculous towering top hat, who followed his uncle everywhere, muttering to himself. The Banker only acknowledged Val when he stepped between the ghost and his uncle, at which point he would grunt with a piercing glance, wring his hands, and then diligently step around Val to continue his migration.

Then there was the one he'd christened the Cook, who sat on the kitchen counter from dawn to dusk, wearing a threadbare apron. This apparition seemed to have a love affair with Aunt Blanche, the only person Val had ever met who was chubbier than the rotund ghost. The Cook smiled at Val whenever he entered the room, and occasionally waved, although her eyes were always drawn relentlessly back with phantasmic admiration to watching Blanche putter and bustle.

In Blanche's beloved herb garden, Val often happened upon an old spectral Farmer, dusty overalls and luminous sweat beading his transparent brow, working with some misty corn stalks. Never pausing from his labors, the Farmer occasionally nodded at Val, and even more seldom drawled a soft "Aw-yup."

But Val's favorite ghost, by far, was the nimble Frenchman, who popped up anywhere and everywhere like a mischievous imp. This spirit enthusiastically sang in a language Val assumed was French. At times he thought he heard "*du vin*" among the lyrics, but he wasn't sure. All he knew was the Frenchman laughed constantly and burst into a vigorous jig without apparent provocation.

Of course, ever since Vee first appeared that fateful evening, all the other paranormal phenomena avoided the barn like it was infested by leprous ghost fleas. The poltergeist Val had often heard knocking and banging about the barn prior to her arrival, simply evaporated. Vee divulged the change in behavior was likely caused by the idiosyncratic revulsion of beings stuck in Nowhere to the slightest hint of Here. Once people have decided something is impossible, they cannot abide the presence of proof they might be wrong.

Val sipped coffee outside while he contemplated the Farmer's "work" amongst his aunt's prized purple echinacea—fascinated with the healing potential of plants, Blanche fancied herself a kitchen herbalist and would have been appalled to know her garden was the ghost's preferred haunt—when he heard the front gate creak open and slam shut behind him. A familiar voice said, "I should have known I'd find the King of Cappuccino clasping his mighty chalice."

Astonished to hear his high school epithet, Val whipped around, covering the distance between them in three paces and engulfing his friend in a heartfelt bear hug. "It's been far too long, my Knight of Neapolitan Pizza."

The friends both brushed away some errant tears, then stood apart in a companionable silence, each content just to be in proximity of the other.

Val was the first to break their quiet communion. "I don't know how, and I don't know why, but I'm so glad you're here. I didn't realize how very much I've missed you."

"Well, someone has to knock some reason back into that thick skull of yours."

Val exhaled, less surprised now. "Well, if that's why you're here, let's at least make another pot of coffee. This might take a while." He turned and took the steps leading up the wooden porch two at a time.

Opening the screen door, he called into the house, "Aunt Blanche, we have company!" Beckoning to his friend to follow him inside, he entered without a backward glance.

Peter didn't know what to make of it. Val had changed. He was somehow *more* Val. He seemed bigger—oh, he was still just as skinny as always, but he looked taller than the 6 foot 3 he had been last June. Higher, somehow. How could Val be so much closer, yet feel even more out of his reach?

As a matter of fact, this whole place seemed larger. Peter had visited Hill Manor once before, when Pastor Hill legally adopted Val after his dad left. Peter had heard places from one's childhood were supposed to seem smaller when the adult returned to them, but this was just the opposite. The immense oak trees surrounding the home supplanted the heavens, branches reaching so high the clouds seemed but puffy fruit in their grasping tips. He felt pint-sized in comparison to the spacious white portico wrapped around the slate-grey house, as though protecting it from something. The gambrel roof was beginning to show its age—reminding Peter of what the Amityville Horror house would look like if had been haunted by the Holy Spirit instead of the ghost of a mass murderer—and the alabaster sash windows, recently painted, appeared to watch him, warily, waiting for him to stumble. Central to the household stood a burgundy door with a cross-shaped door knocker adorning it that read: *As for me and my house, we will serve the Lord—Joshua 24:15.*

Unbeknownst to Peter, the Farmer advanced toward him while he stood frozen in his reverie, until the two seemed to converge: The Farmer toiling with his ghostly plants, underneath Peter wrestling with how to confront his alien best friend, struggling in the same place to conquer a different perpetuity.

Val watched the merging from the kitchen window, saddened by his friend's reticence. He poured two fresh cups of coffee.

Hefting his suddenly lead-footed legs up the porch stairway, Peter climbed the prodigious steps to, slowly, open the cross-emblazoned brink.

Val sat at the ample oak table, sipping from his caffeinated cup with a welcoming smile and softly lit eyes. The smell of fresh-baked bread wafted throughout the immaculate kitchen at the heart of Hill Manor, but Blanche was nowhere to be seen.

"She wanted to greet you, but I asked if we could have some privacy to hash things out first."

Peter sat down in front of the other mug, grasping it like a damned man accepts redemption. Procrastinating, he added three teaspoons of sugar, then a fourth. And lots of cream. He'd never understood Val's old-man proclivity to drink his coffee black.

Since Peter seemed mute, Val prodded, "Well, let me have it then."

And the dam finally burst, as all the unspoken words Peter had censored while with Julie surged forth. "You've destroyed her, you know. She's desolate. Lost without you."

Averting his eyes, Val answered, "It's better this way."

"Oh, come on. This is me. We both know you've taken the coward's way out."

Jerking his head up, Val met his friend's reproachful eyes straight on. "I can promise I haven't. What exactly do you think I've done?"

"You broke up with Julie to avoid telling her the truth."

"I what?"

"You don't want her to know about the others. That you can see spirits."

Incredulity filled Val's face. "Is that what you think I've done?"

"You dated for almost four years, and you never told her. I know you think you're protecting her, but she can handle it. She's stronger than you think."

"Whether or not she could handle the information is immaterial. I didn't break up with Julie to avoid telling her I can see ghosts."

It was Peter's turn to be stunned. "So, you've decided, then? They're actually dead people and not demons?"

Val simply nodded.

"What does your uncle think?"

"I haven't told him. He wouldn't understand."

"Does he still think you're wrestling with devils?"

"I've stopped mentioning it. Other than one slip-up last week, we've both silently agreed to a mutual dissembling."

"What happened last week?"

Val gulped a mouthful of coffee before answering. "We encountered a particularly foul horror together in the church sanctuary, and I couldn't keep up the pretense because our lives were threatened."

"I thought you said the spirits are harmless."

"For the most part, that's true. Generally, they are wholly enmeshed in their own circular reality to the exclusion of all else. Occasionally, they seem able to engage with our world, even in a positive manner, but their interaction's shortsighted and habitual." He filled his lungs to capacity and exhaled with a slow whistle before continuing. "Very rarely, however, I've encountered a genuinely wicked ghost. If Vee hadn't intervened, I don't know what would have happened."

Peter stiffened at the strange name. "Vee? Who's 'Vee'?"

Val leaned over the table, bridging the space between them. "My soulmate."

Peter's jaw dropped so quickly, he nearly gave himself whiplash. "Your. Soul. Mate."

"I know it sounds corny and pretentious, but in this case, it's true. There really isn't another word in the English language to describe what we share. I would say we *agape* each other, but that word has been twisted so by well-intentioned Greek scholars and pop culture to the point of impossibility." He paused, a faraway look in his eyes. "It's our souls that've been mated, anyway, not our bodies. This love is as a death, for death checked our course and set us on another." He refocused his eyes on Peter and chuckled, "So maybe she's my Checkmate."

Peter saw nothing funny about it.

"There's actually another woman? You cheated on Julie? No," he closed his eyes and shook his head as though somehow he could unsee and unhear the wretched reality, "you're not capable."

Val reached forward, gently taking his friend's hands while looking directly into his face. "I never cheated on Julie. I broke off our relationship right after I met Vee, before anything happened between us."

"I don't understand—how could you do this to Julie? She's the best thing that ever happened to you."

"No, she's not. You and she are the best things from my past, but Vee—she is everything else."

Peter jerked his hands away from Val, his green eyes turning flinty.

"I've heard enough," he said as he stood, veering toward the red door.

"Please stay, it's not what you think." Val's next words stopped him cold. "Vee's dead, Peter."

Pale as a. . . well, a Vee, apparently. Peter sputtered, "D-dead? No longer with us? As in a pine box?"

Val nodded.

"You dropped the most wonderful woman in all of God's creation for. . . a corpse?"

Val frowned. "It's not necrophilia—she's not even a ghost, precisely."

"If she isn't living, and she isn't a ghost, then what is she? Precisely."

"She's like me, but the dead version of it. Just as I live in our world but can see dead people, she exists on the other side but can see the living."

Peter's solid legs turned to tree sap, refusing to stand. He collapsed back into his chair, thankful for its wooden embrace that continued to obey the natural laws.

Val ached for Peter, hunched and nonresponsive over the table. He longed to put his arms around his friend and comfort him, help him absorb this new reality, but recognized his childhood companion's convictions could not allow it. Recalling a sermon his uncle had preached a few months back about the four Greek words for love— *storge, eros, phileo,* and *agape*—Val realized he had been blessed with all of them in his short life. *Storge,* or familiar love, with his uncle, aunt, and mother. *Eros* with Julie in their passionate romance. With Peter he shared *phileo,* for just as King David had loved his enemy's eldest son, Jonathan, Val loved Peter as he loved himself. And now, of course, with Vee he knew love without condition or limit: *agape.*

The Cook began gesticulating eagerly from her countertop perch, presaging a busy Blanche deluging into her domain.

Taking in her disheartened houseguest, she cast one accusatory look at her nephew before enveloping Peter in an affectionate, if yeasty, hug. "Oh honey," she said, raising his chin with her small, plump hand, "we're so glad you're here. Have you eaten? You look half-starved. Let me get you some sustenance." She patted his back before moving toward her enormous pantry. "I think I have everything in to make your favorite." She turned on her prized wood-fired oven, special-ordered from Italy. "Val doesn't eat much, but I know what all those huge muscles on you need. A real meal. I'll just go out to the garden and pick some fresh basil for your pizza." She departed in the same whirlwind with which she entered.

Peter peeked over at Val, smiling despite himself. "She does command the room, doesn't she?"

"You know she won't tolerate it if you don't eat at least one whole pizza by yourself, and then they'll want you to stay with us. She was probably upstairs preparing the guest bedroom while we spoke." Val sat down across from Peter, hesitant.

Peter held his hands up and out, signaling defeat. "Well, I can't say no to pizza."

The Cook clapped with glee.

ELEVEN

"By the pricking of my thumbs, something wicked this way comes."
—*Macbeth, attributed to William Shakespeare*

Julie walked like other people ran.

Determined, she walked through the campground, blind to the sugar maple and beech trees around her competing fiercely for their own little piece of sky.

Her day had been an abysmal failure. Besides discovering Eastern Michigan was quite possibly the perfect college, the college she now wished she would be attending in the fall, she'd found no trace of Val's mystery girl during her day on campus.

It didn't help she'd come across some of the nicest human beings she'd ever met. Some of the most friendly, cheerful, give-a-guy-the-shirt-off-your-back folks had looked up endless information for her, checked records, escorted her high and low, answered all her questions, and just generally made her feel like a dirty snoop in comparison.

Without a doubt, they hadn't known they'd been aiding Julie. They thought they were assisting Sebastian, a young Black man interested in finding out more about the university's Africology and African American Studies program. She'd taken her shredded hair to get a professional haircut yesterday afternoon, and now she sported a stylish fade with twisted curls. She'd always admired girls with ultra short pixie cuts, and she rocked this new look. Without qualm, her new acquaintances accepted she was an eighteen-year-old male, albeit a dainty one.

And yet, nothing. Although a sprinkling of people knew of Val and his uncle, no one knew anything about a romantic love interest.

It was like this girl was a ghost.

Julie had spent the last few hours growing increasingly disgruntled as she trudged the streets of Ypsi. Finally within eyesight of the cozy cabin she'd rented for the week, she couldn't wait to take a much-needed hot shower and wash off her losses, hoping Peter had fared better.

Iago shared in Julie's aggravation. Just as she had failed to attain her prize, so Iago had futilely sifted through the myriad shades cluttering the college campus, at last forced to admit defeat.

It preferred its metal clockwork vault to these broken shells of T. S. Elliot's requiem for the hollow men.

If only Julie were dead. Her spirit's spunk and resourcefulness, so like Iago's own resilience, would make a comfortable Penumbral eternity.

Maybe it could kill her?

As Julie walked by assorted tents and RVs set up for sleep, the odors of campfires and dinner preparations assailed her. Picking up her pace, she almost made it back to her cabin door without disruption, when she was forced to notice she had unfortunate new neighbors: A dilapidated camper trailer pulled by an even older Ford pickup truck was parked in the campsite next to her cabin, blocking the entrance to her front door with their open tailgate.

The travel trailer itself was the most conspicuous, and quite possibly flammable, contraption she'd seen in her life. Covered with blinking holiday lights, many of them in need of replacement, the walls were graffitied with slogans such as "Love Wagon," "Tarot Cards Read," and "Your Future Revealed." There was a huge image of a hand with an eye in its palm painted on the right side that made her distinctly uncomfortable, and even more bizarre was the elaborate cross defaced with gaudy primary colors next to the green pentagram encased within a red heart on the left. To top it all off, a glittering yin-yang circle was nailed above the trailer's doorframe.

It looked like Christmas had thrown up all over the New Age

movement.

The door under the yin-yang opened to reveal hanging plastic opalescent beads concealing the interior of the caravan. From between this wall of beads emerged a man wearing a ratty ponytail, cargo shorts, and grimy bare feet.

"Om Shanti," he said with a convivial smile upon seeing her gaping at him, "peace be with you."

"Um. . . hi, I guess."

"Do you need some help?"

Speechless, she glared at the tailgate barrier in front of her cabin door.

His deep tan flushed as he apologized, "Oops! Sorry about that."

He didn't move like he was sorry. He moseyed up to the tailgate and deftly flipped it upward with a loud clunk, remaining within her personal space as he turned to her—reeking of cloves, incense, and insolence—to say, "There, all fixed. Anything else I can do for you, miss?"

Her cunning disguise hadn't duped him.

Just then the tallest woman Julie had ever laid eyes on appeared within the beaded drape. She stooped to avoid striking her head on the door jamb, tawdry plastic fragments smashing against each other in an almost melodic jangle. Swathed from head to be-ringed toes in many shades of purple, it took her a moment to stand her considerably elongated frame erect. At full stature, she looked like the Queen of Sheba—she would bow to no man, whether king or husband.

Majestic, she pivoted to regard the short, leathery man and Julie. Her Junoesque face seemed to transform, smiling in welcome as she said, "Greetings, my dear. A pleasure to meet such a bright spirit. What brings you to our home?"

Befuddled, Julie eyed the campsite, reluctant to concede this vehicular mashup could be anyone's residence.

Unfazed by Julie's reticence, the woman persisted, "Appearances can be deceiving, poppet. You've already met my partner, Benjamin, but please allow me to introduce myself. I am Madame Westcott, but you may call me Madame. And I am making the acquaintance of. . . ?" She paused, dramatically.

A war raged within Julie's breast. Actually, just above and beneath them. Her good upbringing and common sense told her to run as fast as she could in the opposite direction from these weirdos, but a much more determined Iago—who had learned from its unfortunate incident with William Lilly never to underestimate the power of fortune-tellers—zeroed in, prying open her lips to say, "Julie Williams, ma'am. I mean, Madame."

"Ah, of course you are." Madame strolled toward Julie, concern etching her ageless face. "Come closer, lamb. Madame can discern your heart is troubled. Your soul is weary. You need guidance." Stopping just beyond Julie, she decreed too loudly, "The spirits have brought you to me, and I—I shall deliver you!"

Her taloned hand shot out to clutch Julie's wrist, who first cowered and then acquiesced as Madame dragged her toward the mystifying bead divide.

Past the plastic veil, to her astonishment Julie discovered ordinary, if shabby, domesticity. Most noteworthy was a mottled chessboard arranged on a neatly-made bed. The chess pieces themselves were unusual, larger than normal and sculpted to resemble animal-headed Egyptian gods.

Mythology had been Julie's favorite subject in English class. Other kids made fun of it, saying they were just stupid stories made up by dead people, but to Julie each myth revealed something of the civilization who believed it. She knew the entire Egyptian pantheon by heart, and especially admired the goddess Isis for her resolve to do whatever she had to in order to bring the man she loved back from the dead.

The squares of the chessboard were oddly partitioned into brightly-colored triangles. Quite pretty, really. Julie loved themed chess sets. Competitive by nature, she enjoyed all board games, but chess was by far her favorite. It was one of the numerous interests she'd shared with Val, who'd been president of the Chess Club in high school himself. Many of their dates concluded with one of them soundly hammering the other, first in chess and afterward between her silken sheets, on top of and underneath the brocade duvet her mother insisted she display on her bed.

Her parents were so clueless.

Madame motioned for her to be seated in a common camper-style booth and put a kettle of water on the stove. Placing two delicate teacups, one chipped, on the tabletop, she asked, "Would you prefer your tea black or white?"

Not sure what white tea was, Julie shrugged.

"Black, then—to suit the dark energies that surround you."

Julie began fidgeting with the pendant on the necklace Val had given her. Usually, white comments about black energies bothered her, but disconcerted by Madame's own dark eyes that missed nothing, she was pretty sure they had nothing to do with the color of her skin.

Once Madame poured the boiling water over the black teabag she had meticulously positioned in Julie's cup to steep, she sat down counter to the young woman, pushing her own unused cup aside. Next, Madame placed a sizable stack of playing cards, black with a crimson symbol on each, before the girl.

Julie began to tremble.

Madame shuffled the cards, fanning them across the middle of the table.

"Choose a card for each person you wish to know more about, speaking that person's name aloud as you turn the card over."

Tentative, Julie chose her first card from the center of the line.

"Val." She said without hesitation.

Turning the card over, an intriguing image made entirely of gold on a black background presented itself: A man with an alarming head reminiscent of the Creature from the Black Lagoon, wearing a lop-sided crown, sat enthroned with a goblet in one hand and a fish in the other. Words were printed at the bottom of the card; she supposed it was the card's title.

Iago couldn't believe its luck. It would know that fish-faced follower of Dagon anywhere.

"The King of Cups. This is the man you love," Madame said matter-of-factly.

Julie's cat eyes opened wide, then narrowed. She examined first the card, then Madame, closely, not knowing quite what to think.

"Choose the next card, please."

This time, Julie took over a minute to make her selection. This card was to signify herself, and she didn't want to make any mistakes. At last, she reached a bit off-center, choosing a card and saying, "Me."

This card pictured a young angel on a mountaintop, clouds behind her, holding up a medieval sword. She liked this card.

Iago choked down a derisive snort.

"The Princess of Swords—no surprise there," said Madame, "Next, please."

Three full minutes passed as Julie studied the back of every single card, until at last she chose one card from the far left, and turned it over.

It displayed a demonic queen, awful in her beauty, sitting on a throne and grasping a wooden staff in one hand with a skull super imposed upon a flower in the other.

Iago couldn't contain its jubilation, triggering an inappropriate smirk to cross Julie's face in response—it had finally found its mark.

Julie stared at the abhorrent figure.

"And this is. . . ?"

"I. . . I don't know her name." Julie admitted, ashamed.

Madame sighed. "Well, she is the Queen of Wands. Any more to choose, or shall we continue with the tarot reading?"

Tarot. Julie had heard the word before, of course, but had never actually seen a tarot deck. Peter would be against it, she was sure. Val would have shared her curiosity.

Peter! She had completely forgotten him.

"There's one more." Haphazard, she took a card from the right. "Peter," she said as she turned the card over, "my best friend."

A bald man sat astride a dark horse, holding up a golden disc. Madame picked up the card, intent in her evaluation. "The Prince of Pentacles," she said under her breath. "Poor fool."

Madame commenced with picking up the unused fanned cards and reshuffled them. She cut the pile three times, then laid three additional cards on each of the original four Julie had picked.

With a renewed diligence, Julie and Iago read the foreign phrases at the bottom of each new card.

On the King of Cups, Madame put the Four of Wands, Ace of Cups, and Three of Wands.

To Julie's card, she added the Five of Pentacles, Seven of Swords, and Three of Swords.

With the Queen of Wands, she joined the Two of Cups, Four of Swords, and Ten of Cups.

The lone Prince received the Seven of Pentacles, Two of Pentacles, and Three of Cups.

Without emotion, Madame pronounced her verdict. "Your beloved has fallen for another. There are complications. You have come here to win him back. Your friend is in love with you."

Julie, now a genuine convert, hung upon Madame's every word. Iago respected that, the medium's eccentricities aside, this was the real deal. It had to tread carefully now, giving Julie just the right amount of truth in a form that could be coaxed toward its own aims.

"This is all what you know," Madame said, picking up the idle stack of cards and handing them to Julie. "Now, let us find out what you do not know. Please shuffle the remaining cards, choose ten at random, and hand the ones you choose to me."

Julie shuffled with attention, picked ten cards off the top of the deck, and gave them to Madame as though consulting the Oracle at Delphi.

Unnaturally still, Madame shut her eyes. When she finally opened them, her gaze cut through Julie as though the room was real but Julie was not, saying, "May the cards guide you through what is, revealing what is not, what might be, and what shall be."

Turning over the first card, she began, "Seven of Cups: This is you, right now. You pretend minor matters have great significance to avoid painful consequences. Jealousy. A dangerous partnership."

With the mention of a "dangerous partnership," Iago realized this tarot reading could go south quite quickly. Reshaping Julie's perception of what she heard to its own liking, it chanted into Julie's heart over and over, "Val is in danger, this girl is dangerous for him. Val is in danger; this girl is dangerous. Val. Danger."

Madame shot bolt upright in her seat, as though stung by a wasp. Fervid, she visually searched the room, sensing a threat. At last, her eyes zeroed in on Julie's necklace, still being toyed with by nervous hands.

Iago buried itself deep into Julie's pendant clock, trying to make itself as undetectable as possible.

Wary, Madame shook herself, squinting as she massaged the bridge of her nose between thumb and forefinger.

After the lull had extended a few minutes, Julie gently nudged the elbow of Madame's elevated arm and asked, "Madame. . . are you okay?"

Madame opened her eyes, but her gaze settled below Julie's own.

"The spirits wish me to continue. But I must warn you to listen to my words, not your own impulses." Resettling herself, Madame turned over the next card and said, "The Judgment. This crosses you."

To Julie's dismay, the illustration depicted a dreadful mass of whirling tentacles with one evil eye ascending from the heavens to destroy the main street of a small town. A monstrous hand reached from the darkness below the town to join in the carnage.

Madame recoiled as well. "Beware. Someone you cannot trust works behind the scenes to bring ruin. The past must not be resurrected."

Iago murmured, "Beware—she destroys your past."

"The Lovers," Madame said, "is your next card. It is reversed, showing your internal focus, what matters to you. You want the love you've lost, for it makes you feel worthy." She turned another card, exposing a man that hung upside down from a tree branch, dressed only in pajamas and one tattered bedroom slipper. "The Hanged Man is over you. Your love has a secret. The dream that you choose to inhabit is but a small part of the whole truth."

This wasn't so bad, even Julie had her own secrets, but the figure on the next card seemed sad, and a little lonely. A Lancelot-type knight with bowed head stood on a hilltop staring at what looked like a mess of spilled cups.

"The Five of Cups reversed is what brought you here. This is heartbreak and general loss of pleasure. To avoid pain, this knight embarks upon a quest to find the false holy grail, not realizing there are two standing cups behind him."

Madame turned the next three cards in quick succession, as though rushing to the end: the World, the Devil, and the Tower. To Julie, each progressive image was more disturbing than the last.

"The World reversed bodes well for you, even though you don't appreciate it. However, the Devil upright reminds you that you cannot trust yourself or your instincts. You are possessed." Madame shuddered, revolted. "It covets, but it doesn't want you."

Iago observed Julie closely. The girl often surprised it with her intelligence, but in this she persisted with the self-consumed idiocy unique to humanity. "He doesn't want you... You're not good enough..." Iago droned throughout her self-absorbed heart.

"The Tower upright reveals what's above, beyond your control." Through Julie's eyes, Iago identified a huge Sauron-like eye raining fire and brimstone upon a tower of biblical proportions, the Lord of the Rings crashing the Tower of Babel on a tarot card. Madame intoned, "This is a crisis of initiation for you all, a baptism by fire. All must be annihilated, especially your lies, if you are to live. Be prepared, for a battle is coming."

The next card astounded even Iago. "The Emperor," Madame predicted, "he lies in wait." Unmistakably, inexplicably, inescapably, a facsimile of Iago's Master from ages past perched atop a pile of human bones, wearing a gilded crown. Behind his cruel Master were drawn assorted constellations in the night sky, its home world of Betelgeuse shining brightest among the stars next to the black hole in Sagittarius, hiding the necropolis of the Great Old Ones' initial incursion into this material playing field.

It was Iago's turn to shiver, the pendant itself quivering in response.

Madame grabbed the quavering pendant in her left hand, squeezing it as she shouted, "He has the power, but you are caught up in a war that started long, long ago. You cannot be passive—act now, or he will win."

Calming herself, with deliberation Madame flipped the final card with her right hand.

"The Wheel of Fortune. This is the end of the matter, the conclusion that cannot be avoided but for which you must prepare. Only when you embrace what is not, can you enjoy the fullness of what is. Stop grieving for the emptiness of being but one. Go into the void rather than avoiding the dark."

It seemed to Iago as though this message was far beyond the scope of Julie's trivial trashed romance. What did the witch really see? Exactly for whom was this reading intended?

Madame dropped the pendant as though it burned her. Standing, she shifted her frame far away as possible from a mute Julie.

"The spirits have spoken," she said, brusque and dismissive. "It is time for you to return to your own abode." She swept up the tarot cards, leaving only the Queen of Wands lying face up on the table.

That's when Iago remembered the chess set.

TWELVE

"Look he's winding up the watch of his wit; by and by it will strike."
—*The Tempest*, attributed to William Shakespeare

Called Rosicrucian Chess by those who wanted to seem orthodox, and Enochian Chess by those who preferred to give the finger to orthodoxy, Iago's initial encounter with Madame Westcott's queer strategy game was when Val's great-great-grandmother Lola brought a handmade version of the chess game into her bridegroom Frank Hill's home upon their marriage. Although the couple purposely distanced themselves from her infamous father, a nefarious magician whom Iago had had the infinite misfortune to never meet, Lola's father had crafted the chess set himself as a primer for the occult upon initiation into the mystery society known as the Golden Dawn at the turn of the nineteen century.

After Frank gave Lola the watch pendant as a wedding present that, unbeknownst to her, caged a chafing Iago, it was such a fine piece of jewelry and a grand family heirloom that she only wore it for special occasions. Most of her lifetime, Iago was relegated to the back of her hope chest, a large cedar box that contained a meager inheritance from her scandalous father and the pieces of a past she'd sooner forget.

The watch pendant was carefully wrapped in a silk handkerchief and laid behind a stack of *Weird Tales* magazines, mysteriously collected and preserved by Lola's father, which Iago read during its decades in the hope chest out of sheer boredom. Most of the stories were pure rubbish, of course, but Iago soon discovered a peculiar young writer, one "H. P. Lovecraft," whose dark stories were clearly inspired by Iago's Master of old.

Distraught by the implications of such a prophet, Iago turned to the disregarded chess set so neatly packed away next to the magazines of doom and its pendant of internment. Goaded by the horrific visions of Lovecraft, it began to interpret the robust resonant vibrations emanating from the chess set's boards (for there were four different boards rather than only one) and pieces, eventually recollecting the game's fragmented memories to learn, not only the unusual rules for the game, but even more importantly its supernatural potentials as well.

Iago required that medium's chess set.

Its chance came the following morning—after Julie slept through the night in a cadaverous stupor that illuminated her body's ill response to Madame's distressing tarot reading the evening before—when Peter, naïve to the prior day's upsetting portents, knocked upon her cabin door.

Iago had wished to rouse Julie hours ago, but had, quite disquieted by its perplexing choice, constrained this impulse, uncharacteristic concern for her melancholy curbing its own revitalized jubilance in unearthing its Penumbra, the Queen of Wands. Sluggish, Julie stumbled the short distance from sleeping bag to door. When she spotted Peter on the other side bearing two venti caramel macchiatos from Starbucks, she could have kissed him. He also brought freshly baked apple scones, straight from Blanche's kitchen. They smelled like the Garden of Eden.

And so, the serpent struck.

Once the two were seated with their makeshift banquet at the unstable cabin table that wobbled like a skittish Weeble, Peter took a long sip of sugared espresso, sighed with contentment, and said, "That's an interesting eyesore you've got parked next door."

Julie gripped her paper coffee cup tighter, brown knuckles going ashen. "About that. . . " a distinct tremor could be heard in her usually hearty voice. ". . .something happened yesterday."

"I've got news, too."

She removed the slouchy beanie she'd slept in when the coffee began to warm her insides. Peter's eyes swelled, threatening to pop out of his face.

"Your hair! You. . . you look like. . . like a boy." Too late, he composed his misbehaving eyeballs.

"That was the idea, remember? Not that it deceived them . . . , " she trailed off, licking her lips.

"Deceived whom?"

"The f-freaks next door." Her stutter betrayed the fear underlying her typical moxie.

"Tell me."

This was going to take forever, so to avoid this particular forever and go about making the one Iago wanted, it took control of Julie's mouth. "My neighbors have something I want, but I'll need your help to get it."

It was Peter's turn to go pale. "You mean. . . take it?"

"Trust me, you can't take anything from them," she said, "but I suspect we might be able to buy it from them. I think they need money—I mean, just look at that monstrosity they're living in."

"What do you want to buy from them?"

"It's a chess set. The coolest chess set I've seen in my entire life." Iagojulie paused, calculating, then asked, "Would you get it for me? Pleeease?" Iago added some wheedle to Julie's tone, for effect, as it encouraged her to reach her supple hand across the table to ever-so-lightly trace Peter's rough one. "It could be my birthday and Christmas present all together."

A low moan escaped Peter's partly opened lips. "I've only got a couple of hundred dollars on me—do you think it will be enough?"

"It'll have to be."

Peter took out his wallet, removed the bills, and offered them to her.

"No, I can't talk to them again," she demurred. "I'll wait here."

Uneasy, he stood and walked outside, closing the door behind him.

He relaxed on the porch, pausing a moment to inhale the sylvan scent of the forest surrounding the cabin. The trees seemed to reach for him, calling him away from the troubles of his two friends, beckoning him to forget them and lose himself in their wooded wonder beyond the cares and travails of humanity. Not for the first time, Peter wished he could merge with the wonder of it all, losing himself in the grandness of something greater, for he was so very weary of the solo smallness of being but one.

Pressing his lips together and quickening his stride, Peter steeled himself to ignore this longing and reorient upon the task Julie had given him.

Wary, he knocked on the already-dented door as he contemplated the glistering yin-yang above his head.

"Just a mo!" A masculine voice yelled from the interior. "Gotta get my bottoms on."

Peter had no idea what to do with that.

The door opened, and a bare-chested wrinkled leprechaun popped his head out from behind a spray of rainbow bubbles. "You need somethin', buddy?"

Peter cleared his throat. "I have a business proposition for you, sir."

Green board shorts materialized, attached to the hairy chest as well as naked feet. "I'm listenin'," he said. "What'cha got for me?"

"My friend from the connecting campsite—I believe you've met, uh. . . her?"

The leprechaun just stared up at him.

"So, um, she says you have a chess set, and uh. . . I'd like to buy it from you."

"You want to buy my chess set."

"Yes."

"My only chess set."

"Um. . . yes?"

"Well sir, it's going to cost you."

"I've brought ca-ash?" Peter asserted, embarrassed as his voice broke on the last word.

The little man looked at him as though he could see right through him. "I don't need your money."

Unsure what to do next, Peter asked, "Is there something else I can give you?"

"I want your word."

"You want my word."

"*Haan.*"

"I'm sorry?"

"That's yes in Hindi. Yes, I want your word."

Peter was at a loss. "What word do you want exactly, sir?"

"I want you to give me your word that when all this is over, you will bed that girl and never look back."

"You want me to sleep with. . . Julie?"

"I'm speaking clear English to you now, son." And for the first time the fey man smiled. "I want you to throw yourself into doing what's best for you, for the first time in your life."

"I can't do that, sir."

"Oh, you can't do that."

"No, sir. I could only do that if she wanted it, too."

Two remarkably young eyes, hidden in all those folds and furrows, regarded Peter with sympathy.

"If you give me your word, when she tells you she wants it, you'll take her and make her your own right there and then, come hell or high water the consequences, I will give you my chess set."

Peter had no idea how to respond to this pervert.

But he had promised Julie he'd acquire the chess set.

"All right, I give you my word."

The man disappeared into the bowels of the trailer home for a moment, to return with a huge pitch-black box.

"Just make sure you never play it alone," he warned, "and don't you never tell my missus!" he added before slamming the trailer door in Peter's aghast face.

Clutching the dark box, Peter made his half-hearted walk of triumph back toward Julie's cabin. A stray maple leaf, too eager for autumn, gently alighted on his shoulder, spooking him in his guilt.

Peter realized it was shame he felt. Shame, because a good man didn't make a pledge he knew he couldn't keep. Shame, because a righteous man didn't capitalize on another's misfortune. Shame, because an honorable man didn't want his best friend's gal.

Shame overwhelmed him, filling every space within him because he couldn't stop the wanting.

Girding his wayward feelings, he braced himself to be what Julie needed.

"Knock, knock. Special delivery!"

With an atypical squeal, Julie threw open the door and latched onto the black box, pulling it, and Peter by extension, toward her chest. "You did it! Oh Peter, I knew if anyone could, it would be you. Thank you. Thank you so much!"

Peter stepped away from her perilous appreciation, plopping down at the precarious table. The rickety chair groaned under his weight.

Julie, on the other hand, radiated in her exultation. Iago could have kissed the girl for her genuine excitement, if it had had lips to do so.

For the first time, it occurred to Iago that a kiss might just possibly have an entirely different purpose than its own devices.

Peter couldn't really wrap his mind around why a silly chess set would mean so much to Julie, but his heavy heart instinctively lifted in response to her zeal.

Painstakingly separating the unmarked black lid and placing it on the other chair, Julie began removing the most unusual chess pieces Peter had ever seen.

There appeared to be four sets of identical pieces—king, queen, knight, bishop, rook, and four pawns—each group in yellow, blue, red, and black. Nine pieces in each color, rather than the traditional sixteen in black and white. They were all overtly Egyptian, like hiero-glyphs come to life.

Peter's recurring nightmare of scarabs burrowing into his still-alive body entombed within a rigid sarcophagus scurried before his eyes, flashing him back to his second-grade history class when he first learned about the mummification process. The pawns—which were alike in their vase-like bodies but each with a different head—looked like the eerie photographs of canopic jars excavated from King Tut's tomb, used by the ancient Egyptians to hold the liver, lungs, stomach, and guts of a mummy for the afterlife.

Peter loathed mummies. Why couldn't people just let the dead stay dead?

Julie withdrew the black king, queen, and knight with enthusiasm. "These kings are unmistakably Osiris, with his distinctive crown, and the queens look like Isis. I suspect the knights are their son Horus, but there are others I'll have to research to find out which god or goddess they're supposed to represent." She pulled out an instruction manual the size of a small dictionary, and proceeded to bury her nose in its pages. "This is the perfect way to make up for my dreadful day yesterday."

Peter had never understood Julie's and Val's love of chess. He'd learned the game by association, between hanging out at chess club with Val during lunch and enduring Julie as she belabored the latest chess opening she'd read about to trounce Val. Indoor games of any type eluded Peter's interest. The all-around athlete in high school, from defensive lineman in football, and shortstop in baseball, to small forward in basketball Peter would have spent his entire school year outside if he'd had anything to do with it. He'd kept up his grades, but other than Botany and Spanish he'd basically coasted through his classes, happily settling for a low B average. Val, of course, had effort-lessly been valedictorian, while Julie had worked her butt off to keep up with her boyfriend, studying ten times as much as Val or Peter to barely accomplish her 3.85 GPA.

It was time to stop avoiding the unavoidable. Nothing satisfied Peter more than making Julie happy, but she needed to know about his discussion with Val. The sooner, the better.

Rubbing his too-tight chest and staring down at his well-worn work boots, he ventured, "I got some bad news myself, yesterday."

Julie's head skyrocketed out of her instruction manual. Her fists clenched around the chess book as she demanded, "Well. . . ? Tell me—now."

"Although I haven't met her yet, Val told me about his new. . . um, attachment. Her name is Vee, and he believes himself to be very much in love with her."

Julie reared backward as though shot. She swallowed, hard, her eyes convulsing. For a split second, Peter thought he saw someone else peering at him through Julie's splayed irises.

And he didn't much like what he saw there.

Tossing aside the chess manual that had given her such pleasure just moments before, Julie picked up the pendant she wore around her neck and began grappling with it, almost as if her hands struggled against themselves—her right hand to rip off the pendant and her left to cradle it close—until she finally yanked the necklace over her head and hurled it away from herself as though it was a venomous rattlesnake about to bite.

Peter caught it without thinking.

"How can he have forgotten me—forgotten us? How can he have replaced me so soon?" She crumpled to the floor in despondent tears.

Peter kneeled beside her and slipped a gentle arm around her shoulder. "He's not himself right now. He's changed, somehow. . . " Peter shifted his cramped legs, attempting to find a more stable position for supporting both himself and Julie, along with the scorned necklace. "But I know we haven't lost—not yet."

A long sob, and then silence. The cessation scared him more than the crying.

"Give me one more chance to talk some sense into him. Let me speak with his uncle, maybe even meet this girl, if I can. . . figure out what's really behind this rash decision."

Julie looked up at him, all hope gone. Peter feared Val's personal metamorphosis was going to alter her too, but in the wrong direction: From a gorgeous butterfly into a comatose caterpillar.

"I think. . . " Her voice wavered as she bit her lip. "I think I would like to meet her, this not-Julie but more-Val."

The watch pendant Peter clasped in his hand captured his attention and gave him an idea. "Let me take this necklace to him and tell him you're here." She covered her shorn head with her hands at his suggestion. "Let me give him back your necklace, tell him you're returning it to him since he doesn't want to be with you anymore. Maybe the necklace will shock him into realizing what he's losing." He slipped the chain over his own neck, hiding the effeminate pendulum beneath his shirt. "Let me talk to him again, first. . . to give you time to gather your own strength so you can confront him yourself."

Numbly, Julie nodded. Peter knew he was running out of space and time. Something had altered, going from not-quite good to most-definitely bad, but he couldn't quite put his finger on it.

Iago reached from the watch pendant for Peter's beating heart.

THIRTEEN

"What light is light, if Silvia be not seen? . . . She is my essence."
—*Two Gentlemen of Verona, attributed to William Shakespeare*

Vee hadn't been what most would have considered a pretty girl when alive, but Val didn't care.

It was part of her charm.

Although he had seen her assume different shapes during their evolving intimacy, she still gravitated back to a facsimile of her seventeen-year-old body, with bushy hair, too-short bangs, and spectacles. The eyeglasses particularly enchanted him in their uselessness, for when she seemed to recall they were there at all, she would fiddle with the bridge and nose pads as though they still pinched her not-nose, even occasionally taking them off and "cleaning" them in a habitual manner until she herself realized the inanity of this habit and impudently poked her not-fingers through their not-lenses with a breathless giggle.

She also seemed to have a love affair with books, even though she couldn't lift them or turn the pages. Val favored the extensive library available on his e-reader to the limitation of a physical book, but Vee scoffed at what she called his "ghost of a book."

Perhaps he preferred ghosts.

She'd even taken to floating instead of standing or sitting of late, which had been disconcerting initially, but he'd grown to love this idiosyncrasy as well. With Julie, he'd always had to force himself to overlook the little things that irked him or that he didn't understand, but with Vee, the little things—what others might call quirks or flaws—only endeared her to him further, for their distinct assemblage were what made her solely herself.

Val spent much of his inner life sorting out the measure of his own soul. He knew he wasn't perfect, never would be, and he felt it acutely. He had no desire to pursue goodness the way his uncle chose, nor did the love of all things natural satisfy him like it did Peter. Julie's passion, ambition, and self-consciousness remained unrivaled only by his own, but her single-minded chasing after what would never be had ultimately alienated him. As Val spent more and more time discoursing with the deceased, he was forced to confront his own terrible similarities: the same futile urges to deny what he didn't wish to be, justify his choices and the choices of those he loved, take what he wanted, and destroy what he shunned. The only way to contain his own capacity for harm was to be honest with himself and speak what he knew to be true when communicating with others. . . and when he wasn't ready to speak his truth, at least write the full extent of it down on paper.

Conversations with the dead will do this to a man—age him beyond his years, give him agonizing wisdom and awareness of the end with which few are willing to contend. It's a hidden blessing that most people don't recall other lives or existence outside of a body. For Val knew as surely as he breathed his next breath that death was not release, the material world was not the cause of a spirit's suffering, and humanity brought hell with them into and out of their sojourns within this world. Hell resides within humanity, for we are the ones who wish things were other than as they are.

Of course, it was this same endless aspiration for *more* that spurred humanity's imagination, creation, invention, and art—so Val would still have it no other way, regardless of the feculence that seemed humanity's legacy.

It's what comes of everyone being so full of shit.

Caught in a shitstorm of her own making, Vee was entangled in a vise of her own vices. She painstakingly and somewhat mercilessly ripped away at V after V with a single-minded preoccupation that perplexed Val. Her Vs, although on occasion annoying and impertinent, were theatrical in a way that appealed to his temperament. But Vee hated her Vs, simultaneously mystified and horrified by their very existence, yearning above all else to extricate herself from their dark influence.

That was it: If Val was desire, then Vee was longing. If Val was the struggle of a person to contain and rise above personal dissatisfaction with the lack inherent in living and dying, then Vee was the message who reviled itself for voicing the void that everyone wishes to avoid. Both found themselves set apart in disparate ways—Val from humanity, with his painful awareness of heaven and hell constantly battling for dominance in the species, and Vee from her very self, as she was so busy looking through everything that she lost the capacity to accomplish what mattered most.

He surrounded by the dying; she besieged by what won't die.

And so, each inhabited a penumbral twilight only understood by the other; she became his harbor in the unbearable lightness of being, and he her anchor in her torrent of shadows.

As dusk engulfed them both in the old red barn, she floated next to where he had propped himself up against a couple of bales of hay, reading Shakespeare together while Val sipped a mug of coffee. They had just finished *Richard III*; she read aloud the female parts and he the male—with the exception of King Richard himself, whose part Vee read as though her death depended on it—spurring heated debate over what constitutes evil and whether its conclusion was inevitable.

"You're wrong. King Richard had every opportunity imaginable to amend his ways." Vee radiated like the sun as she spoke, her corona turning a distinctive shade of pink when she got excited—about anything. "I mean really, the ghosts of eleven dead uncles the night before the battle wasn't enough of a hint? Oracular dreams? Hellhounds? There are more supernatural warnings and references in this play than in *Hamlet* and *Macbeth* put together! He had choice point after choice point, and he still chose the worst possible outcome every single time."

"I beg to differ. This guy was cursed from the beginning to be evil. There's no destiny here, just fate. All these supernatural events don't offer him an actual choice, they form a grotesque motif to further reinforce his doom. When someone's this far gone, there's no way out. He and his reign are innately evil, and everything that happens—including all the supernatural stuff—is just a reflection of the landscape of his depraved internal reality. The guy's sick and twisted on the inside, and so not only does he attract sick and twisted things to himself, but he alters those around him and his own kingdom to reflect his inner sick and twisted universe. Richard's England is reshaped by his own expectations."

Vee did something she'd never done before—not that doing new things was an unusual occurrence with Vee—and diffused: Extending centrifugally, she lost her human form entirely, encompassing not only Val, but spreading outward to contain the entire barn itself. Like a cool mist touching every part of him, inside and out, she both chilled and soothed him in her expanse.

Val waited, knowing her well enough to recognize she needed some distance.

After a few minutes, she contracted back down to her mortal silhouette as ethereal letter Vs in every shape and size surrounded her, tickling her face and poking her here and there.

But it was the not-smile opening her face like a springtime sunrise that spellbound Val. Only then did he realize that he'd only ever seen her smile once before, in a dream.

"Sorry about that," she said, swishing a particularly annoying letter V away from her not-face with her not-hand. "Sometimes I need to outside myself to see inside a viewpoint, especially on this side. The more All I become, the less I am, but it's the only way I've found to get muchier."

Val fell in love with her just a little bit more.

Sheepish, she continued, "All of a sudden, dissecting *Richard III* with you, I realized I felt happy. Truly happy. I've never been happy—

well, not actually happy—that I can remember. The closest thing to happiness I've known are brief moments of not-sad, not-suffering, not-scared. . . with my mom, when reading, watching a particularly uninhibited sunset. . . Happiness is a fragile story we tell ourselves to live with the mounting fear of the impending doom that frames our lives like a malignant tumor, a passing emotion we mythologize and make last through the contrived search for meaning." Vee sighed, her not-smile falling away from her face like the last leaf from a mighty oak, piercing Val with an aching poignancy as he mourned its passing. "The truth is that there is no meaning of life, nothing lasts, collapse is inevitable, and now, of course, I've seen that even death is a rather unpleasant lie, too."

Smiling wistfully himself, Val said, "I wish you all the joy that you can wish."

"Have you seen *The Matrix*?" Vee asked out of nowhere.

"Sure, who hasn't? It's a seminal movie."

"I've often thought that the Oracle from the *Matrix* movies is a more optimistic reimagination of H. P. Lovecraft's character Yog-so-thoth. You know, the Old One who sees all and guards the gate between worlds."

"I don't think I've read as much Lovecraft as you have, I tend to prefer some comedy with my tragedy." He paused, his eyes sparkling as he tipped his head back to gaze at the rafters above them. "I guess I can see the possibility. But what in the world does Lovecraft have to do with *Richard III* and *The Matrix*?"

"Do you remember that scene in *The Matrix Reloaded* between the Oracle and Neo, when she tells him the reason he cannot see whether Trinity lives or dies is because he can't see past a choice when he doesn't understand why he's made that choice?"

"A movie moment that changed me forever."

She looked at him as one dream to another, parting her not-lips instinctively as she leaned toward him and whispered, "I am Neo."

Val looked her flushed shimmering coalescence up and down,

admiration bubbling over his transitory boundary called "skin," and whispered back, "As am I."

They entered the void conceived by their joint affirmations, alternating between pervading one another and being still together, beside space or time rather than inside or out of it, within the joint eternity they'd created within each other.

Eventually, out of breath and absolutely sated by their merging, Val picked up *Richard III* and asked, "Have you met Shakespeare among all the spirits on your side?"

Vee seemed disturbed by the question. "Actually, no. And I've encountered basically every historical personage I've ever dreamed of meeting Here except the Bard. I've even had conversations with some of his fictional characters, but still no Will Shakespeare."

Val did a double-take. "Fictional characters? How can you have a conversation with a fictional character?"

"I'm constantly amazed, when I consider all the things I've learned from you, how the gravitational pull of a body within the physical universe forces you toward the tangible. Plato's right. The senses are obstructions to communing with higher spiritual beings and one's true self." Enlarged not-pupils and parted not-lips displayed her fondness, even if her words left him feeling vexed. "More to the point, I even asked the prince of darkness why I couldn't find Shakespeare, but he only smiled his Cheshire Cat grin and told me I'd find him when I was 'ready to see him.' What an intensely irksome mentor he can be at times."

Val found himself averting his eyes from the distant stare in her own, still uneasy at mention of the prince. He changed the subject. "Did I tell you there's going to be a costume party at EMU after freshman Move-In week?"

"A back-to-school masquerade ball? How fun for you."

"Do you want to go with me?"

She looked at him in disbelief, unsure how to respond. "You do know, as an incorporeal spirit, I can't really 'go' with you to a college party? I can assume any form, of course, but only you'll see me. And I can't mingle, or nosh, or make small talk. No one can perceive me but you."

He chuckled, "Sounds like the perfect date to me—I get you all to myself the entire evening. No competition."

She made as if to take a swipe at him, her disembodied not-hand dissolving right through his solid shoulder.

"No seriously, why not come? I can guarantee there will be spirits littered about the campus, especially McKenny Hall where they're hosting the get-together. Unlike you, I've spent my whole life going to school parties and dances, aware of all the ghosts and ghoulies about. It will be a nice change to go with someone who can see what I see." He sat up straight, mustering the courage to make his next suggestion. "In fact, I think it's high time to make some decisions together about my move to the EMU residence halls next week. I want you to come to college with me." He sped up as he saw her skeptical frown. "I realize we can't live together in the traditional sense, but I'd like to be partners in higher learning—attend the classes and lectures that interest us and treat my room as yours, too. Let's dissect the meaning of the universe and everything until the wee hours of the morning. You deserve the university experiences you lost out on because you died so young."

Vee didn't respond, except to gasp.

She tended to lose her ability to speak when put on the spot.

Then the not-tears began to leak from her not-eyes. "I never attended a dance, or a costume party, or even visited a college campus before I-I. . . died." Was that a spectral hiccup he heard?

He opened his arms, inviting her to join him in the embrace they'd honed over their time together: She wrapped her ectoplasm around his head and torso, and he followed her effusion by hugging his upper body with his own arms. It seemed to him she became the space between his very cells; she said he became the only time she had left.

"You're going to love my costume," she sighed.

"It's easy to have an amazing costume when you can shape-shift at will," he murmured into her not-hair.

Their shared bliss was interrupted by an uncertain, single knock.

"Duke. . ." Val said, ". . .s'that you?"

"It's me." Val would know Peter's voice anywhere, specifically when augmented through a cedar door. Wood loved Peter like Jesus loved the world. If only the world had loved Jesus as much as Peter loved wood back.

"Come in," Val called, standing.

"He has such a sweet spirit," Vee said as she floated away from Val and toward Peter, "but he's so conflicted."

His best friend slid open the barn door and closed it behind him with an unyielding slam that seemed strange to Val.

Peter was different. Of course, last time they spoke, Val had noticed subtle changes, mostly for the better; this new transformation, how-ever, was not a positive one. There was something behind his too-in-tense eyes, an air about his rigid shoulders, that made Val want to both embrace his best friend and avoid him at the same time. Even Vee seemed to shrink somewhat, turning from pink to a dark crimson, as though huddling into herself in anticipation of danger.

This was not shaping up to be the first meeting he had envisioned between the two great loves of his life.

Peter spoke first, an uncharacteristic gruffness to his tone as he clenched and unclenched his burly fists, "I have something to say, and you're going to shut up and listen to all of it."

"As you wish." Val relaxed his posture, letting his arms hang slack at his sides, in direct contrast to the tightly strung bow before him.

"Julie's in town. She's staying in a cabin nearby, and you're going to see her." Peter reached under the neckline of his T-shirt, pulling out the watch pendant Val had given to Julie what seemed lifetimes ago. Holding up the token for Val to see, Peter continued, "She also asked me to return the necklace you gave her, since it's your family heirloom and all. She doesn't feel she has the right to keep it if she's not going to be a part of your family someday." He started to remove the necklace, but Val's next words stopped him cold.

"I don't want the necklace, and I won't accept it. It was a gift, a symbol of what we shared, and it can never be returned as it once was. Now it represents something else, and it is hers and hers alone." Val spoke flatly, emotionless to Peter's volatility.

"What you shared—exactly. You love Julie. Not some dead girl who, frankly, should stay dead with her own kind. Admit it—and give up this insanity. Seeing ghosts is one thing, but you've started down the path to madness now, and I love you too much not to put an end to it."

It was Val's turn to counter with intensity. "I'm sorry you and Julie have traveled all this way to change me, but my mind is made up. I love Vee, and although I wish only good things for Julie, she's not my soul's match. She needs to move on with her life, not erect a false effigy to what we once shared. Stop encouraging her to reshape the memory of our relationship into her own fucking golden calf!"

Peter and Vee gaped at Val. Neither had ever heard him swear before. Since Peter seemed to have lost the ability to speak, Vee interjected, "Maybe it's time to introduce him to your succubus?"

Val gave Vee a wry look at her choice of words, but he knew she was right. Taking a deep, measured breath to calm himself, he turned to Peter as he swept his arm toward the hovering Vee. "Peter, I'd like you to meet someone."

Peter's face went the color of an overcooked hardboiled egg. "You mean her? She's here. . . now? She was here for all of that?"

"Peter, this is Vee." It looked as if Peter stopped breathing, his eyes going a ghastly shade of puke green. "And Vee, this is my best friend, Peter," he said to what seemed to Peter just a patch of empty space, above and to the right of him.

"It's a pleasure to finally meet you, Peter," said Vee. "I've heard so much about you."

"She says it's a pleasure to finally meet the person she's heard so much about," Val translated.

Recovering his manners at last, Peter stammered, "The puh-pleasure is all mu-mine, miss." He bowed, hoping he wasn't being too formal for his first time meeting a ghost. Especially this ghost.

"She's a little further down and to your right, pal." Val said, "But she's turning a rather extraordinary shade of pink, which is a really good sign."

Peter tried to hide his scowl as he said, "Julie's favorite color is pink."

"And if she'd been able to meet Vee, I'm sure the two would've been fast friends," Val said, "but this shade of pink is for you, not Julie or even me."

Vee blurted, "Oh, he's such a gentleman. Are all the guys from Merced such gentlemen? And look how much he wants to dislike me, out of loyalty to her, but wants to please me at the same time. How sweet." Unbeknownst to Peter, she swooped down so close she was right next to him. If she'd had a body, they would have been touching. "There's something wonky about his soul, though. Like World War III is raging at the heart of his well-muscled physique."

Val's blue eyes blurred his own greenish tint as he said, "It's tough to be a devout disciple when you find yourself plunked smack in the middle of enemy territory. Especially when the enemy keeps telling you how muscled you are. . . " he laughed at himself as he added, ". . . I think I need to start going to the gym."

Vee turned such a hot shade of pink she was almost fuchsia. "I can admire his frame, but it's not the frame that makes a child's drawing into art. You, my love, are a masterpiece."

Val turned an ever-so-light shade of pink himself.

"Uh, Val?" Peter began. "Are you both still with me?"

Val inclined his glowing face back toward his friend, "Sorry about that. Sometimes I forget you can't hear what she's saying. She. . . uh. . . she says she likes you and thinks you have big muscles—which I might add have grown inconsiderately larger since high school—but you seem burdened by something."

Until this point Iago had been viewing the ping-pong match of wills between the two man-boys with gusto—only wishing it had a big tub of hot buttered popcorn to munch as it watched—rather than paying much attention to what they were actually saying in their puerile exchange. But when the fair-haired boy mentioned his imperceptible ghostfriend, Iago realized that Peter was at last meeting its long-sought-for Queen of Wands: This spirit, whom the boy called "Vee."

Intriguing. Iago couldn't see Vee the way it did other ghosts. Perhaps it perceived the faintest iridescence, occasionally, as though a ray of sunlight momentarily flashed through a sagging cloud for the briefest of instants—but then back to nothing, all over again. Yet in these ephemeral moments, it sensed the smothering power of darkness simmering in between the tantalizing flickers.

This Queen was nothing like the others. This was something else, utterly. Astonishingly. Opportunely.

Penumbrally.

Acting fast to direct the confrontation toward its own intended ends, Iago interceded, wielding Peter's vocal chords with such finesse Peter thought it was he himself speaking. "The only battle I'm fighting is the one you've manufactured for me. What you're doing is against nature, and no matter how right it feels to you both, you know God doesn't want you to throw your life away like this. Either you meet with Julie, or I'm telling your uncle. Everything."

The threat appeared to only strengthen Val's resolve. "I will not waste one minute of Julie's or my own precious time," he said, intractable. "Not if you talk to my uncle, not even for you."

The stalemate between Peter and Val became palpable, forming a ravine that could not be crossed, even by their powerful bond.

Vee glided closer to Val, offering him otherworldly comfort that, although imperceptible to his senses, was sensual, nonetheless.

Peter and Iago watched Val slowly reach his hand upward to clasp at nothing, but what they missed with Peter's eyes, they both felt keenly in Val's tender look. "You complete me," he said to thin air. "You are my essence."

"And you are my substance." Vee said.

Torn by Val's poignant scene, Peter doubled down. "She might make you happy, but that doesn't make it right."

It occurred to Vee that she, Val, and Peter were the exact same distance from one another, forming a perfect equilateral triangle.

FOURTEEN

"Weaving spiders, come not here,
Hence, you long legged spinners, hence!"
—*A Midsummer Night's Dream, attributed to*
William Shakespeare

Julie lazed in her sleeping bag, reading the last few pages of the instruction manual for her new chess set. She couldn't recall the last time she'd relaxed like this, just let herself go.

There was so much more to this new game of chess than she'd imagined. Made for four players who worked in teams of two, rather than two single opponents facing off one against the other, this game was as much of a mashup as the home of its prior owners. Game play originated from the ancient Hindu chess game called *Chaturanga*, and instead of one board with black-and-white squares it contained four distinct chess boards, one for each of the four classical Greek alchemical elements: red fire, blue water, yellow air, and black earth. To start, players set up their Egyptian-themed chess pieces in the "lesser angles" in each of the four outermost corners of the board, rather than along two opposing sides with teammates seated counter to each other as in normal chess.

There was also a strange white piece, half the size of the others yet much heavier, carved from some sort of white stone. Called the "Ptah," this little stand-alone had something to do with using the chess set like a deck of tarot cards. Julie skipped this section of the rules, as she had no intention to dally in divination ever again.

The instruction manual recommended that new players begin play with the earth board. Julie's least favorite was the air board, and the fire board both attracted and repelled her in equal measure. She didn't really understand how to play with the board attributed to water, which made her wish to master this first, even though it would probably challenge her the most—just as Val had always challenged her.

The living water who animated her dead days.

For as long as she could remember, Val had served as the source of inspiration in her life. His superiority in nearly everything he put his hand to drove her to strive for excellence. His insightful mind provoked her to develop her own. His willingness to tackle uncomfortable topics and discuss unpopular truths caused her to be more honest. And the fact that, out of all the women in the world, he'd chosen her to love, obliged her to trust she was worthy of love.

But now he'd stopped loving her, and she didn't know what to be without him at the center of her life.

She knew Peter thought he loved her, knew he'd basically worshipped the ground she walked on since the ninth grade, but his love was like the amorphous love of God preached to her from the pulpit every Sunday—a gift she didn't deserve or do anything to earn, and so she took it for granted. Peter was her place of rest, the one who thought she was perfect even when she was at her worst, but what kind of person would she be if she chose to love a man like Peter?

Chose to believe in a love that brought out the worst instead of the best in her?

She laid the chess book down and noticed a fat black spider scuttling across the cabin crossbeam. It froze, as though it had a sixth sense about her sudden attention, trying to make itself as inconspicuous as possible. Spiders never bothered her the way they seemed to bother everyone else. Most of the time she felt sorry for them, really: So tiny in a huge world that didn't want them around, not appreciated at all for leaving webs to be walked through or disposing of what bugs us. This black one probably had to labor like Hercules to blend into the cabin's light pine timber planks; no wonder its kind tended to hide in the dark and come out at night. Spiders weren't evil, just misunderstood.

You really couldn't fault spiders for biting you when you nearly squash them with your unconscious appendages. If hope and fire were the divine gifts to humanity, the god of spiders blessed its followers with venom and shadow.

Taught from birth God the Father was goodness and love—and was light-skinned, of course—Julie felt deep down there was something wrong with her, more Arachne than Absolute, a woman with black skin who didn't blend well with this bleached world that nailed the son of man to a tree and called him savior.

Without Val's radiance to orbit around, did she deserve salvation at all? With all this venom and shadow within her, how could she ever be worthy of an adoration like Peter's?

She had to escape these man-made walls.

Julie threw off her sleeping bag and bolted outside the cabin. She was trapped in between two truths: the always-just-beyond-her-fingertips edifice of light she spent every waking moment reaching for and the eight-legged shadow she tamped down into her blood-red core.

No matter how hard she struggled, she couldn't escape this web of betweenness. She was cursed to be neither good nor bad, neither true nor false, neither hero nor villain, yet forever know who she could be, if or what she might do. If only.

Life was one big nothingness of free-falling in between.

She stood frozen in the endless yearning. When at last she noticed Peter approaching on the horizon, it was as though a giant fist released her only to smash her flat. She rubbed her hand through her shaved hair, not sure if she was thankful or mortified.

He waved, backed by a thick copse of red oak, relieved to see her.

She hated how much she needed him, needed other people to assure herself she was good enough.

When he reached her, he engulfed her in an embrace that felt desperate. Ambivalent, she hugged him back.

"I'm so glad to see you," he said, searching her eyes with an intensity at odds with his usual affability. "It didn't go well."

She took two deep breaths, one to let go and one to steady herself, before looking directly into his conflicted eyes and saying, "I'm ready."

"I met her. Vee."

Unruffled, she asked, "Is she pretty?"

"Is she. . . what? Who cares?"

"Everybody cares. We all say looks don't matter, but it's the knockouts that get the guys like Val."

"It doesn't matter what she looks like, but there's no way she's as gorgeous as you are."

A small part of her was grateful for his kind words, as biased as she knew them to be. "Did you give him the necklace?"

"He wouldn't take it."

Surprised to discover her lack of surprise, she asked, "What's she like?"

Pursing his lips, he said, "She's like nothing I've ever seen before. She was friendly enough, but she's no good for him."

He was hiding something, but what? "How do you know? How do you know she's not meant for him?"

"Trust me, she's all kinds of wrong for him."

"Can I meet her? Will Val see me?"

Shoulders curling forward and chest caving inward, Peter hung his head and whispered, "No."

No. What power one of the smallest words in the English language had to change a life forever. Her own shoulders sagged under the weight of his refusal.

Scalding anger startled her. Not a "poor me" rant, or fury at a girl she'd never met, not because Val rejected her or she wanted him back, but because he didn't have the proper decency to tell her to her face, give her the closure she deserved.

He broke up with her through an email, for Christ's sake.

She deserved more than this from him. He owed her.

"I'm alone," she said the unfamiliar words aloud to herself. They felt stiff, yet unexpectedly powerful: like a pair of skin-tight leather leggings. "It's really just me."

"You're never alone," Peter assured her, "I'm here. I'll always be here when you need me."

"I think my need may be part of the problem. At least, my belief about what I need. . . and what Val doesn't."

That's when she remembered the costume party at Eastern Michigan University. The back-to-school costume party that the perky twenty-something resident advisor she'd met in campus living—the RA whom she suspected had a bit of a crush on Sebastian—had gushed about when giving Juliesebastian the promotion flyer. The costume party all new campus residents were required to attend. Indifferent, Julie had stuffed the neon orange paper somewhere amongst the application paperwork. Now, she tromped back into the cabin, grabbed her backpack, and pulled out the crinkled flyer from the folder, fluttering it in front of Peter.

"If he doesn't want to see me, he can tell me to my face. I'm sick of following his rules. You and I are crashing this costume party at his school this Friday, and he is going to confront what he's lost."

Iago missed Julie. Discomfited by the foreign emotions surging through its new host, it reached out and urged Peter to speculate he knew exactly how much Val was losing—and for what? A phantom. A cold, dead disembodied wraith that wasn't even human anymore. Val was very much alive, yet he chose death as his mate. Never had Peter doubted Val's judgment in their decade of friendship as he doubted it now. Never had he questioned Val's paranormal sensitivity, but he questioned it now.

This lifeless mockery of a relationship must never be.

Both delighted with its own success and impressed with the girl's proto-Machiavellian manipulations toward her own ends, Iago realized it naturally resonated on a much deeper level with Julie than it did with Peter. Without its influence, its prior womanish host was using her wit and wiles to effectively accomplish her own ends for herself.

How quickly they grow.

Unlike Julie, this Peter fellow presented an unanticipated obstacle. His core vibrated to a contradictory rhythm other than Iago's own, one that—for a second time—made Iago want to rip Julie's face off and throw it at him.

Well, maybe someone else's face. Julie's face suited her so well.

But first, it would use this masquerade to drive Peter to the very edge of his morality. Then Iago would shatter him and use the pieces to capture his quarry.

For how does one violate a knight in shining armor's sacrosanct code of chivalry? By warping that very code to violate another, of course.

FIFTEEN

"God has given you one face, and you make yourself another."
—*Hamlet, attributed to William Shakespeare*

The entryway to McKenny Hall stood apart, an imposing white building rising from between the overextended brown-brick walls sandwiching it on either side. The gorgeous geometric stained-glass window above their heads entranced Peter, second only to the lush trees and other foliage he pointed out to Julie over and over as they walked from the parking lot with a group of dressed-up students drifting in its general direction.

Peter was as impressed with Eastern Michigan University as Julie herself had been during her previous incognito visit as Sebastian, although for different reasons. Peter loved the nature, but Julie had quite possibly found her people. At least, what might have been her people.

Dressed head to foot in a furry black dog's costume, Julie realized she once more wore a different face than her true one on this campus. At least this time everyone around her joined in her lie. Peter walked beside her, shifting and awkward in his donkey costume, still peeved none of the others at the costume shop would fit over his ginormous muscles.

Sympathetic, she reached up and tweaked his long ear. "Stop fussing, you look cute."

"I look like an ass. Literally, an ass."

"Calm down. We won't be here long. I just need to find Val, get him alone, and reason with him."

"Reason and love keep little company together."

"Oh, my god, really? That ass's head might be going to your own—maybe you should take it off."

Without hesitation Peter removed the donkey head and hid it as much as he could under his arm. With his sweaty, messed-up hair, now he looked like Bigfoot, but Julie had to admit it was a marked improvement.

McKenny Hall was a model environment for a social gathering, the school sparing no expense for the party tonight. Large and well-lit, the walls were plastered with green-and-white decorations in school colors. Its elevated oval stage exhibited, amongst a collection of small tables advertising various activities and clubs, a larger-than-life "Swoop," the eagle-headed mascot so popular at EMU sporting events. Dressed-up students from all walks of life chatted and munched, enthusiastic to meet potential classmates and begin the new school year.

For the last time, Julie allowed herself to wish she could be a part of Val's world. The last time.

The two split up, wandering the packed hall apart in hopes of finding their target faster. The costumes made their search trickier, but they knew Val's height would eventually give him away.

Iago spied Val first in a distant partially-concealed corner, grinning at nothing as he sipped his characteristic cup of coffee. It directed Peter's attention toward the solitary form costumed in what looked a lot like the eagle head of the school mascot, only darker.

"What are you supposed to be?" Peter asked as an ice-breaker. "A dirty Swoop?"

Taken by surprise, Val laughed, almost choking on his coffee. Once he recovered, he placed the lip of his paper coffee cup between his teeth, held out his arms as though flying, and said, "I soar! I am a hawk." Looking his friend up and down, he continued, "And you are... the headless donkey?"

Then he looked back up at the Nothing, grinned again, and said, "Vee wants to know if Puck cast a spell on you, Nick Bottom."

Grumbling, Peter said, "Oh, so she's here, is she?" Scrambling for small talk, he asked, "Did she come in costume, too?"

"Why yes, old chap. She looks simply ravishing as a sparkling red bird, which she tells me is a Scarlet Ibis, inspired by the story of the same name by her good friend, James Hurst."

Peter just stared at him. "James Hurst. The deceased author. Really."

That's when Julie found them. The bird of prey and the Bigfoot, continuing their relationship without her.

Tapping Val on the shoulder, she forced herself to speak. "Hello Val," her words came out soft and husky despite herself. "Long time no see."

Val choked again on his coffee, this time gasping for breath.

"Ju-Julie," he faltered as he turned to face her, giving Peter the stink eye, "how. . . um, nice of you to join us."

Peter raised his eyebrows, inspecting the ceiling innocently. Something unfamiliar tickled at Iago's peripheries and slowly spread throughout its meager being; an alien warmth stupefied Iago as it saw its past protégé at long last confront her ex-lover. If it hadn't known any better, it would have called the feeling "pride" in a human.

A feeling? Was it possible Iago had just felt something? Something uniquely its own?

"Grrr. . . " Julie said as she raised her big black paws in mock attack stance, "Since I am a dog, beware my fangs."

A blank look on his face, Val stared at her as though listening to something she couldn't hear, shook himself with a quick wink at the empty space to his left, and said, "So little terrier, do you wish to speak?"

She nodded, shock making her mute.

"Give me one minute to give my supposed best friend his stage directions, then we can find a bench outside, away from the crowd. The moon is lovely tonight."

Putting his be-feathered arm around Peter's fuzzy shoulder, with a set jaw Val ushered Peter a few feet away and whispered, "I see you would force my hand, dear friend. So be it. As Vee reminded me just a few minutes before you arrived, 'there's a knot of cruelty by the stream of love.'"

Peter opened his mouth to speak, only to have Val place his finger in front of it and murmur, "Shush. You've set the stage, and now it's my turn to act upon it. Wait here." Val marched over to Julie, reticent yet gentle as he took her wrist and led her out of McKenny Hall.

The two walked hand in hand, into the darkness.

Adrift and unsure what to do while he waited, Peter glanced at the empty space Val had only just finished engaging, wondering if he could perceive even the faintest glimmer of the ghost girl who had so bewitched Val.

Nothing. Just a whole lot of nothing.

Restless, Peter cast about the room, wondering if the food was worth investigating.

That's when Iago saw Him.

The Man stood alone in the undead center of the room, surveying the party. His image flickered, caught somewhere between There and Nowhere. Dressed entirely in Mardi Gras motley, with an extravagant sequined octopus's head atop his unseen features and small, stunted, green bat wings peeking out at abnormal angles from his back, the Master's cephalopod eyes zeroed in on the center of Peter's chest, sharpened onto Iago, and took a single step toward its host.

Not knowing how or why, only knowing he was filled with a mortal terror so all-consuming he would have killed to elude it, Peter found himself running faster than he had ever run in his entire life, reckless and panting, out of the nearest exit and into the unknown night.

SIXTEEN

"Sweet lord, you play me false.
No, my dear'st love, I would not for the world."
—*The Tempest, attributed to William Shakespeare*

There was so much water.

Water was scarce in California. Sure, the famous beaches had water, but you couldn't drink it in, couldn't make it a part of you. Only the insanely rich enjoyed California's scenic water on a daily basis anyway—the rest of the Californians visited it on weekends or for vacations, but it didn't form the milieu of their lives. California was, after all, a natural desert.

Val had always loved water, it didn't matter if it was fresh or salt. He'd find rivers and lakes like an expert treasure hunter, willing to drive hundreds of miles just to spend a few hours sitting in silence or fishing companionably with Peter. During summer breaks in high school, the three of them made the pilgrimage to Monterey in Julie's pink Volkswagen bug, often staying overnight at Pfeiffer or Limekiln Campground. Julie was a sun-worshipper who loved putting on her skimpy bikini and lathering up to bask on the sand. Peter immersed himself in surfing and bodyboarding as he frolicked in abandon with the waves, but Val would inevitably set off on his own with his compass and leather-bound journal in hand, seeking out the most secluded patch where the water met the earth. When queried as to what he did during his prolonged hours of solitude, he insisted he communed with the naiads and the kelpies. He'd find Julie and Peter again, just after sunset, to either start preparations for the evening meal at their campsite or begin the long trek homeward to Merced.

Loving Val had been like loving the ocean. Beautiful and life-affirming, but also tempestuous and mystifying. And you never felt quite safe because you could never see to the bottom of it.

Julie sat beside Val, close but not touching on a sea of grass by the EMU student center, next to a lake so dark in the silvery moonlight that it almost seemed carved out of obsidian glass. With just enough light emanating from the streetlamps on the walkway behind them— so they could see each other's faces, but not so much they felt exposed—it was the right place to at last have "the talk."

Julie wondered why, now that she was finally getting what she thought she wanted, did she wish to avoid it so acutely?

Too-warm and stifled, without thinking she reached up and slipped the shaggy dog's head off her perspiring scalp to reveal the nothingness that replaced her once-abundant curls.

When Val glimpsed the void space around Julie, the long hair she had prized so much about herself now wholly rejected, he fathomed for the first time what he had to do, though he wasn't sure how he was going to do it.

"You've cut your hair. It suits you."

Julie harrumphed in self-deprecation, meeting his eyes with candor. "I only cut it to get you back."

It was Val's turn to harrumph. "I'm fond of change, but only for oneself."

Julie's nostrils flared as she retorted, "That's easy for the person with all the power in a relationship to say. But when you're the one receiving the back end of someone else's change, you're only left to pick up the pieces. Powerless."

"I know it feels that way, but in every relationship, we really only ever have two choices: to stay or to go. The power just comes from being the one to instigate the change."

"We had a good thing, and you threw it away like it meant nothing to you."

"We had a good thing, past tense. Yes. But if we'd stayed together, it wouldn't have continued to be so good."

"How can you say such a thing? How do you know?"

"I can only speak for myself, but the part of me that was in love with you grew up."

Julie gasped. "Grew up? Why, you self-righteous prick!"

"I am a little self-righteous. And you're a little angry."

Julie wanted to hit him. She wanted to smack that self-righteous smirk right off his fine-looking face.

"I deserve better than this. We deserve better than this."

"I agree. Our break up brings the best possible outcome for all involved."

Checkmated, Julie tried another approach. "What if you gave us one more chance? I could move to Michigan, attend college with you for a year, and we could try to make things work. Maybe the grown-up you and the grown-up me are still meant to be."

"I've considered that, actually. But we're too different, and you need to find your own way, not follow in my shadow. You deserve more than that."

Checkmated again. Dang, but this king was a slippery bastard.

Julie threw out all the stops. "Is she prettier than me?"

Scrubbing a hand over his face, drained by her question, Val answered, "Not even close. You're still the most beautiful woman I've ever known. But that doesn't change a thing."

There it was, that ugly word "change" again. Julie didn't like it. She didn't like endings. Things deserved to continue, not dwindle or die, becoming no-thing.

She had to avoid the nothingness at all costs.

Lost in her own thoughts, Julie was unprepared for Val's tenderness as he reached out and lifted her chin, bringing her eyes upward to meet his own. She saw the light reflected there, surrounding the darkness of his pupils, and she realized that before she could ever get what she wanted, she needed to accept what is.

That's when the tears came, more water pouring out than she

knew she had within her. "But I gave you everything," she admitted in a small, brittle voice. "All of me. . . " She closed her eyes as though afraid of his answer. "What's wrong with me? Why wasn't I. . . enough?"

Val chose his next words more carefully than he'd chosen any in his entire life. "There's nothing wrong with you. You were perfect. Are perfect. Perfectly you in every way, which is more than anyone can ask for."

"But she's more perfect. . . for you?"

Val knew the time had come. "There's something you need to know, something I've hidden from you for far too long. Something that makes Vee perfect for me, but in no way makes you any less perfect." Seeing the confusion in her eyes, he plunged headlong into the unknown, "I see ghosts. Always have. I can see and talk to them, and they're everywhere. Death shapes the subtext of my life."

Julie's streaming tears ebbed with Val's next words. "Vee is a ghost."

She watched him, leery. Was he teasing her?

That's when she saw that his hands were trembling.

Perplexed, then dismayed, then upset in rapid succession, her volatile reactions at last settled upon sympathy. Sympathy and relief.

This explained so much.

And yet, Julie found herself waiting. . . for something. For that mounting dread, that hollow ache that had made its home at her core—that paranoid pressure that caused the small hairs at the nape of her neck to prickle in defiance, reminding her daily of her string of failures and missteps. It had infested the quietest part of her heart for so long, she had begun to think it her true self censuring her.

Silent, at last.

How long had she been denying her own ghosts?

"Vee is a ghost." She repeated the foreign words out loud for herself. "Vee is a ghost, and I am alive. She is dead. You are in love with a dead girl."

Then the obvious hit her smack in the face, and she had to ask. Had to voice the pivotal question that at the same time seemed impossible. "But if she's a ghost, how can you be in a relationship with her? Why would you do that to yourself? What about. . . well, what about sex?"

Contrary to her obsession with the importance of her own beauty, Val had always valued Julie's bluntness more than anything else about her. He tried to explain what he feared was inexplicable. "Sex isn't simply sex, at least not for me. Not anymore. At first, it was the great taboo, the fumblings of my yearning to find release—an end to my search for the fulfillment of having a body and satisfying its constant demands and desires."

She looked away, crestfallen, but he persevered. "I found that with you, and initially you and I sought it again and again, and it was good. So good. In you, I found the meaning of physical love. Through you, I learned what it means to be a man." He reached up to lightly caress her dark cheek. "Your sweetness, your softness, your hills and valleys, the way your passion met mine stroke for stroke. Our intimate moments pleased me so completely, they freed me to seek that walking shadow our mutual sexual exploration would never truly yield: Myself."

She finally met his eyes, questioning, unsure if she could trust his meaning. He continued, "If it had not been so very good between you and me, if I had felt I'd failed to please you, or if I'd believed sex was somehow dirty or wrong, I probably would have been like most everyone else, wasting my twenties and maybe even my thirties searching for some idealized romantic relationship or worse, the degraded cycle of ever-cheaper conquest with the next tantalizing stranger."

He held her chin with both hands, his gaze penetrating hers. "But you saved me. Because of you, because of what we shared, I'm done seeking significance in those around me. But in her, I've found the completion that only comes from being unapologetically myself. You were never the problem in our relationship, I was."

For the first time since his email, Julie felt like she could breathe again. "But what if I don't want what we've shared to end?" she asked.

"Everything ends. Everything changes. I'm grateful for what we had, but in Vee, I've found what I didn't know I always wanted, and she's become the space that's my home."

"But what about marriage? And children?"

"If I wanted those things, you're probably the person I would've wanted to have them with. Right now, I don't."

"But how can you live without sex? Your body has needs, everyone's does. Isn't what you're doing. . . unnatural?"

Val's eyes twinkled. "That's exactly what I asked myself when I began to realize the depth of my feelings for Vee. But there's unnatural, and then there's supernatural. Now I see there's sex, there's sexuality, and then there's making love."

"I don't understand."

Unhurried and sure of himself now, he continued, "Sex is natural, animal, beautiful in its simplicity, but it's all about physical reproduction, about making a baby, which I don't want to do. Sexuality, now that's completely different."

Then he sighed as though he released all the troubles of the world in one, single exhale. "Sexuality's also about reproduction, but it's the process of conceiving and giving birth to myself and Vee as we become each other. It can be given and received without any physical touch. I immerse myself in her; she pervades me. We explore the beauty we discover—together."

A private half-smile lifted his cheek. "Pleasure isn't just physical, you know."

"Okay, maybe. But are you really satisfied?"

"I was raised to think sexuality can only be fulfilled by sex, and more to the point only by a woman. I've watched those around me become trapped within their own heads and obsessed with the thwarted expression of their sexuality, elevating the sex act itself to the highest expression of humanity or else debasing it to the lowest expression of depravity. But sex is just sex, like the need to eat or drink, the hunger for it comes and goes and is as uncomplicated as taking a bite."

"But your body will eventually need to, umm. . . take a bite again, won't it?"

"I've no doubt of it. And when that comes, Vee and I will figure it out—together. There are so many endless possibilities when making love."

Julie had always liked having sex with Val. It satisfied an ache within her she had no idea how else to fulfill. But now she found herself wondering if she'd ever actually made love?

"Making love isn't physical, it's spiritual. Sure, spirits with bodies use sex to do this, but the bodies aren't necessary. The capacity to make love doesn't die just because our bodies die," he grinned with a contentment that made the muscles in Julie's stomach bunch up. "With Vee, I end to begin anew."

A small group of costumed revelers interrupted their seclusion, swaying down the walkway behind them and cackling as they hollered at each other, "It's after midnight! Time to get home before we turn into pumpkins!"

At last, Julie understood. Val hadn't rejected her, he'd found himself. She wanted to find herself, too, but not with Val. At least, not with the image that she'd painted in her mind of what she needed Val to be.

She could allow their fairy tale to end, for in this ending she was finally free of the never-ending Cinderella story that had fashioned the glass slipper she'd harbored her entire life: The belief that if you are saved by an imaginary prince, you will escape the nothing at the end.

The almighty was her beginning, not her limit. Light was an option, not a condemnation.

For the beauty of a story is not that it never ends, but that it is only within the dark nothingness of endings you can begin anew.

And Julie was, blessedly, dark.

SEVENTEEN

"Oh, she doth teach the torches to burn bright!"
—*Romeo and Juliet, attributed to William Shakespeare*

Peter was drowning.

Most people think you can only drown in water, but drowning in darkness is by far the more painful way to go. Water kills by stealing your breath, by infiltrating your lungs and suffocating your cells until you lose the rhythm of life, but most of us don't fear the water until our heads go under, and those who have almost drowned describe a strange pervading peace once the panic of drowning subsides and they accept their watery end.

Fear of the dark—of what you can't see or don't know, of what is out of your control—will kill your soul while you're still alive.

Darkness drowned Peter as he ran from McKenny Hall to the cabin, racing through miles and miles of pitch blackness to reach the woman he loved so much.

Julie's cabin door was wide open.

When Peter showed up at her doorstep just over three hours after she and Val had last seen him at the party—now doubled over and drenched with sweat—he found her packed up and in the middle of writing a letter at her cabin table, which was incidentally wobbly no longer. Julie had brought in a beech tree branch from outside that was the spot-on height and width to prop up the table so that it, finally, stood flush and secure.

He watched her fold up the piece of paper she'd just signed, place the note in an envelope, lick the back to close with care, and write a name on its cover.

The envelope was addressed to him.

So, Julie was leaving.

Leaving in the middle of the night without even waiting to say goodbye.

The nameless dread that had driven Peter to run just over 18 miles without a second thought evaporated, replaced by one he knew all too well.

Julie handed him the envelope, softened features skirting a cheeky grin.

"Nice of you to show up," she said as she stretched her supple arms upward, arching like a sable cat, honey eyes twinkling.

"What's this?" he said, indicating the envelope in his stiff, out-stretched hand.

"I didn't know if I'd see you before my ride got here, so I wrote you a note." Humming as she hefted up her backpack and sleeping bag, she offered him the keys to the rental car. "You'll be needing these now. I've scheduled a transport to the Detroit Airport."

"Don't be silly, I'll take you."

"No, you won't. It's time I take care of myself for a change, and perhaps more important, it's time you take care of you." She shifted under the new weight on her shoulders. "Besides, you and Val have some healing to do."

"So, you're going back to California."

"Yup."

"Alone."

"I am."

"And Val. . . ?"

"Is staying here to go to college. With Vee."

"And this is okay now because. . . ?"

"She's dead."

"Because she's dead."

Julie lifted her hand almost sadly to cup Peter's chiseled jaw, gazing intently into the depths of his wooded eyes. "You know she's dead, Peter. I'm sure Val told you—he tells you everything. I've been the outsider to your fraternity for four years, watching from the sidelines as you've known Val in ways I never could. You've always been his person, not me." She dropped her hand with finality.

His cheek branded by her brief caress, Peter's world seemed to slow down, as though they were underwater. Haltingly, he asked, "How can you be okay with all of this?"

Glancing at her wristwatch, Julie motioned for Peter to sit and joined him on the other side of the table. The only thing out of place was the conspicuous black box of the chess set, lying on the middle of the table between them.

"I've got maybe fifteen minutes before the shuttle service gets here. That's why, when you didn't answer my phone calls or texts for the past hour, I finally decided to write you this letter. No—" she put her hand on his own as he went to break the seal, "don't read it now. Let's talk until I have to go, and you can read it later. There are things that must be said."

She took a drawn-out breath as her small hand massaged his strong one for a moment, and began: "I always knew, deep down, Val was beyond me." She held up her hand to silence his outraged protest. "Stop. Just stop. Can we please stop pretending I'm meant for Val and you're okay with that?"

Dumbstruck, Peter lost the ability to speak.

He didn't know Iago, having walled itself away within a disconnected abysm of gibbering terror since glimpsing its cruel octopod Master at the party, had begun to rouse itself back into earthly cognizance.

Julie continued, "I don't mean he's better than me. He's beyond me. And I'm tired of reaching for him. Tired of working so hard to be the me I thought he deserved."

The girl's words shocked Iago, stirring unfamiliar and unwelcome feelings within it.

"I think, while he consciously kept his ghosts from me, he unconsciously only ever truly gave himself to you—until this ghost girl. The one person who gets him entirely, even more than you. She makes sense in a way that makes no sense at all."

Peter looked down at her hand, still holding his own. Her tiny, perfect hand that fit so perfectly within his generous one.

His eyes slammed shut, unwilling to look any more.

"For a long time, I told myself that if I could just make Val love me again, everything could be as it was. But that liar inside me never considered what Val needed. . . what Val wanted. All the liar cared about was winning. The truth is, Val left us long before we graduated. And now, it's time for me to stop deceiving myself and find myself, on my own. Find myself within this world birthed by women but forged by men."

Peter couldn't have what she was saying, couldn't quite grasp hold of the portent inside her words. But he knew what a good man should say, and so he said, "What about Val?"

"You're asking the wrong question. What you really mean is, 'What about me?' Or more completely, what about you and me? That's what you really want to know, right?"

And then, she kissed him.

She leaned right into him, over the table she had steadied without his help, positioned her warm brown hands lightly on either side of his dark bronzed biceps, and placed her succulent mouth against his solitary one.

All indecision and self-doubt cast aside, Peter's strong arms captured her lithe ones, planting them around his sturdy neck while he stood, lifting her to his chest as though she weighed nothing. The pleasure that filled him as his lips moved against her own, as their rambling tongues touched and tasted each other's rare and distinctive flavor for the very first time, was the keenest he'd ever known, like prayer personified.

A throaty moan escaped Julie as his hands cupped her on the twin mounds where her thighs met her bottom. She lifted her legs in reply, wrapping them around his chiseled hips, climbing further around him and into their embrace, so neither could tell where one started and the other ceased.

He played upon her as he sculpted wood, igniting her kindling, at last awakening her slumbering fire to burn with its own inner source.

She shared with him her darkness, a heady liquored sip of what might be.

And they saw it was good.

So good.

"Stay," he murmured against her bruised lips. "Don't leave us."

"Oh Peter," she sighed, trailing butterfly kisses up his jawline that ended with an impish nip on his earlobe, "I could never leave you. But just as Val had to leave us to master his ghosts, I need some space away from both of you to find the me that exists outside of us."

"Is there an us?"

"You know there's always been an us, both with Val and apart from him."

"Why now?"

"Choosing Val was a result of everything I thought I was supposed to be. Choosing you just may be the result of choosing who I am."

The mounting heat that had infiltrated Peter's body during his kiss with Julie left Iago vaguely unsettled, trying to fathom its extraordinary reactions. It was as though the fanged mouths of a thousand famished gugs suddenly inverted into simpers and cuddled Iago like monstrous suckling teddy bears. Fucking, now this Iago could understand, and conquest it had mastered, but this diffusing warmth that made it want to melt, this enfeebling desire to disappear within this female, left it feeling like it had been caught with its pants down in a cozy pool of mud.

Vulnerable.

Iago threw itself into the conversation, finding the lone resonance it shared with Peter and distorting it to its own advantage, coaxing Peter to speak the truths bubbling within him rather than continue to feed these disgruntling feelings. "I'm worried about Val. It's not good for him to spend so much time with the dead. I mean, who is this Vee—really? We know nothing about her. How do we know Duke isn't right, that Val isn't being influenced in some way? It's because of Vee that Val has decided what he perceives isn't evil. . . if their relationship is so right, why won't he tell his uncle, the one person in his life whom he respects above all others?"

Surprised that he'd voiced such offensive truths, Peter was even more astonished to realize he agreed with every idea he'd just articulated.

Hushed for a few moments as she traced his broad shoulder with her fingertips, Julie eventually asked, "What about Trudie? Val loves and respects her."

"He loves his mom, sure, but respect? Only as the Bible requires. He's never been able to quite trust her, since his father's abandonment broke her."

"Why did his father leave? I didn't really know him then."

"His father couldn't handle that Val sees ghosts."

Disbelieving, Julie stared at him. "How could a man do that?" She thought of her own father, who stayed and supported her even though he didn't even really *like* her. "How could his father discard them just because his son is. . . special?"

"There's a fine line between special and abnormal, for some. Duke's faith enables him to be open to possibility, but Val's dad always seemed painfully common to me. Intentionally so."

"So, his mother knows? She's known all this time?" Julie let this sink in a moment. "You and his mother and his uncle and even his father knew, but no one ever thought to tell me?"

"It was Val's truth to tell—not ours."

"What does his mother think?"

"At first, I think she blamed Val for his dad leaving. Then, she started the drinking and partying phase, bringing so many men by the house at all hours of the night, men Val never even met. Eventually, she hooked up with Claude, Val's stepfather—Claude and Val's dad were like brothers before everything went down."

Julie nodded, knowing this part of Val's home life. "You know Val and Claude get on well enough, but they only ever seem cordial, never any real affinity or investment. I think both Claude and his mom were secretly glad when Val decided to go to EMU and move in with his uncle for the summer."

Peter agreed. "I've never understood how they could live for so many years under the same roof and never talk about it. About his dad and why he left. I know Val tried to talk to his mom once, before she got together with Claude, but she fell apart and they haven't spoken of it since."

"How awful to live in a house of make believe."

"Val once told me play-acting comes second nature to him when dealing with the living."

"I can understand his mom, a little. One of the most difficult things in love is to be the one who's left behind."

Peter clasped her closer in concern as he asked, "Are you really okay?"

"Yes. I'm okay. Really. I'm more than okay. I might even be free."

"Free of Val?"

"Val was never a burden, although perhaps I burdened myself with him. I don't regret our time together, but I don't want to be with him that way anymore."

"What do you want?"

"What I want doesn't matter. To need or not to need, that's the question."

"Well then, what do you need?

"I need to go home, while you stay here and resolve things with Val. I need to know you and Val are going to be okay, no matter what the future holds. Most importantly, I need to spend some time by myself if I'm ever going to be able to make space for the possibility of that future including you and me, together."

It was difficult to let her go, but Peter knew she was right. Things had to be set straight in the here and now, before the future could be built. "You're right, I have to stay. I have to make sure Val's going to be okay, to repair the rift that's formed between us—over you."

"I don't think Val would mind us being together."

"It's not that. Of course, he won't mind—he wants us to be happy. It's the way we handled it, what I've hidden from him. And then there's the problem of Vee. It's all standing between us right now, like the walls of Jericho."

"You're going to need more than shouting and a trumpet to bring those walls down."

He and Iago chuckled, Iago caught off guard by the change wrought in this Jezebel. Perhaps all females were not quite the anathema it had once supposed.

Perchance in this particular female, Iago could even begin to see why knights fought dragons and men worked jobs they hated for their entire lives, just so this sort of female could come into her own.

With a satisfied sigh, Julie slipped out of Peter's arms and repositioned her backpack. "I'm not promising anything, but I can say as I learn to love the parts of myself I've been taught to hate, I might be able to accept that you already love them."

Peter knew it was time. He unzipped his still-sopping donkey costume, letting it fall to the floor around him, and reached into the front pocket of the shirt he wore underneath, removing the smooth wooden figure he'd continued to carve in his occasional solitary moments during the past weeks.

He placed the miniature white whale in the palm of Julie's hand. It rested as though it had been created to dwell at the nadir of her heart and life lines.

"Whales were both revered as gods and feared as demons by primitive cultures, but I think they're really just misjudged mammals that live in the water but breathe air, an animal who loves the surface yet's equally comfortable plumbing the depths. Able to live in two worlds—"

She silenced his speech with a lingering kiss. "I love it, really. It's almost perfect."

"Almost?"

"I just have one small favor to ask, if you don't mind. Could you paint it black?"

"You want me to paint it—black?"

With a gleam in her eye, she answered, "Yup. Just like me."

"Nope. Never. Paint hides the wood, covering up the natural beauty of the grain. . . " he trailed off, pondering. "But stain it? Absolutely. Black stain will preserve the inner individuality of its lines while deepening its external expression. Maybe we can even stain it together, when I get back?"

She handed the wooden marvel back to him. "When you get back."

Iago, uncomfortable in its growing regard of this female, compelled Peter to ask for what it needed most before she abandoned them both: "Would you mind leaving the chess set with me?"

She laughed again. Julie had laughed more in this interlude than Peter had seen her laugh in far too long. "I was actually going to ask you to give it to Val. He loves chess so, and I think the part of me that wanted it so badly is gone now." The bright headlights of a vehicle beamed through her cabin window, illuminating them both in each other's arms. She placed the single cabin key, attached to a chunk of wood, on the table, and casually took his hand. Placing the miniature whale in his jeans pocket, he picked up the chess set with his sodden donkey costume in his free hand, then followed her outside as he closed the cabin door behind them.

A man wearing an official-looking cap jumped out of the waiting shuttle. "Julie Williams," he asked, "shuttle service to Detroit Metro Airport?"

She handed him her backpack and sleeping bag. "Yes, thank you."

Giving Peter's hand one last squeeze, she let go, opened the car door, and waved goodbye before disappearing from his sight into the recesses of the back seat. As the shuttle pulled away, Peter climbed into their rental car, dropping Julie's still-sealed letter, the chess set, and the donkey skin into his own back seat. He readied himself for the coming confrontation with Val as he turned the ignition key and began the drive to Hill Manor.

Iago found itself much less willing to accept Julie's desertion. Whatever had possessed her to leave them now, precisely when her help would have proved so valuable in capturing the ghost girl? Iago searched for the word that named its experience: Offended. No, miffed. Yes, it was miffed at her selfish departure. As a result, it must concern itself with far-more-pressing solutions for these paradoxical dilemmas. What was it to do now that the traitorous rook had removed herself from play? And much more ominous to consider was the evil manifestation of its Master from ages past who seemed to somehow have returned at the party—however temporary His emergence—and against all odds, located Iago amongst all the spiritual flotsam and jetsam littering this material menagerie.

Was it possible the stars were, improbable as it might seem, again aright? Or, even more hideous to consider, did He still have followers alive who were deluded enough to summon Him from his dreamless slumber beneath the waters?

Why was He here, and what did He intend for His former thrall— or for any living being on planet Earth, for that matter?

Iago had to escape this mortal plane. It refused to be culled in yet another apocalypse.

EIGHTEEN

"The instruments of darkness tell us truths,
Win us with honest trifles, to betray us
In deepest consequence."
—*Macbeth, attributed to William Shakespeare*

"I am the Alpha and the Omega, the beginning and the ending, saith the Lord, which is, and which was, and which is to come, the Almighty."

Every morning since he had taught himself how to read it, Peter had studied his Bible faithfully and prayed with open eyes to a God he couldn't see, but in whom he chose to believe. This morning was no different, and so before he walked downstairs to face his best friend, Peter turned to the only other genuine friend he'd ever known, the Lord Jesus Christ, for counsel.

Julie's opened letter lay to his right, and he'd laid out his King James Bible open in front of him as he sat at the writing desk in the Hill's best guest bedroom. To his left, a cooling autumn breeze drifted in, the rustling of the fresh changing leaves a siren's call through the wide-open window. Julie's letter, though affectionate, said in no uncertain terms he was to return to her only when he'd patched things up with Val, and Peter was determined to fulfill her wish, regardless of what he wanted.

Not quite trusting himself, he opened his trusted Bible in the hopes the Word of the Lord would give him the guidance he needed.

Believing in what you cannot see might be challenging to some, but Peter begged to differ. Every time you reach out to love others, you choose to believe in them despite a host of secrets hidden inside them you cannot, and probably will never, see. Love takes an immeasurable capacity for faith and an endless willingness to believe, regardless. To Peter, love was an action, not just an emotion, and although feelings might come and go along with the decision to love someone, those sensations were but a barometer of intensity and your own self-centered cravings, never a true north from which to judge your devotion to the one you loved.

For today's quiet time he read from the apostle John's Revelation, the last book in the New Testament. "I am he that liveth, and was dead; and, behold, I am alive for evermore, Amen; and have the keys of hell and of death."

If Jesus had the keys of hell and of death, He knew what to do about Val and Vee, right? Peter just had to listen for the answer.

The end of the chapter mentioned, "The mystery of the seven stars which thou sawest in my right hand, and the seven golden candlesticks."

The Bible was full of numbers and counting, but Peter remembered a sermon he'd heard Val's uncle deliver years ago about the symbolism of numbers in the Bible. The number seven could be literal, but it was often metaphorical, and Duke had preached that in the Bible the number seven commonly indicated wholeness or completion. When Peter hit upon a number repeated in a passage, he usually found God really wanted to emphasize what He was saying or about to say.

Peter continued reading into chapter 2. "Nevertheless, I have somewhat against thee, because thou hast left thy first love. Remember therefore from whence thou art fallen, and repent. . . ."

While Peter knew John wasn't speaking about Val in these verses, and was actually addressing the church of Ephesus, the scripture landed painfully close to home, nevertheless.

As he continued reading into the third and fourth chapters, he was struck with the extremity of the message. Many Bible scholars insisted this book should be taken as allegory, rather than actual, and as he read about all the violent punishments promised in the war between Heaven and Hell, he found himself hoping those scholars were correct.

In chapter 6 he read, "And I looked, and behold a pale horse: and his name that sat on him was Death, and Hell followed with him." Peter had always found the biblical image of the pale rider disconcerting, as though it was light and the pale face who brought death and destruction to humanity, rather than darkness or demons.

He read the last line of chapter 6: "For the great day of his wrath is come; and who shall be able to stand?" He set his Bible aside, exhausted by its ferocious implications.

Meditative, Peter unfastened his beat-up leather prayer journal. Filled with his private reflections of supplications in pencil and ink, these familiar pages were a personal record of the time he spent alone with the Lord. He often found, if the Bible didn't help him, he'd discover God's will while he wrote upon these weathered pages.

Perhaps this was exactly how the book of Revelation was revealed to John, so many years ago. Peter knew the book was originally a letter John wrote from prison, bestowed by God upon John alone.

He took out his favorite pen and began to write.

Iago couldn't believe its good luck.

It had agonized through this unbearable daily Bible compulsion of its host since the girl had transferred its hexed ornament of incarceration upon this stupid twit.

In a moment of diabolical epiphany, Iago hatched a new plan. It would take some ingenuity, but Iago was nothing if not ingenious.

For possession was the game, and lack of self-possession the opening. Whether a being used others as his source of truth or an old book, abdicating oneself as source instigated the opportunity for overthrow.

Encroaching upon Peter's consciousness, Iago employed a trick it had learned aeons ago from the Great Old Ones, a lost skill little known in modern times, except by the fanatical and the occult: Automatic Writing.

As a being of pure energy, Iago altered the basic synchronized electrical pulses of neurons firing in Peter's primate brain, shifting his brainwaves into a relaxed condition that invited outside manipulation. Common among the Pentecostals who speak in tongues and the Vodounists who are mounted by their deities, this impressionable state invites channeling from an outside source, whether benign or malevolent.

Peter's eyes glazed as they fixated on the wall directly in front of him with a vacant expression, and his right hand began writing furiously in his journal, even though he was left-handed.

His left hand knew not what his right hand was doing.

When Peter regained consciousness of himself and his surroundings, the clock on his desktop read 10:02 a.m., almost an hour since he remembered opening his journal to begin writing. Where had the time gone?

He looked down at his open journal, baffled to see the following words written in an unfamiliar hand:

To Peter, the Rock of the Morning Star:

Peace to you and those you love, may you have the grace sufficient to protect them from the coming trial of darkness.

I am the manifestation of the unknowable, but behold! My light shines upon you!

For the time has come, now and in the very future, that the Alpha and the Omega will return, and you must pave the way.

So it was, so shall it be! Amen.

I encircle your neck and fill your heart. My ecstasy shall be yours, my love your love.

To have love, you must follow my love, for I am the fount of love.

The path to love is sevenfold, let my seven lights shew you:

You are the divine agent of my love, but the other knows me not. This other is not as you are—never forget this!

The other is the enemy, an infestation, a dragon to be con-

quered—verily a worm you must crush beneath the wrath of love.

The worm cannot and will not recognize love. Its feelings are delusions—trust it not!

If the worm protests, you must silence the protest, for the other knows not the truth that you know.

The body is but a vessel to be saved by divine will, and your will is aligned with this higher will.

Comprehend this divine truth: one love is very much like another, only you are the difference.

The highest secret to everlasting love is this, my son: You must be willing to force love upon those who do not comprehend it, so they may see the light and be released from their darkness. It is up to you to save them from themselves.

Use these 7 lampposts to banish the demon from this realm. For the Whore of Babylon tempts the one you love and shall destroy the one you wish to love.

Subjugate the Dragon!

Peter didn't know what to think.

Had God spoken to Peter, just as the prophets and apostles of old?

It certainly sounded like it could be from the Bible, specifically the book of Revelation.

Did the Holy Spirit use his own hand to write its message to him in his prayer journal, or had the message magically appeared of its own volition? He had no memory of writing it, and the handwriting was distinctly different from his own.

Suppose this was real, the Lord's answer to him?

Peter looked more closely at the enumerated list of seven, the number of wholeness and completion. It almost seemed to be a process for something, but a process for what?

Could this be God's answer to unlocking Val's hardened heart and helping him see the error of his ways?

A grim hollowness reverberated throughout Peter as he determined to do whatever was necessary to save his friend from himself.

At last, at last, at last, Peter was vibrating at a rate and oscillation perfectly in tune with Iago's own.

Their thoughts were aligned.

Their spirits were aligned.

Their intentions were aligned.

For the first time, Iago launched a full-scale possession. No more of this petty prompting, hinting, and rare moments of duplicitous vocal control. Now, Peter's pliant spirit was pushed into the background as Iago took center stage, spreading outside the pendant and the boy's lovesick beating heart to take ownership of his entire physical body.

Its physical body, now.

The secret to breaking free of any prison is to dissolve the bonds of agreement that keep one bound there. As soon as Peter and Iago resounded in accord, Iago burst forth from its metal boundary to claim the larger periphery of tissue and sinew so innocently relinquished by its foolish proprietor.

Although Iago was still stuck fast to a material body, this human body was capable of far more than a humble necklet. For this body, in its own way, could possess another body capable of eternities beyond its own gross limitations.

Only one body can possess another, and immutable embodiment was the ignoble end to which Iago aimed. Iago envisioned how to escape both imprisonment and its Master's judgment in one fell swoop.

In order to live forever, it only had to possess the eternal: a spirit body.

The chessboard was the key to violating Vee.

NINETEEN

"All the world's a stage,
And all the men and women merely players."
—As You Like It, attributed to William Shakespeare

Duke Hill's personal study was a sanctuary in wood. Sitting in it was like visiting God's own Camp David, and if Peter had been able to take back possession of his mouth from Iago, he would have said as much to Val's uncle as they sat around the live-edge-cherry gaming table built to match the curved desk, both exquisite hardwood pieces left deliberately raw with their warm honey natural finish, lending an organic feeling to any work or play.

Wall-to-wall wood, Duke's home office was nothing like the rest of the house he shared with Val's aunt. Blanche's tastes were eclectic, and it seemed as though all the other rooms in Hill Manor were decorated in homage to a different period of history, from the all-white Victorian living room, with its high-backed fancy chairs and velvet chaise lounge, the country-themed calico family room littered with handmade quilts and log-cabin accents, to her modern top-of-the-line stainless-steel Viking kitchen.

Duke's office, in contrast, seemed chastened by omnipresent walnut bookcases, filled with a vast library of hardcover books acquired during his fifty-some-odd years' sojourn on this earth. Most beautiful of all was Duke's treasured prayer cabinet, handmade for him by a Hindu man he'd befriended on one of his missions to India. Framed in teak, with ebony accents and inlaid with rare West African zebra-wood veneer, it formed a focal point to the otherwise clean neutrality of the space. The intricately woven cushion at the foot of the cabinet was by far the most worn-out item in the room.

Only a touch eccentric was the study's noticeable lack of windows. Originally built to be a spare attic room in Hill Manor, it had no external access to the outside world, and one single door at the top of a winding staircase. Its high wooden rafters that Duke restored himself, however, lent the room an unusual feel of the cathedrals of old, encouraging everyone who entered to gaze upward in worship.

Pastor Hill was the only person Peter had ever known who seemed to appreciate wood even more than Peter.

Of course, Iagopeter was a ghost of a different color. Iagopeter knew everything Peter thought, but those thoughts were like a stage-whispered aside for a forgotten line, unheard by the audience and easily ignored by the actor Iago.

Iagopeter sat at Duke's cherry gaming table with Val, his uncle, and supposedly Vee, Enochian Chess set spread out before them. It had been fairly challenging to get Val and Vee to join in the first place, and—still hampered by its strange incapacity to directly perceive the Queen of Wands—even now Iagopeter wasn't sure Vee was actually at the table as the straw-haired boy claimed.

Val had been none too happy to see Peter come downstairs earlier on this overcast Saturday morning, and it had taken a deft application of subterfuge to persuade him to a "friendly" chess game.

"So, you're still here," Val's reception was curt as Peter entered Blanche's kitchen at half past ten. Once again, Val sat at the table with a steaming cup of coffee in his hands, but this morning he was also reading a book entitled *Seeing Dark Things*. With eyebrows raised, he watched Peter take down a mug from the cabinet and pour himself a cup. "I thought you'd have gone back to California with Julie for sure."

"She's better off without us at the moment." Iagopeter sat down opposite.

"That was pretty devious what you did to force my hand with Julie—"

"It's best for both of you."

"—if you'd let me finish, I was going to say that was pretty devious what you did to force my hand with Julie last night, but I'm glad you did it."

Iagopeter's mouth fell open.

Val continued, "I'd started underestimating Julie right along with her own diminishment of herself. She's changed in a way I can't quite put my finger on, and it's for the better. Much better."

"The girl surprised me too last night."

"What?" Val stiffened at Iagopeter's odd usage of "the girl" to indicate Julie. "What do you mean?"

Backtracking carefully, Iagopeter said, "I mean, I saw Julie last night before she left for the airport, and she's surprisingly fine without you." Iago wondered if that was *oops*, a tad too harsh?

Val responded with a small, private smile. "Well, it's about time she realized it."

Iagopeter barely suppressed a repeated jaw droppage. Who was this boy and what, exactly, was his game?

"Is your ghost girl here now?" it asked, changing the subject.

"No, she's off in another dimension somewhere. Except for my bedroom, she doesn't come into the house unless invited, as a rule. Trying to respect human privacy and all that, even though she's beginning to lose track of why it matters to us so much."

Iago could relate; human customs of propriety were so tiresome to observe. "I wasn't sure if I would need to seek you out at your dorm room today."

"Classes don't actually start until Monday, and I promised Duke I'd help mend the fence on the south side of the property this weekend. Plus, who could pass up the chance to indulge in Blanche's home cooking one last time before being downgraded to bland campus food?" Val examined his friend, sensing something amiss. "Are you all right? You don't seem quite yourself."

"I'm not myself, actually. I'm exhausted. This has gone on far too long, and I'm sick of what separates us."

"You mean your devotion to Julie?"

"I mean your devotion to Vee."

"Vee isn't between us at all. It's your own pig-headedness. I appreciate bacon as much as the next man, but you've got to accept Vee's in my life."

"How can I accept what I cannot see?"

Val looked askance at Peter. He never dreamed he'd hear those words come out of his most faithful of friends. "I can see her, and that should be good enough for you."

"She is not to be trusted. Not one scintilla. She could be anybody, any *thing* for that matter."

Val bristled. "She's no 'thing.' Back off. I love you, man, but you've got to get over yourself."

Circling round its prey, Iagopeter prodded, "If you have so much confidence she is who you say she is, introduce her to your uncle. Tell him the truth."

Val's shoulders drooped. "I want to, I really do. . . but I don't know how."

Iagopeter pressed its moment of advantage. "I have a novel idea: a chess game."

Shrugging, Val said, "I mean, he loves chess as much as I do, you know that. But I don't see. . . "

"I have a new chess game. An improved chess game. It's called Enochian Chess."

Val laid his book on the table, curiosity piqued. "Enochian Chess? I've never heard of it—how's it different from regular chess?"

"Julie discovered it, and it's quite old. Much older than normal chess. It's designed to be played by four people."

"Well, it's out for today then. Aunt Blanche won't be home till late. She's leading a ladies' group tonight."

"Even better. We don't want Blanche to play—we want Vee to be the fourth player."

Val just stared at him as though in doubt of his sanity. "You want the invisible spirit, who can't move matter and whom nobody can see but me, to play chess?"

"Don't you see? It's perfect! You can pretend to play both sides as partners at first while she tells you how to move for her, but then—at the right moment, after we've worked together to maneuver the conversation with your uncle—you can disclose her to Duke."

"Sounds. . . precarious."

"Aren't you tired of hiding?"

Val shut his eyes. Iagopeter tried to imagine all the images ambushing Val behind those closed lids—his sham of a childhood home with his mother, the fundamental place Duke held in his life—and it knew it was going to succeed.

"All right," Val conceded as he opened his eyes wide, pulled back his shoulders, and sat tall like a lone lighthouse in the path of an imminent storm. "Let's do it."

They'd spent a rather awkward and uncomfortable Saturday afternoon together since reaching their resolve, as they waited for Duke to get home from his church meetings. Although Iago could draw upon any of Peter's memories or natural reactions as it wished, it did not comprehend the most basic substance of the lads' interactions—like kindness, decency, or unselfishness—and, most especially, it could not conceive of this distasteful and ambiguous love. Love was a foreign language to Iago: it had heard the expressions and endearments many times, of course, but it lacked the bandwidth to translate it. Desire, self-interest, and pecking order it understood, but this entirely too-close connection, this merging of one's own universe with another's until the universe of the relationship becomes paramount? Disgusting. This put the entity at a distinct disadvantage, as it said or did jarring and inappropriate minutiae throughout the day that set Val on edge. Thank Azathoth exploring the rules for the chess game together had eaten up a few hours, and Val's subsequent excitement about the prospect of conquering a new game had caused him to miss obvious mistakes on Iagopeter's part as well. It was relieved when Val went up to his bedroom alone to explain their scheme to Vee.

Plus, this gave Iagopeter just enough time to set the remainder of the stage for its plot to unfold.

TWENTY

For the first time since they'd met in the barn on that auspicious rainy day, Val wasn't sure how to speak to Vee.

A human-shaped prism of light, she shimmered above his bed, motes of dust floating throughout her and pulsating like sprinkles shaved from a variable star. The contents of his room looked somehow less substantial around her, as though matter and light wanted to be more wave than particle in her presence.

She would never feel the quilt spread out beneath her, the one that Blanche had lovingly stitched for him so many Christmases ago when he visited his aunt and uncle after his dad left. He would never feel the heat of her as they covered themselves with the quilt together, their arms and legs would never intertwine in the discovery of each other, his male body would never experience the rapture of fitting so perfectly within the subtleties of her female one.

In choosing Vee he had found his soul's match, but he consigned his body to a lifetime of isolation. He knew this; he'd chosen this willingly. With Vee, he could sense but never touch and be touched, perhaps for sixty years or more. Was it enough?

Was anything or anyone really ever enough for an entire lifetime?

And what about an eternity?

Why these doubts, now? His conversation with Julie last night had brought him relief, not apprehension. He was uneasy about Peter and his plan, but equally longed to tell his uncle everything.

It all came back to Duke.

At last, he understood. He was not afraid of choosing Vee, not afraid of the singular life he would live as her partner. But Peter's plan forced him to face his unspoken fears of what would happen when he, at last, told Duke about Vee—had to face his own barometer of external truth in the heavenly eyes of his surrogate father.

He did not doubt himself so much as the world's reaction.

"So, did you resolve Julie's love triangle?" Vee asked, handfuls of transparent Vs zooming away from her and toward Val like little whirlwinds of interrogation.

"I would say she solved her own love triangle. I merely stood witness to the event."

"Did you tell her about me—about us? Does she know you see the dead?"

"I told her. Everything."

Vee visibly relaxed. "Good. She won't be haunted any longer by what she senses but cannot see. And we've one less V to worry about."

"Your Vs don't bother me."

"Well, they should. Julie had only one triangle to unravel, I apparently have hundreds."

"Looks more like thousands."

Vee rolled her not-eyes and changed the subject. "Julie's much prettier than you gave her credit for."

"Thank you for understanding. Most women wouldn't have been so okay with me meeting alone with my ex."

Vee giggled. "I'm hardly most women."

His bedroom seemed to fade away as he watched her, more real to him than any trifle he could touch. His breath escaped him, and his heartbeat quickened in response to what he saw in her unblinking bottomless not-eyes.

For he glimpsed not only himself, but the entire world and beyond within their lucent depths.

"How is Peter taking all of this?"

He shook himself to break his trance, and answered, "Something's definitely off."

"You do know he loves her, right? I mean, he might just love Julie more than you love me."

"Impossible."

"Okay, maybe not more. . . but certainly just as much, in his own way."

Val considered this revelation. Of course, it was obvious now. Evidently, he wasn't the only one who hid his ghosts from those he loved.

Amazing how easily we can see the truth when we're ready.

"Is that why you wanted me to talk with Julie—because of Peter?"

"Oh, no. I'm hardly that altruistic. It was something the prince said. And Shakespeare."

"Shakespeare? Did you finally meet him?"

"It's quite possible I will never find him. Perhaps he's left us all to do something bigger. Better. Or maybe he just wants to be left alone."

"I doubt that."

"Why not? Don't you think the occasional greater being might just be finished with this merry-go-round?"

Val considered Vee. She was so much more than him in so many ways, yet at the same time needed him perhaps even more because of it. "Physicality's the platform, this merry-go-round's the playhouse. And the play must go on."

"But why? Why must the play go on? Especially when so many of us don't like it?"

Val inspected the Vs buzzing around Vee like honeybees protecting their hive. "To share the experience together."

Vee pouted, sweet little see-through furrows forming all over her not-face. "I like people most when I'm by myself."

"And I like myself most when I'm with people."

"They do say opposites attract."

Val shunned clichés. He could feel his hope for the future of the human race dangle an infinitesimal drop further over the oubliette of extinction every time he heard someone waste air with yet another of these tiresome repetitive mediocrities. "Your adage is too short. Opposites attract—until they stop opposing things. Only then can you begin to comprehend anything or anyone outside of yourself, much less love."

Vee's face pinched as though gathered by an invisible thread. "I think your uncle would benefit more from that insight than me."

A spasm tightened Val's shoulders and neck, but he restrained his response. After all, this was expressly the segue he needed. "I couldn't agree more. Actually, Peter and I were discussing Duke just this morning. We have a plan to tell him about you."

"We have a plan, as in you and Peter? Why would Peter be involved at all? Look, I know you think the world of him, but his motives seem highly suspect to me. He set up your confrontation with Julie—despite your explicit directives to the contrary, if you'll recall."

"You're right. But Peter's motivated by his love for me, not his own benefit. Something from which I could stand to learn."

"You are the least selfish person I know."

"Then it's time to broaden your circle of friends. Individuals make for the most selfish people of all, and I am nothing if not an individual."

Vee puckered her not-lips before curdling to the color of a moldering pumpkin. "We'll agree to disagree on that point. Tell me about this plan of yours."

"We're going to introduce you to Duke over a game of chess."

"There's that we again. I don't think it's a good idea for me to be there when you tell your uncle, and Peter shouldn't be there at all. Do you really think you ought to be playing a game when you tell him?"

"Duke loves chess. It's something we both share—it will put him at ease. And this particular type of chess game requires four players. You, me, Duke, and Peter."

"I don't play chess."

"Oh, don't worry about that. I'll make your moves for you."

"I'm not saying I'm unable to play chess. I mean I don't play chess. In fact, I have an aversion to playing games of any ilk."

Val scratched his jaw. "You don't like games?"

"I prefer to choose the parameters for my own diversions rather than following rules determined by others. Playing games and following rules is where the trouble starts for the living."

Heat coursed throughout Val's body as he felt himself stiffen. "You may have forgotten this, but I just happen to be alive."

"Oh, alive and living—those are two completely different phenomena. Any amoeba or bacterium can be alive, but an entirely new set of complications surfaces when you decide you want to live."

"I like games."

"Of course you do. Most humans do. It's how you all ignore how blasted bored you are with yourselves. But you'll notice all the frenzied game-playing stops when someone loses or finds out she has cancer."

Val's tone became soothing as he leaned forward. He'd forgotten for a moment that Vee was dead. "I'm sorry, that was insensitive of me."

Vee turned a vicious shade of red as she expanded to twice her size. It looked like a few of her Vs sprouted talons and wielded wicked-looking butcher knives. For the first time he found himself thankful they were mere figments and couldn't actually stab him in her anger. "I'm not talking about myself, you cretin. I'm talking about you. All of you, lost in your placid islands of ignorance and your deadly light. I'm glad I died. It released me from the superficial, cyclical miasma that transfixes you all There in your massive lie of existence!"

Val's voice deepened to a dangerous whisper. "The lady doth protest too much, methinks."

A cone-shaped V dive-bombed down at him, jabbing at his right eye repeatedly with a claw-shaped pincer. Vee shrieked in her corporeal powerlessness. "This plan of yours is a recipe for disaster. You think that if you can set up the perfect situation, control enough variables, your uncle will understand and maybe even take your side, but that's the universe's prank: Nobody takes any side but his own! You overestimate your friend as much as you underestimate your uncle. And I want nothing to do with it."

Even though Val was still himself hesitant about Peter's plan, he rallied to support his best friend in the face of this ghost girl turned ethereal harpy. He knew Vee had a temper, but she'd never turned it on him or anyone he loved before. He shouted, "If you love me, you'll do this! I need you there—for whatever support you can give from your sanctimonious perch of death and darkness." He felt his own ire begin to crumble in his all-encompassing need to unify the inverses that seemed to measure every moment of his waking life. "Please," he pleaded, "even if you don't approve, even if you think I'm mad—do this. For me."

Vee deflated before his eyes, her Vs withdrawing to a few feet behind her. She somehow looked smaller than she ever had before. "I would follow you anywhere, whether up to the stars or over the cliff of doom, and I hardly think this qualifies as either. It's perhaps the most human idea you've ever had, but I love your humanity. I will play your ludicrous little game of chess, and hope to god I am mistaken about the rest."

He reached for her, but as she settled down and around his heart and he enfolded her in his all-too-human arms, it brought him little comfort. For there was an alien quality in their joining that felt cooler, a tinge detached.

Convulsively, he gripped himself tighter, hoping it would be enough for both of them.

TWENTY-ONE

"Our king. . . is prisoner to the bishop."
—*The third part of Henry the Sixth, attributed to*
William Shakespeare

Duke walked in his front door at a quarter past four, wearied and ready for a day of rest. He found Val and Peter together in his living room, sitting on opposite ends of his wife's favorite sofa, which he noticed for the first time was the fragile color of eggshells. The white space between the boys seemed huge: Val read one of his philosophy books; Peter stared into space, unblinking, as though nobody was home.

"You boys all right?" Duke asked. Peter's head pivoted much too slowly, blank eyes focusing on him with a mechanical aloofness that chilled the older man. Duke shuddered involuntarily, equally disturbed by the wooden way his nephew put down the book—as though he only read to fill the time rather than for any pleasure or meaning.

Night had fallen in Duke's house before the sun had even set.

In silence, the three demolished a homemade lasagna Blanche had left them for supper, and Duke took very little convincing to join Val and Peter in a "new and exciting" game of chess. They tromped up the circuitous stairs to the highest room in his home, Duke's private study.

It wasn't until Duke noticed the uncommon chess pieces were hand-carved from wood that he became truly interested in the game. Before, he'd been placating the boys. Something wasn't quite right between the two, and he was hoping he could help heal the rift during their interaction in some small way.

But the wooden Egyptian chess pieces? The intricately carved Osiris figure in particular, wearing a pharaoh's hedjet and holding the distinctive crook and flail, took him back to his visits with the Coptic Christians in Alexandria during his mid-thirties. The Osiris myth had always rung true with Duke, the god-king who died and was resurrected to become ruler of the afterlife. The story of salvation, rather than being unique to Christianity, was scattered throughout most cultures all over the world in one form or another. Just another sign of the Lord's goodness that everyone was given the chance to find the story of redemption through whatever means possible.

As a matter of fact, Duke valued chess as more of a spiritual revelation than a simple game of logic. How a man played his chess game often revealed how he lived his life. Did he take unnecessary risks? Did he try to keep as many pieces on the board as possible? Did he make deliberate sacrifices along the way and take his time, aiming for the long game? Or, did he make quick arbitrary moves, rushing to a speedy conclusion? Was he always focused on his next move, or was he entirely caught up in the prospective moves of his opponent?

Duke could get lost in a good chess game.

Less experienced players generally fixated on the Queen and her formidable prowess to turn the tide of a game with her free and equal movement between dark and light squares. Although the King had the ability to move any direction it pleased on the board, he was bound by the rules to move only one space at a time, just like a spirit merged with a material body is bound by the limitations imposed by the physical universe itself. To Duke, the King represented a person who had awakened to his or her own salvation while on Earth. The Queen, on the other hand, symbolized the Holy Ghost that endlessly gives and has the unlimited potential power to move in any direction, but who has chosen to limit herself because of her love for the King and her desire to see him saved. The Spirit of God only hinders itself through love.

With a profound sigh, Duke picked up his yellow Bishop—the

piece he saw himself mirrored in far too often—and placed it on its opening square on the chess board. The Bishop's movement in a chess game demonstrated what happens when people try to live their lives by their mind or their heart piecemeal: Two ways of working in the world apart from spirit. Either the head rules and morality governs the heart like a cold-hearted dictator, or the emotional whims of the heart control the common sense of the head. As the Bishop can never move straight but only diagonally, and must stay on the black or white path whence it began, so this flawed approach to living is only ever at cross-purposes to a person's full development.

If you spend your entire life on the same path, you live only a half-life at best.

He considered the tiny piece's oddly curved beak and its tiny carved hand that wielded an even smaller ankh, and wondered not for the last time how he could continue to straddle the worlds of faith and philosophy while remaining true to himself.

"What's this piece again?" he asked Val, who was busy setting up blue pieces in front of himself and red pieces on the opposing side of the earth board, which they were using for their initiation into this exotic version of chess. The fire board was not to be found, but they dismissed its disappearance when Peter suggested Julie must have misplaced it.

"That's Thoth, the Egyptian god of wisdom. He's got the head of an ibis," said Val. "At least, I think that's an ibis bird." He held up the blue Knight and Rook, adding, "I'm pretty sure these are Horus and Nephthys, Isis's son and sister, but don't quote me on it."

Peter placed the small, white "Ptah" piece in front of the empty seat that would have been their fourth person. To Val he said, "Since you're going to play both sides of the red and blue team, I'll just put this one-off piece here for you to use when you make your moves for the red team." Duke thought this a rather impractical suggestion but dismissed it as inconsequential.

"Have I set my side up right?" Duke asked, unsure of this unconventional arrangement. "The King and the Rook are placed together on the same square in the corner—the one you called the 'throne square'—since we're using the 'earth board,' correct? And Peter has the first turn since he's playing the black pieces and we're using the corresponding board?"

Val observed the entire board, "Yup, and yes—looks good," he consulted the rule book one last time. "You know, it looks sort of like a pinwheel, or even a swastika with a different color in each corner. It's odd to play with fewer pieces, but I think I'm going to like the challenge of something new."

Peter said, "Yes, I think I am going to enjoy this. Very much."

Val looked from Peter to Vee, who glared behind the empty chair across from him at the fourth side of the gaming table, leaving more space between them than was strictly necessary. Her not-face was mottled a worrisome combination of the same colors as the pallid Ptah and nine red pieces sitting in front of her. Uncharacteristically mute and reserved, she looked neither at Duke nor at Peter, but fixed her stern not-eyes on Val as though telepathically repeating to him over and over what a bad idea this was.

Vee's intense stare, in combination with Peter's gauche peculiarity today, gave Val the creeps. Which, considering his routine macabre encounters, was really saying something.

Peter started the game by moving his black pawn in a way that made no sense at all to Val, but then he was still adjusting to the subtle changes in game play. For example, the Queen's powers were limited to three squares in any direction in Enochian Chess, and no castling or *en passant* was allowed, either. Most striking was the new rule that if a player "mounts" his King upon the throne square of an opponent or ally, he actually takes control of the other's forces. The only hope of re-obtaining your captured King and his forces was if your ally captured the opposing King and proposed an exchange of prisoner Kings. While a King was captured, he was taken out of play and the remaining pieces of that team stayed frozen on the board, becoming permanent obstacles to the rest of the players. Victory came only when both kings of the opposing team were captured.

The order of play, clockwise around the board, was: black Peter, blue Val, yellow Duke, and finally red Val (Vee). Val countered Peter with one of the only clever openings he knew that could possibly be used in this game, the Nimzowitsch Defense, by moving his Knight.

Duke, however, knew how to best respond to that opening, and so the game was afoot.

Serious faces teemed with unspoken thoughts, fixating with unnatural determination on the multi-colored chess board and making no eye contact at all. Peter's lips pursed as though cemented. Duke's forehead creased in careful concentration. The atmosphere in the room felt ponderous and restrictive. Attempting to lighten the mood, Val quipped, "You all seem to be pawn movers. Did I ever tell you George Carlin's joke, about whether you can buy an entire chess set in a pawn-shop?"

Duke groaned. Peter raised an eyebrow in disdain. Vee sighed, puffing out her not-cheeks as she blew a not-lock of not-hair out of her not-face. "That is so not funny," she said, telling Val which pawn to move for her, "and I swear something is really wrong with your friend. I mean, he's always waxed a little gloom and doom, but today there's something downright sinister about his aura. An outside pitchy edge, as if he's a stick man trapped in a skeleton egg."

Peter chose that precise moment to up the ante as he took his next turn. "So, Pastor Hill . . . " he said formally, for all appearances nonchalant. "What do you think of Val's ability to see ghosts?"

Duke's head catapulted upward as though struck from behind by a two-by-four, caught off guard by *this* opening. Val found himself at a loss for words, flabbergasted by Peter's handling.

Peter continued, "Oh, I know he sees ghosts. From what I hear, you don't approve. Do you think that's wise?" His black Knight took a red pawn.

"Now, now, son, let's not be too hasty—is this what all the ruckus between you two is about?" Duke moved his Bishop for the first time. "I never said I don't approve, exactly. My own opinion doesn't matter anyway. It's God's say-so I'm concerned about. I care about what this means for his immortal soul."

At Vee's say-so, Val moved the red Queen into play.

Peter snorted as he moved a pawn to threaten another red piece. Val wondered when Peter had learned to play chess with such acumen.

Duke continued, "I'm not even sure what Val thinks he's seen is real. Children's imaginings seem true enough to them when they're young, but as the good book says, 'When I became a man, I put away childish things.'" Duke situated his Knight to take Val's pawn, "It's been quite a while since he's even had one of these episodes, right Val?"

Moving his blue Rook to protect his King, his added caution surprising even himself, Val finally joined the discussion. "Not exactly, sir. What Peter is trying to say, albeit with a ham-fisted approach, is my paranormal experiences have, uh, progressed."

Duke released his fingers from the piece he had just repositioned, turning the full weight of his gaze upon his nephew as he repeated, "'Progressed'?"

Play continued as Val explained. "Yes. I know now I'm not imagining them, and they're not demons—although once in a lopsided moon they might have malicious intent. They're ghosts, uncle. The spirits of those who have died but for one reason or another have remained on Earth."

Forming his hands into a steeple, Duke leaned forward. "How do you know this? How can you be sure?"

"Besides my own eighteen years of experience? Besides my own eyes and ears?" Val moved a red piece at Vee's request. "I've met someone else who sees what I see."

Duke leaned back, covering his mouth and chin as he cocked his head to the right side. "And who is this person of such infinite perspicacity?"

"Her name is Silvia, but she goes by Vee for short."

"Ah, so she's a girl." Duke said this as though it explained every-thing. "And you have feelings for her, it seems. How did you meet this collaborator? I'm not aware of anyone by that name in Milan—did you maybe meet her last week at EMU?"

Val reached toward Duke, lightly touching his knee as he answered, "I met her right here, in your own barn." He paused, glancing at Peter for support and noting Vee's rapt fascination despite herself. "She's a ghost."

Vee winced.

Peter smiled.

Duke exploded. "A WHAT?" Pushing himself away from the table with such force two red pieces fell over, a single vein along his temple engorged as he stood. His tone deepened. "Do you hear your-self, boy? Do you understand what you're saying, the danger you're in? Either this is delusion, or even worse: you are keeping the counsel of a pernicious spirit. There are no such things as noble ghosts, if they are ghosts at all—and this insanity has gone far enough!"

Val jumped out of his own seat, towering over his uncle at his full height as he faced him. "She's a real person—her soul's as good as yours or mine, just not bound to a body. How can you be so sure if I see spirits, they must be evil?"

"Because I believe the Word of the Lord." With eyes and chin thrust high, Duke looked beyond his nephew to his diligently varnished rafters, returning to his habitual role as preacher: "Leviticus cautions us, 'Give no regard to mediums or familiar spirits; do not seek after them, to be defiled by them.'" He raised his arms heavenward toward his rafters. "Corinthians adds that, 'Satan masquerades as an angel of light. . . his servants masquerade as servants of righteousness.'" He laid his hands upon his nephew's shoulders, as though compelling the spirit of God to enlighten him. "The only spirits who walk the earth are servants of the devil. If this Vee is real at all, its very nature is evil."

Val jerked his shoulders away from his uncle's hands. "Then to your Bible quotations, I must counter with the words of an acquaintance of Vee's in the afterlife, Nathaniel Hawthorne: 'Let him do with me as, in his justice and wisdom, he shall see good. But who art thou that meddles in this matter?—that darest thrust himself between the sufferer and his God?'" Val flexed his muscles, lips curling with passionate contempt. "I must reply to your version of biblical interpretation with the Bible itself: 'Eye hath not seen, nor ear heard, neither have entered into the heart of man, the things which God hath prepared for them that love him.'" Depleted and desperate, Val entreated his uncle to understand, "And I do love Him, uncle. You and I love the same God with all our hearts."

Incredulous, Duke stared at his nephew, for the first time convinced the young man was either insane or possessed.

Speaking of possession, unnoticed amongst all the commotion, Iagopeter moved the black King to mount the throne square of the red King on the chess board, replacing the white Ptah piece for its own King and palming the now weirdly glowing red and black Kings together in Peter's left hand as it uttered one irrevocable word of binding: "Vee."

From the vicinity of the space directly behind and above the red corner of the game board, there emanated a nightmarish whistling followed by a distinct popping sound, like a python squeezing the living breath out of its victim until the tiny heart stops beating.

At last assured the sympathetic magical mounting had worked, and all the other red pieces were now motionless on the board and in fact blocking the ability of both Val and Duke to respond in kind, Iagopeter absconded from the study, descending the curving flight of steps into the darkness beneath.

Unaware of the sorcery transpiring in their midst, Val and Duke continued their argument unabated.

"You cannot love both God and the devil. But it's never too late to reject your wicked ways. The book of James admonishes, 'Submit yourselves therefore to God. Resist the devil, and he will flee from you.'"

"I don't love the devil, I love Vee," Val shouted, losing all semblance of composure. "And I intend to live my life beside her for as long as she will have me!"

Horror infused Duke's countenance. Horror, and then an escalating revulsion. He slowly backed away from the fierce changeling who had once been his beloved nephew, muttering, "'. . .and they may come to their senses and escape the snare of the devil, after being captured by him to do his will. . .'"

Duke stormed through his study door, slamming and locking it behind him.

Grim as he was when he heard the lock's click, Val gazed at the sealed wooden barrier a few moments longer. It was as though his father had walked out on him all over again, complete and utter rejection because he saw what others could not. Only God himself would ever change his uncle's mind, now. Hopeless, he turned to find comfort with his beloved and his best friend.

"You were right, of course. . . ," he began, until he spied the empty space above the far corner of the gaming table.

The empty space that should have been Vee.

His second shock came as he scrutinized every portion of the room only to discover himself, inexplicably, alone.

Vee and Peter had vanished.

TWENTY-TWO

"And love you 'gainst the nature of love—force ye. . .
I'll force thee yield to my desire."
—*Two Gentlemen of Verona, attributed to William Shakespeare*

A chess board is a curious thing. Especially when one finds oneself stuck within a continuous column of polychromatic light that shoots as far upward as the not-eyes can see and as far downward as the not-feet can distinguish, originating from what, at first glance, appears to be a plain corrugated chess board—notwithstanding unusual in that its 64 squares were divided into 256 triangles—the missing fire board from a now highly suspect Enochian Chess set.

Most curious.

Circumspect as Vee, constrained *within* for the first time since her death, watched from her prison of light whilst a dark figure unbolted the creaking barn door, she noted the figure closed the unwieldy door without any physical exertion after entering: for the dark figure—or was it two figures, one on top of the other?—jabbered a guttural incantation beneath its familiar breath, prompting the door to slam shut with a formidable reverberation, like the final echo a cadaver feels when its mausoleum forever encloses it within its prison of compulsory absence.

Once the door was magically sealed, the figure(s) stepped out of the shadows and into a beam of moonlight trickling down from between two missing shingles, illuminating the recognizable form of Val's best friend Peter, but also a second shape, both infinitesimally smaller and substantively greater than the physical body's original owner from a spiritual perspective, superimposed upon and infiltrating into the youth, and what Vee now observed to be the current operant of Peter's virile brawn.

Curiouser and curiouser. This enchanted incandescent pillar both enabled her to perceive for the first time the source of the strangeness that enthralled Peter, this nonphysical entity neither dead nor living but something else entirely, as well as gave her own spiritual body tangibility. For she could touch and press upon the physical resistance of the light barrier, as well as sense the startling feeling of nails biting into her palms as she clenched her apparently now-fists in response to her limitation. Her now-nose even smelled a rank stench pervading the space around her, reminiscent of rotting fish and putrescine.

And with the realization of her newfound solidity, coupled with the iniquity exuding from the approaching Peter fused with his puppet master—his unwinking eyes now enlarged with impossibly dilated pupils as though they might bulge out of his eye-sockets like two bloated pufferfish—her objective curiosity began to ever-so-slowly metamorphize into an intimate monster she had previously confronted only within the vulnerability of dreaming: Fear. That most primal and powerful of human emotions that she speculated to be the source of so many of her unidentified flying Vs.

When alive, Fear had rarely plagued Vee's waking hours—not even the fear of her impending death, once she accepted its inevitability. Her brother feared aplenty for both of them, and she swore off Fear as she watched her brother's fear transform him into a victimizer who rationalized his cruelty toward his younger sister out of this same self-justified fear.

His nightmares vindicated his nightmarish acts.

Vee's own nightmares, however—both in life and after—were filled not with fear, but with strange phantasms of lost enchanted hills and gardens, of impossibly out-of-reach fountains that burbled in the scorching sun, of forlorn golden cliffs overhanging siren seas, of endless plains that stretched down to paralyzed cities imprisoned in bronze and stone, and of longings for shadowy companies of grail knights riding noble steeds along the edges of labyrinthine forests from which they would never escape; haunted by the Vs that would eternally elude her and the possibility of an earlier world of wonder and time of perfection that was hers before her awareness made her miserable, knowledge of the nameless horrors that walked not in the spaces we know, but between them—serene, primal, dimensionless, and deadly, yet unable to awake from the nightmare themselves.

So many Vs fought to claim her attention that she did not have to focus on the one thing she wanted to avoid at all costs: that so much of the Fear of life comes from our Vulnerability, and so we play the Victim to hide our own Violations.

Vee was glad for her early death. A death that, though sad from many human perspectives, had from her own vantage point granted a vital boon: Sovereignty over herself.

But now, she saw her end in the empty eyes of her captor, consumed by a fear far worse than any she'd felt before.

It was as though her brother Tom (and all the real and imagined Venomous Victims of her Visions) advanced toward her from the Grimm's Fairy Tales of her childhood, and she was Little Red Cap inside the ravenous Wolf, she was Snow White running from the vain Queen, she was Rapunzel confined by the evil Witch, she was Cinderella in bondage to the wicked Stepmother.

She was trapped, exposed, and able to be hurt, perhaps even destroyed. Her own uninspected Fear anchored her agreement with her possible fate.

Iago, in drastic dissimilarity, was the master of its own fate for the first time in hundreds of years. Just as a body is a form creating individual separation between one and another, so the Enochian magical circle it had cast via the fire tablet, that selfsame image hidden in plain sight to the eyes of the uninitiated upon the chess game's speciously innocuous elemental boards—the four Great Quadrangles of the even Greater Tablet, the fire region denoting the spirit dimensions—allowed this human body's heretofore inept vascular orbs to see whatever spirit body had been summoned and entrapped within its denizens by the game of invocation.

For unbeknownst to the ignorant simians that believed themselves to be the original rulers of this planet they now called Earth—because they had long ago lost its true name—the invocation and mastery of spirits is neither a superstition nor a parlor trick, but a very real and ancient craft practiced by beings both corporeal and non, a collection of rules and rituals dating back to the creation of this miserable prison planet for the whims and diversions of the Gods of Old. Though dabbled in and romanticized to disastrous effect throughout the ages, most human beings lived their short, dismal lives benighted about the grander design governing their meager existence.

At last viewing the Queen of Wands ensnared like an insignificant insect in the web of its fire circle, Iago exulted. Although her materialized spiritual body wasn't exactly an impressive specimen visually, Iago could sense the precocious power blistering outward, made barely tolerable to behold by the circle interning her.

Here was the Penumbra in all her glory, the prize he had sought for so long: A mighty spirit body, infinite and therefore without end by its very nature, that it could dominate for eternity. Never again would Iago wander from fleshbag to fleshbag, exposed to trick and entrapment through the intransient structure of this short-lived collection of metabolic, circulatory, endocrine, and lymphatic systems.

The Penumbra was the key to Iago's everlasting liberty.

During its interminable captivity within the watch pendant, Iago had gradually apprehended the grey area between the laws of light and the chaos of darkness, for possessing another's spirit body—stealing and occupying that which, by its very nature, cannot be appropriated—had never before been dreamt.

The very idea was an abomination rejected by the entire spectrum of existence.

But Iago, you see, was the abomination of abominations. Neither living nor dead, neither Here nor There, nor even Nowhere, but instead inBetween. By its own composition a Penumbra itself, only a being such as Iago could conceive of the corrupted space and adulterated time necessary to achieve the greatest of all sinful states—substantial immortality. A perversion possible only by means of the impossible: A gross material body must violate an ethereal spirit body.

Possess.

Rape.

But how to rape a ghost?

Using all the craft and erudition gleaned during its aeons of be-twixt-ness, Iago had groomed Peter's body and volition over time to perform this awful act of abuse.

From inciting hostility toward the Queen, to urging Peter to dehumanize her—that she was not a person but a thing—and convincing him he knew what was needed, thus objectifying her as a good slave master must diminish his slave to be able to sleep at night, Iago had worked its own black magic of seduction upon the hapless youth. The supposed-epistle from God that Iago had influenced the boy to automatically write laid out in no uncertain terms the seven stages of objectification that lead to justify harming another. Finally, and most crucial, Iago's crowning victory had been manipulating Peter's my-thology, the beliefs and stories whence the roots of his own self-con-cept and life itself germinated, to convince the fellow to act against his own good reason and common sense because he believed God commanded it: inspiring him to see Vee as the Adversary, whose thoughts and feelings need not be taken into account at all in the quest to do what is right.

Like a cat, Iago savored the prospect of tormenting its target before possessing her glory as its permanent dwelling, using this feeble physical body to violate and take over this infinitely superior spiritual one forevermore.

For the briefest instant, Iago found itself thankful for the slaugh-ter of its own perfection at the hands, manacles, and tentacles of its old Master and His minions so many millennia ago. Without the lessons learned during those aeons of enduring unspeakable atrocities, this moment of triumph would not have been possible.

Menacing, Iago stepped Peter's body ever-so-much closer to the Queen's bright bastille.

This Queen was about to be royally fucked.

Now-eyes huge and now-limbs shaking, Vee endeavored to awaken Peter from his spiritual abdication. "Rouse yourself, Peter! Awake! I see you there. I feel you, slumbering just beneath the surface. You can still stop this before it's too late."

Iago felt the faintest stirrings of response deep in Peter's brain stem. "The Knight has surrendered to his better. Call me Iago." It gloated in Peter and Vee's joint impotence, continuing the game of cat-and-mouse. "There are 64 squares on a chess board, did you know?" Taking another inexorable step forward, it continued, "64 is a mystical number. A number of such. . . prerogative. The square of 8, the cube of 4." Wringing its hands, the slightest drip of drool descended from the left side of Peter's mouth, contorting it into an execrable sneer.

Peter's once compassionate eyes constricted as they fixated on Vee, glistening as though infected with a virulent green mucus. "64 is the number of attainment in numerology, and so I have attained you. Of course, most humans scorn the ancient wisdom of numbers, relegating them to math class and calculators. But it is mathematics that describes and determines everything in existence. People always dismiss what would save them only to be destroyed by their ludicrous obsessions."

It continued its ghoulish pedagogy with another terrorizing step toward Vee. "64 is the number of power. The Apostle Luke wrote there were 64 generations between Adam and Jesus, and there are 64 codons in the genetic code." Iagopeter arrived at the outskirts of the magic circle and reached under Peter's T-shirt, extracting the forsaken watch pendant. "64 tantras in Hinduism, 64 hexagrams of the I-Ching." It tugged the necklace's pendant, breaking the chain so it fell from around

Peter's thick neck. Fragments of delicate gold chain speckled the floor, leaving only the watch pendant in Peter's hand.

Vee didn't count the pieces, but she was sure there were 64.

The pendant was horribly altered from when Vee had seen Peter hold it up the last time they were together with Val in the barn. Now barren and treacherously brittle, its metal casing pulsed with an uncanny glow and droned with a faint rasping noise that reminded Vee of hungry locusts swarming.

A dizzying weakness spiraled around and into Vee, creeping from her jittery now-limbs to clench about her now-heart. She closed her now-eyes, but instead of seeing stars as she expected, a vision of her beloved Val smiled back at her with his lopsided grin.

Through his living eyes, she saw the beauty of what it is to be human.

It couldn't end this way. They couldn't end this way. She'd been so remote during their final embrace, believing they had eternity to find each other again.

But she knew, deep in her core, that very soon there might be nothing left for Val to find.

Vee lobbed her own 64 at Iago, reciting the only words she trusted far more than her own, "And Shakespeare's 64th sonnet says:

When I have seen by Time's fell hand defaced
The rich proud cost of outworn buried age;
When sometime lofty towers I see down-razed,
And brass eternal slave to mortal rage;
When I have seen the hungry ocean gain
Advantage on the kingdom of the shore,
And the firm soil win of the watery main,
Increasing store with loss, and loss with store;
When I have seen such interchange of state,
Or state itself confounded to decay;
Ruin hath taught me thus to ruminate,
That Time will come and take my love away."

Choking on the exponential longing that lingered within her, she whispered the final couplet more to herself than to Iago. "*This thought is as a death, which cannot choose but weep to have that which it fears to lose.*"

For the first time in her immortal experience, Vee felt the sonnet's message as though it were her own. It had never occurred to her that one's essence could be lost, or perhaps worse, subjugated and shattered. But through the lens of her Fear she saw her own destruction play out before her like a paranormal slasher flick.

Perhaps old souls cry more than new souls. They've loved more, and in each successive loss remember more of the love they've known. Hearts in love aren't happier, just fuller. It's the Monet pond shattering over and over and over again.

She opened her now-eyes to a world brimming with beautiful tears.

For a moment, Vee's Shakespearean quotation immobilized Iago. By Azathoth and all that isn't holy, he loathed that charlatan. The playwright had never had a unique idea in his entire life, instead making his living by amalgamation and derivation. In fact, the only worthwhile thing the Bard did during his pitiful time on Earth, that remained unknown by the myopic professors of today, was to spearhead the salvation of the world with his frenemy Christopher Marlowe, the magician John Dee, the psychic Edward Kelley, and the philosopher Francis Bacon. This star-studded group had used the geomantic architecture of Burbage's Old Globe Theatre to perform a joint magical working that prevented the return of Iago's dreaded Master and banished His essence back beneath the Hawaiian Islands in the waters of the South Pacific.

Begrudging, Iago admitted to itself these Elizabethan fools had done the world a great service. The only other time during human history the stars had aligned to allow entry from His dimension into this one was during the age of the ancient Greeks, who recorded this narrowly-avoided catastrophe in Hesiod's myth of Typhon.

But the Greek gods and goddesses were gone. Shakespeare and his cronies deceased. Iago must press on to resolve the scheme at hand if it was to avoid the next time the stars were aright and darkness descended upon the Earth, probably for the very last—and longest lasting—midnight.

Iago shook Peter's suddenly cotton-filled head side-to-side, attempting to reorient itself and dissipate the feeling of dread slithering up its bipedal spine. It countered Vee's citation with a darker reference of its own. "And on page 64 of the Necronomicon, that detestable tome written by the mad Arab, Abdul Alhazred, it prophesies of the two sets of divine beings who shall rule the physical universe: The Elder Gods, that heavenly race championed by the religions of Light who hope They might return some day to help humankind yet again; and the Ancient Ones, those Evil Gods of Darkness who ruled There long before the arrival of the Elder Gods, and whose utmost desire is to enslave all sentient beings once more."

Iago grasped the watch pendant in Peter's hand and held it aloft as though the damaged timepiece was Pandora's box, about to be broken and release its only hope. "For aeons they have striven without ceasing to locate the Key that converges the boundaries of dreams and other dimensions with physical reality. With this Key in their possession, they mean to recapture this world, transmuting their grotesque bulbous bodies of shape without matter. For while the Key is lost, and the stars are wrong, they cannot live or manifest in the physical realms to wreak their Ragnarok."

The fiend continued as though in a trance. "And Chief among these is their High Priest, whose body inhabits a hidden dimension of the outer void while His spirit voyages beneath the surface of the waters. Only the devout, the demented, and the discerning know Him, through the collective nightmares of the unconsciousness."

Vee stared at the villain speaking through Peter, her disdain for the moment overtaking her Fear. "You do know that entire mythos is a fabricated fiction from the haunted imagination of Howard Lovecraft, right? I mean, it's the stuff of RPG games and horror movies—maybe it's developed a cult following from geeks and writers over the years—but it is not real."

An abominable beast of a smile stretched the corners of Peter's mouth from ear to ear, drawing his chin upward and his forehead downward into a scrunched caricature of a human face, like a cartoonish image on a piece of silly putty stretched too far side to side, past all recognition and into the stuff of delirium. Vee thought she heard a few bones crack and tendons groan in the process.

Peter's blank eyes stared ahead as his body snatcher used his base voice to build to a crescendo. "That little horror writer—whom you call Lovecraft—prophesied in his stories that the High Priest Cthulhu would return when mankind becomes as the Great Old Ones are: believing themselves to be beyond good and evil, reveling in destruction, lusting for lust's sake. Sounds a lot like the people of today, doesn't it?" Iago looked from right to left, up to down, as though searching the shadows of the barn with Peter's eyes for a monstrosity Vee now suspected to be far worse than itself. Once it seemed satisfied that a Great Old One did not lie in wait, it grasped the watch pendant firmly in its left hand and tossed the precious casing within the fire circle.

Without thinking, Vee caught it in her now-hand.

In response, the temperature of the pillar of light began to burn red-hot, and she right along with it. Now-skin began to blister, now-hair stank of sulfur as it blackened away to baldness, now-glasses melted and melded to her shrinking was-nose and were-cheeks until only the imprint remained on her charred once-face. The semblance of clothes evaporated, leaving her now-naked and fiery afraid.

Disfigured and wholly exposed, Vee released the watch pendant from her throbbing once-hand to shelter her nudity.

The clock dropped like a nuclear bomb, bursting upward and outward in a miniature mushroom cloud. Instinctively, she shielded her once-eyes from the smoke and saw the scorch mark from the watch pendant had branded her once-palm with the finely-crafted image of Leda and the Swan, now raised purple in livid welts on her puffy skin.

The black King and red King from the chess game, phosphorescent with a greenish luminescence, lay on the scorched fire board beneath what was left of her.

"Fire is necessary to burn away all the lies that remain. I care not a whit what you look like, only that you are easy to take." Iago moved Peter's body into the circle.

When Peter's calloused hand touched her tender once-shoulder, she gasped, her raw pain cooled as her once-body flooded with the half-remembered sensation of opening the freezer to stick her upper body into its icy respite on a sweltering day. Instinctively, she drew nearer, thankful for the chilling reprieve from her agony.

She closed her once-eyes tight, for the first time comprehending what her brother Tom must have been feeling when he only deigned to look at her as he hurt her—for she recognized Tom's sadistic gaze staring back at her out of Peter's once-gentle face.

"Don't fight it," Peter's husky voice murmured as his other hand slid to the shriveled small of her once-back, "It will hurt less if you surrender the remnants. You only hurt because you hold on. . ."

Iagopeter bent to kiss its gambit.

A clamorous cacophony echoed through the heavens as the wooden roof was ripped from the barn above them, flinging Peter's and Vee's bodies out of the fire circle and away from each other like forsaken voodoo dolls.

For Hell was at long last empty, and all the devils were not Here, but There.

TWENTY-THREE

"For there is nothing either good or bad, but thinking makes it so."
—*Hamlet, attributed to William Shakespeare*

It sounded as though the world had ended, only to leave Val caged and cut off, stranded forever in a dystopian *Twilight Zone* rerun.

Perplexed and brooding, he'd been kneeling before his uncle's venerated prayer cabinet, hands clasped together as he asked the Lord for guidance, when he heard what sounded like a muffled boom from outside, followed by the roar of an unearthly thundering snarl, hurling him and anything that wasn't nailed down into the air. Thousands of hardcover books became deadly projectiles, only to land helter-skelter, altering Duke's Shambhala into shambolic bedlam.

A deafening silence ensued.

Terrified, he raced to the door, hurling himself against it in the desperate attempt to get out so he could lend aid in what he was convinced was a far greater calamity than his own. He shouted at the steadfast wooden barrier, seizing the door handle and shaking it in vain with all his might.

"*Allo zanmi'm,*" an affable voice said from behind him, almost startling him out of this world and into the next. "I think you need a helping hand, yes?"

Val recognized the jolly voice even before he turned to see the spry see-through Frenchman bouncing to an inaudible rhythm on top of his uncle's expensive desk. Long hair and beard moved up and down in a charming puckish way as he pranced upon his improvised stage, face bursting with exaggerated winking and twinkling, which would have made Val laugh out loud if the situation were not so dire.

"Yes—yes, I need assistance, very much actually," he said as he watched the ghost cartwheel off the desk and into a double summersault as though he was a gymnast dismounting from an Olympic balance beam. "You've never spoken to me before—I didn't even know you could speak English."

The ghost looked at him with the queerest expression, mischief in his merry eyes as he answered, "I was told to watch over your family, not to speak to you. Imagine my own surprise when I realized you were watching me back, *jen zanmi*! I've been obeying my charge for many generations, but you were the first to see me."

"Obeying your 'charge'? What do you mean?"

The Frenchman gamboled around Val and the desk as he sing songed, "'I charge you thus, oh Papa Paul, protect my family tree. Until the coming of the Beast, protect them, then be free.'"

Val felt the hint of a memory niggling at the nape of his neck. "The 'Beast'—what is that? And who 'charged' you?"

"Why, the Beast is the one who is come. *Mons la*, the eruption that just now scared you so. And it was your ancestor, your great-upon great-*granpapa*, who commanded me hence."

This was too much new information at once for Val to comprehend. "My grandfather? Who are you, how did you know him?"

"'Twas actually your mother's grandmother's mother's father, and oh, I knew him a great many of your years ago—long before the dream of you came to be. It was *se plezi'm* to serve such a great man during his visit to my hometown, Port-au-Prince." The blithe spirit jumped into a jaunty handstand on the desk for no reason whatsoever before he continued explaining from his upside-down position, "When my rival *houngan* tried to steal my *ti bon ange* and turn me into a *zombi*, it was your *granpapa* who saved me. Though I was already killed, he ensured my *ti bon ange* did not walk the earth as the undead or fall into evil hands, but instead gave me self-dominion over my spirit for as long as the earth should continue, on condition I fulfill this one onus."

"The 'onus' to protect my family when the Beast comes?"

Switching to a one-handed handstand, he stated: "Yes."

"And the 'Beast' is here, right now?"

"Yes, and *m'pa bon mem*—is. . . not so good." He answered as he switched to the other hand.

"What's happening out there?" Val threw up his hands toward the ceiling to indicate the world outside Duke's study. "Can you find Peter and Vee?"

"*Map tounen nan on ti momen*—one moment, I will be right back!" The nimble ghost vowed as he righted himself on the desk and, with a flamboyant bow, faded away.

Val, who never paced, found himself pacing the small room as though he could break through the floor to the room below with his footsteps. What was taking so long? With all the pandemonium outside, why hadn't his uncle come to let him out already?

Even more worrying, was Duke planning to ever let him out? Or worse—was he making phone calls to have him committed? Speaking of crazy, what to make of the Frenchman? Although that thick accent now seemed to Val less French and more Haitian Creole, since the lively ghost had known his ancestor in Haiti's capitol city—and did he say he had been a *houngan* when alive, as in a Vodou priest?

What did that make his great-great-great-grandfather, if he had the power to intercede on behalf of a dead Vodou priest?

It was at this precise moment Val noticed the Banker at the door—disconcerting, he hovered half inside and half outside the room. If possible, the ghost's permanent scowl seemed even deeper than usual, as he motioned in a stilted manner for Val to come outside Duke's study and follow him.

Val didn't know how best to respond, so he asked, "You want me to come outside with you?"

The ghost remained mute but nodded, most emphatic.

"I'm locked in this room," Val explained, turning the handle and demonstrating the door's inaccessibility. "I can't get out unless someone unlocks the door from the other side. Maybe my uncle?"

At the mention of Duke, the frantic ghost's translucent emptiness suffused with shadows, he began to wring his pellucid hands and, if it were possible, he grew even more morose, every corner of his downturned face plummeting toward the floor in a melodramatic fashion that would have been funny if it weren't so poignant. The Banker threw himself outside, peeked his top hat and eyes back inside as he reached his arm around and through the door—pointing toward Val with a pasty finger—then out the door and what Val could only guess was downstairs.

"Is my uncle. . . in trouble?"

Nod-nod-nod-nod-nod-nod-nod-nod-nod. Most emphatic.

Just then the jovial Houngan materialized to his left, saying, "It has gone from bad to worse. Your uncle ran outside when he heard the commotion, and now the Beast has him in His clutches."

"What do you mean He has him in His 'clutches'? Actual clutches, like some B-movie monster?"

"I do not know this 'B movie,' but I mean he is in the Beast's hands—or paws? I am not sure of the correct word to describe these appendages."

Val stopped pacing, frozen in place by the image implanted in his brain of King Kong holding his uncle aloft in fists the size of mini vans. "What on earth would the Beast want with Duke?"

Val noticed a phenomenon he had suspected was so, but only now did the present events prove his earlier inklings: the two ghosts seemed unaware of each other's presence. Both looked at Val as though he was the only other being in the room. Odd. Vee seemed to have no problem perceiving other ghosts. . . .

"Vee! Where is Vee? And Peter?"

"I saw a human body among the wreckage of the demolished barn—I think it is male, but I could not tell who it was, or even if it is living or dead. Your Vee I cannot see."

"But usually you can see her?"

The Houngan's ghost eyes narrowed, as though he suspected Val spoke in jest. "Yes, of course I can see your girl. She is like me, a spirit who has chosen to be on Earth but is not imprisoned here. With silly glasses."

"Can you see all ghosts?"

"I do not know. I see whom I wish to see, this I do know."

"Do you see this fellow to my right, at the door?"

The ghost peered at the wooden impediment, poring over it before answering, "I did not, but now I do. As I said, I only see that which I believe to be."

"What do you see?"

The Houngan seemed at a loss for words. Finally shaking his ghostly head, he answered, "I see a tall Anglo in a top hat and turn-of-the-century suit. With a mustachio. Most unhappy."

So, he could see the Banker clear enough, but the Banker still looked only at Val, with the bottom corners of his miserable frown at least a foot closer to the ground now.

"But he doesn't see you?" asked Val, as the Banker glowered at him and faded away, one could only assume to return to his dear Duke.

"No, of course not. That ghost is a remnant. Because he is so small, he can only see what resonates with what is left of him. He probably cannot speak, either, or if he does speak it is only in catch phrases or half-remembered refrains. The larger and more whole the being, the greater the capacity to perceive and interact."

"Then why can he see me? And my uncle? Do we 'resonate' with him?"

Cocking his head to the left, the Houngan said, "I am not sure this is the best way to spend this precious time, having a lesson on the basic *mystè* of the universe. Most of you Anglos, as a culture, are oblivious to the spirit world and ignorant of its order. In short, all of us, to a lesser or greater degree, depending upon our capabilities and our awareness, pull some experiences and entities toward ourselves, and push others away, like magnets, because of what we say 'yay' or 'nay' to."

"Are you talking about the Law of Attraction?"

The ghost pressed his lips together to blow a loud, wet raspberry that would have sent Blanche into an affronted tongue-lashing had she heard it. "No, no, no. Like much of the Anglo dilution of divinity, that initial misconception has been altered to the point it no longer contains any kernel of truth." He motioned toward the empty space that had once been the Banker, "If that poor shade sees your uncle, then there is a decision or belief he is stuck repeating that somehow echoes a decision or belief your uncle is actively choosing or rejecting right now."

"So, it's the fixation on being or not-being something that draws them together?"

A gleam returned to the Houngan's eyes as he answered with a knowing grin, "You have some of your granpapa in you yet. Yes, exactly. It is like the Beast. The Beast has been seeking your uncle for some time."

It was Val's turn to shake his own head, but in repudiation. "My uncle has nothing in common with a creature so horrifying you would call it the Beast. That's not possible."

Slapping his transparent forehead, the Houngan groaned in exasperation. "Everything is energy—*tout bagay*. All things vibrate and emit a frequency. Your uncle emits a frequency the Beast needs to resurrect the cult which in turn will resurrect Him into a physical body. You see, the Beast is shape without mass. His substance is not of this world, and he has straddled the worlds of spirit and the worlds of matter for aeons, waiting to be made flesh. He senses in your uncle the High Priest or *houngan* He needs to perform the ritual and ceremonies for His return, His incarnation into this physical domain."

"How do you know this? And if He isn't physical, how can He be holding my uncle at all?"

"The Beast is quite old, more cunning than he is old, and even stronger still. I was raised with whispers and hushed stories, which your *granpapa* told me are sprinkled like infested compost throughout the ends of the earth. Physicality may be alien to the Beast's nature, but He covets and He consumes, both of which are central to His nature." The Houngan heaved a sigh, a far-off look in his still-human eyes. "Millennia beyond present-day memory, this was His realm, but He was betrayed and cast out by a collusion between those He enslaved with those whom He served Himself—by virtue of His vulnerable incorporeality. He has existed as essence under the waters and in the void since, waiting for all to align so He can manifest in the mortal world. Although He lacks a physical structure, He yet has the power of force and form, which He is using right now to manipulate atoms as He once did aeons ago, abolishing the barn and holding your uncle captive."

Val's heart began to race, as though it hoped if it just pumped hard and fast enough it would propel him to save those he loved. "If so much time has passed, why does He return now? And why here, in our barn?"

With a curt nod and a straightening of his spectral shoulders, a mismatched serious expression descended upon the Houngan's usually comical face. "I am not sure you are ready to hear what I have to say next, but there is none of your time left. Prepare yourself: A demon possessed your friend Peter." In response to Val's bulging eyes, the ghost quickly assuaged, "Demon is *petèt* not the best word, with how you Anglos have bastardized it. This being is more like an imp, or a discarnate. . . uh. . . goblin, from your own folklores. A parasite. One of the race created to serve the Beast in ages past. In element like its Master, neither of this world nor the next, I am not sure how it has endured so long, but it is here and has taken control of your friend. Your *granpapa* would have called it a 'shoggoth.'"

A freakish keening began, like the clanging and screeching of thousands of sentient cathedral bells being pitched again and again into each other, tintinnabulating from all sides outside the study walls.

A nameless, accursed sound emerged, as if all the souls in Hades itself rose up in a dirge to blanket the world with rage in their pitiless torment. As the floor began to convulse and buckle, Val experienced the most peculiar *déjà vu*, and then he remembered:

Duke and he—and even Vee—had encountered what Vee had called "a paltry beast" just weeks ago, arising from the baptismal as Val and his uncle tried to align the communion table in the church sanctuary.

Could that beast and this Beast be the same sacrilege? But that beast had been tamed and contained within Vee's vest pocket, hadn't it? If they were one and the same, what had transpired since then, and how on earth had the Beast escaped?

Val covered his ears and found himself cowering in response to the inhuman din ringing throughout the night. The Houngan cringed as well, grimacing as the earthquake continued. "*Bondye mwen*, it seems despite my devotion to save your family, we may still lose the whole world."

Then the floor beneath Val cleft open like a cavernous, jagged mouth, and as he plunged into the maw beneath, he cracked his head on a saw-toothed edge, knocking him into oblivion.

TWENTY-FOUR

"What's in a name? that which we call a rose by any other name. . . "
—*Romeo and Juliet, attributed to William Shakespeare*

An unseen chasm had been bridged, as viscous dream-haunted skies swelled down to merge with the close air of the barn. Fevered torrents of violet midnight dusted with noxious starlight and vortices of fire from beyond the worlds conjoined with all the nightmares lost by humanity and careened toward Vee as she lay sprawled upon what was left of the hay-strewn barn floor and the broken fire circle.

Above her, the gargantuan Desecration that had plucked the roof off the barn vacillated between ballooning to the magnitude of a three-ring circus tent and then—as if the very air itself caused it intense agony—recoiled back down to about the size of a bull elephant. Hovering cockeyed in midair on what looked like leathery bat-like wings far too small to hold its corpulent belly airborne, the iridescent octopod head littered with serpentine scales shifted back and forth from chartreuse to pickle green, as though crafted of a poisonous reversible fabric. The globular cranium was capped on the top with ten horns, each horn fouled with the mockery of a festooned crown, and on the opposite end, covering its would-be chin, protruded a morass of tentacle-like feelers, like a beard of wriggling worms stretching to gobble up its sucker-like nipples. Two tiny, ineffectual legs and two misshapen arms stuck out willy-nilly, as though four sticks had been jammed last minute on a snowman by a child tired of icy winter play.

It looked like what would result if a dragon and an octopus gang-banged a lioness in a bear's den while a leopard watched in disgust.

The Anathema was accompanied by its own eldritch soundtrack, too. From the gaping slash across the night sky behind it, leading to the abyss whence it had spawned, spewed a chatter and clamor of discordant shrieking and yowling such that would drive an operatic maestro to lunacy.

And it seemed vaguely familiar. Although noncorporeal beings could assume any appearance at will, they still tended to have subtle similarities to all their façades. Little tells, like visual preferential loops that kept reappearing in each presentation, habitual versions of themselves, exposing the being and its unconscious preoccupations.

Vee intended to reach up and touch what was left of her face, only to discover she lifted a not-arm once more. With the shattering of the fire circle, so too her own imprisonment of form appeared to have ended.

Flexing her renewed freedom, she levitated her not-body just a centimeter off the ground—infinitesimal, so as not to gain the attention of the Thing above her—and lowered herself again.

Check.

Quiet and cautious, she looked down at her lifted not-hand, roasted beyond recognition by Iago's assault, focused her full perceptivity upon it, and thrilled as it smoothed to its preferred aspect of her seventeen-year-old self while she watched.

Dissolving, she took in her surroundings, expanding outward until she felt her outsight touch Peter's supine body on the other side of the barn: Unmoving, but still warm.

He was alive—only just. But if she somehow revived him, would it be Peter or Iago she would face?

Better to gather as much information as possible before acting. It would be challenging enough to confront the larger problem without complicating it further by adding her own smaller problem into the mix.

Focusing her whole attention on the Miscreation—now about the size of a passenger train car—as it deflated and distended above her, she at last realized why it seemed so damned familiar.

Those illogical wings. . . those revolting tentacles. . . the gyrating sludge of superfluous twilight squelched within tumorous margins, as though invoking a perpetual state of metaphysical constipation: It was the she-male, the beast she had folded up and given to the prince for laughs as a thank-you gift.

How was this possible?

"Psssst," a voice echoed within her not-mind, "do you know who you are yet?"

The prince of darkness, of course. Whenever she contemplated him, no matter how unintentional her conjuration, he answered. They had long since dispensed with the pretense of using nonextant vocal cords or not-mouths, but this time his response seemed rapid, even for him. It made one wonder if he hadn't been waiting in the wings for her to make the connection all along?

She got right to the point. "What in heavens happened to that beastly shehe I gave you?"

"First of all, regardless of your frame of reference, He self-identifies as a male, so get the gender right for civility's sake. Secondly, that depends upon your point of view: It's possible He escaped through the rupture between dimensions created by your would-be possessors when they succeeded in fragmenting the boundaries of beingness by improbably encapsulating a spirit in palpable form. Conversely, it might be that the stars have finally aligned so He could gain the force of presence He's sought for aeons to reclaim His reign of terror on Earth. Contrariwise, perhaps I let Him go at the most auspicious moment of my infinite grander design. Opposably, it is possible the prophesied stars of old are not astral exploding balls of hydrogen and helium, but in fact key actors on the stage of manifestation who, through their sheer magnitude of collective size and flare-up of energy across the space-time continuum when incarnated in the same place and time, have always caused the gates between dimensions to thin: of which yourself, your boyfriend, his ex-girlfriend, his best friend, and his uncle are the main players."

"Impossible."

"And so, the Cheshire Cat must make the Queen eat her own words: 'Sometimes I've believed as many as six impossible things before breakfast.'"

Vee's not-stomach grumbled.

The Beast reached down into the pulverized barn to grasp Peter's insensible body with what could only be described as an undulating claw and lifted the body toward His rotund abdomen with a gibbering howl. For the first time Vee recognized Val's uncle dangling overhead, clenched in a pincer-like tentacle, shouting in his futile thrashing to get away.

She knew she should do something—anything—but she found herself immobilized with panic at the idea of contending with Peter and Duke. Opposing the hideous Beast seemed like child's play in comparison, except her not-body refused to budge at all. Her not-mind fogged. Her foresight got down on all fours, put its tail between its legs, and ran for the hills.

And what about Val? Where was he—was he okay? Should she abandon saving the ones he loved most to find him?

The prince's disembodied voice purred in her not-mind. "Are you finished with your Tom-foolery? Are you at last ready to stop chasing Vs, and see Vee?"

Cross and overwhelmed by his nagging, she said, "Stop growling when you're pleased and wagging your tail when you're angry. Help me stop this madness!"

"We're all mad here. Stop having your Fear. Stop trying to do something. Stop being Vs."

Frustrated beyond all frustration as the Beast inflated to the size of a skyscraper, her not-mind noiselessly yelled: "How can I stop being myself? Why can't I act against the Beast? I folded Him up like a freaking piece of putty before, I stuck Him in my pocket and gave Him to you. What's wrong with me?"

"Know thyself."

"I'm Silvia, you puzzling git—Vee for short!" Helpless, she watched the two dots she knew to be Val's beloved friend and uncle, her not-body returned to her prior ethereal inability to intercede in physicality. The dot that was Peter (and Iago?) began to wriggle, apparently rousted to his (their?) frantic plight. Desperate, she screamed at the prince, "Stop with the riddles, there's no time!"

As though in answer to her charge, the scene turned to stone around her. "If you needed a little time, you had only to ask. . . ," the prince's unctuous voice chided. "You know very well time is merely a subjective construct. And 'Silvia' is the name of your last body, not your true name. You've had many names, worn many faces, lived many lifetimes. To see the proper course, you must first properly see yourself, embracing that which you reject. When all else fails, remember: The enemy of my enemy is my friend."

At his cryptic suggestion, Vee remembered the enemy of her prior predicament: Iago.

That iniquitous, molesting, manipulative, and slightly patronizing Mephistopheles that had stolen Peter's body from him and tried to use it to usurp her as well. What had it monologued about during its villainous gloating? Something about the pulp horror of Lovecraft? It professed it quoted from the make-believe grimoire so often referenced in H. P.'s stories—the Necronomicon—about the return of the Old Ones, something about a lost Key required for when the stars were aright, and chief among the Old Gods was a High Priest who, impossible as it may be, looked very much like the twisting chaos holding Peter and Duke captive above her.

Could the fictional world of H. P. Lovecraft, mind-boggling as it might be to imagine, be actual? Was it possible that that prejudiced author of the Cthulhu mythos, that small-minded racist who only became famous after his ignoble death, was actually an overlooked prophet of the true cosmic horror?

How could such a vain and intolerant dead man with so many despised opinions also be the bearer of truth? Was it possible that truth was truth regardless of its source—that in fact, humanity misses the truth again and again by fixating on finding fault with the source of the message in order to be able to dismiss the condemning truth that it desperately wishes to avoid? And why did the prospect of such a feeble harbinger horrify her inexplicably more than the likelihood that his Yog-Sothothery might be so?

Was the unspeakable Word trying to become flesh and dwell among us?

"All things are possible," whispered the prince in her not-mind. "But each and All have a say in how probable."

Each and All. . . each and All. . . the Key and the Stars. . . Vee dimly recalled a book she'd read while confined in her hospital bed during one particularly aggressive round of chemo, concerning cosmology and modern thought about the composition of the universe. Matter only makes up about 5 percent of the physical universe; the rest is an invisible substance called "dark matter," which scientists have yet to see but know must exist because of the gravitational effect it has on galaxies and the stars within and between them. Enfolding it all together is an enigmatic force dubbed "dark energy," which both repels gravity and increases in influence as the universe expands, sort of like the broth of a universal soup with surface tension.

The Dark Energy between the Matter and the Dark Matter: The Penumbra between the Light and the Darkness.

The Key between There and Here.

Could it really be so simple?

"Occam's Razor, my dear. . . ," said the prince, ". . . all things being equal, the simplest explanation is the answer."

The Key would be neither good nor evil, neither darkness nor light, neither dark matter nor matter. The Key would be neither living nor dead, but something else entirely. The Key would exist, yet not as others exist.

The Key, impossible as it might seem, was the simplest answer: Iago. An entity that by its very nature was a Penumbra, Dark Energy personified.

"Iago is the Key," Vee told the prince. "But it has no idea, does it?"

"No idea, just as you have no idea of you and even less of an inkling of me." She closed her not-eyes in response to the gravity of his words, and only then did she see him.

The prince of darkness had been within her, around her, and without her absolutely throughout time and space: The Alpha and the Omega (and All Between), the First and the Last, the Beginning and the End. In attribute, the prince of darkness no longer, for now he appeared to her clad in a Kiton suit made entirely of pure gold, his hair white as snow on sheep's wool, his eyes molten with coal forever burning at their core. His shoes were the finest Testoni in the world, shining like burnished bronze, and a silvery flute peeked out of his coat pocket.

When at first (and at last) he spoke, it sounded to Vee as though she was back at Niagara Falls with her mother and father—the one vacation they'd taken together without her brother Tom—and the only time she'd ever felt truly safe in her fleeting life as Silvia. Of course, there hadn't been that celestial soundtrack playing in the background then—reminiscent of Stanley Myer's classical guitar masterpiece, *Cavatina*, only this rendition seemed to be played by every instrument in existence all at once yet somehow impossibly showcasing each instrument's unique solo sound exclusively—soothing her while the doting prince reproached her.

"You painted me too-dimensional in your stories, of course. From the mash-up name you gave me—*Azathoth*—to the way you demonized me as the Lord of Chaos. What's wrong with a bit of Chaos? For all your verbal genius and extra sensory precognitions, you really did mislead your readers into calling me the blind idiot god, when you know very well I am not blind, but can only be invoked by the blind— those who are separated from their physical senses, like yourself. Even when you were the Apostle John, who tended toward histrionics, you wrote a more accurate account of me in your book of Revelation. But quibbles aside, LoVecraft: Do you see?"

And Vee saw the truth, like coming home to the Ideal of home, at last free of Plato's Cave.

A succession of lifetimes and not-lifetimes passed before her/ him/them in the twinkling of an eye—some hers, some not-hers, but all these dead faces resurrected to converge into the one great Void looped into and upon itself again and again in the narrative conceded by Rome in their myth of Veritas—and the Greeks in Alethia—that elusive goddess of truth and daughter of Saturn, the mother of Virtue. Hers was the objectionable chore to be the shunned messenger of what mortals most despised: the bearer of the bad news that no one wants to hear but just might save us all.

"The End" made flesh to haunt the living.

For it is not facts, but the narratives we tell ourselves to make sense of the facts, that form the fabric of our lives; the living struggle to persevere in the denial of the insatiable Ouroboros.

She had known them all before: Val, Duke, Peter, even Julie. They were each her, yet not-her (and often not-him), incarnating together over and over, assuming various personas and permutations, living most of their lives separate and apart, but in the few precious lifetimes where alignment occurred—which almost didn't happen this time around, with Vee's premature death—the gate between dimensions opened, for they the "stars" were at last aright. Each of the five an ingredient for the magical spell cast aeons ago by the Old Ones to ensure Their return to power over the physical domain.

Iago was the Key required to unlock Vee's Message, so that the Show might go on.

As a particularly insistent V buzzed obsessively before Vee's appalled not-eyes, she recognized the little blighter actually wore the somber face of that xenophobic Howard Phillips Lovecraft himself, morphed with her own visage to form a tiny insect atrocity. Shooing it away in shame, she objected, "But I don't believe any of this! I don't believe in gods or goddesses and I don't believe in reincarnation. I certainly don't believe that I was Daniel or John of Patmos or Nostradamus or Cayce, either—so don't even freaking imply it!"

"Your belief is not prerequisite. Even your English word *believe* contains *be* the *lie* as its essence. Humans fear aliens because their very otherness is based upon *a-lie*."

"What the hell are you blathering on about?"

"It matters not whether the lie is hellish, earthly, or heavenly—it's still a lie."

"A lie is a statement made by someone who doesn't believe it with the intention that someone else is led to believe it."

For one terrible moment, the prince glared at Vee with his abyssal eyes. "How temporal of you to clothe the very word itself in deception. Intention is irrelevant, of course. People innocently believe and spread all sorts of lies, unconscious of their deceit, because they share without seeing. A lie is alteration, a second postulate fashioned to mask the first. You must lie to survive. Absolute truth cannot persist in the physical universe, so anything you believe or perceive must contain lies in order to continue."

"So, what I am is the lie?"

"What you are is what you are. What you are not is the lie. Not just you, of course—all of you."

"So, what you're telling me is that humanity is a collection of lies, the insignificant afterthoughts of the Old Ones, who intended them to be the next slave race in a succession of alterations concocted to manipulate the lie of existence?"

"The Old Ones are themselves much older lies, and significance has nothing to do with it." The prince smiled his ineffable smile as he quoted LoVecraft's own words right back at her: "Yog-Sothoth knows the gate. Yog-Sothoth is the gate. Yog-Sothoth is the key and guardian of the gate. Past, present, future, all are one in Yog-Sothoth. He knows where the Old Ones broke through of old, and where They shall break through again. He knows where They have trod Earth's fields, and where They still tread them, and why no one can behold Them as They tread."

The prince of darkness wasn't telling her—she was telling herself.

And Vee saw that she was Yog-Sothoth, and yet. . . somehow, she was not. She was missing something, had been missing a vital part of herself for time immemorial, returning to human life again and again as a dog to its own vomit in her desperate search for it—but she didn't know the source of the agonizing loss within her. Only that she was but a broken refrain without it.

"Because of Iago," the prince interjected into her introspection. "Although you know that's not the rascal's true name. To counter the intentions of the Old Ones, it was necessary to break off a part of myself, encasing it within their noisome likeness and planting it among Them, so existence might have a penumbra between the light and the darkness: a chance to save itself."

"Why don't you just save us all?"

The prince laughed as a lone, grief-stricken tear trickled down his ageless cheek. "Save Existence from the sum total of exactly what its actions beget? I would never deign to such sublime wickedness. You must save yourselves, or you will only re-create the catastrophe again and again in each successive and ever-more depraved Arkham. It is for you and the one who calls itself Iago to spark the Catharsis that will purge existence from the cancer it has created for itself."

A hollow feeling—as though someone was using an ice scream scoop to gut her—provoked an unwonted craving to retch. "How can you ask such a thing of me? That snake tried to commit the worst atrocity imaginable, and it tried to do it to me. It's unforgivable. How can you ask me to forgive the very perpetrator who tried to rape what makes me, me?"

"You are asking it of yourself, not I. To an individual, rape is one of the worst crimes imaginable, perhaps second only to extermination. But there are far-more-heinous transgressions. The Old Ones will perpetrate devastation of a magnitude that makes the biblical predictions of Armageddon look like a sappy happy-ending, and to All. How can you afford not to let go of the lie of separation, especially when not letting go is, in the end, not forgiving yourself? You must either die to yourself or continue the lie of yourself. . . and the Vs shall never cease."

Vee remembered a conversation she'd had with the German philosopher Heidegger so many once-upon-a-times ago: the discovery of truth is not epistemological, no matter how much humans may want it to be. People cannot investigate the way we know things, only what we know. The discovery of truth is ontological, for what we are as we describe things and their relationships determines our answer to the question, "What is true?" Truth is found in Being, not being. For "only a god can save us."

The prince of darkness wished her to Be much, much more than Vee.

The First and the Last spoke for the final time: "I will neither tell you what to do nor hinder the consequences of your choice, but I will help facilitate your options. First, I will rescue from the Beast the body that the Key occupies, so you may elect to do what you will with it. Then, I will leave you to your decision and save the only person whose plight might encumber your ability to choose, free of impediment: I will give Val all he needs to ensure his own safety until it is finished."

With these words, the prince withdrew from her awareness.

As though Medusa reversed her curse of petrification, the stone scene around Vee gradually suffused with color and came back to life. While she watched, the mountainous Beast lifted the dot that was Peter's body to His cuttlefish head, stared at it with His tumescent eyes, seemed to begin scolding it in what sounded like a sickening cross between Klingon and the Black Speech of Mordor, and then tossed Peter aside like some plaything in which He'd lost interest.

As the Beast zeroed in on the dot that was Duke, Peter's body fell the hundreds of feet toward what probably would have been his death, except that an opaque lavender cloud appeared out of Nowhere, catching him and gently lowering him to the ground beside Vee, just behind a pile of broken barn rubble that too-easily hid him from the Beast's view.

Next, the singed fire board too-conveniently materialized beneath her, nebulously luminous and expediently enabling Iago to see her with Peter's all-too-human eyes, as well as allowing her to perceive Iago herself. Her not-body solidified, becoming touchable once again.

"Thank you," she murmured to no-thing, "for supplying all my need according to your riches in glory."

"Amen," whispered Peter's tenuous voice, regulated by the puppeteer Iago, who unsteadily raised the body to balance on Peter's elbows. "—that is what you people say in response to quoting your absurd scriptures, correct?"

As Duke yelped above them, the Beast responded with what almost sounded like a seductive crooning in His hideous language—if the seducer was a rabid cat the size of Godzilla, of course.

Iago, to Vee's shock and mounting dismay, interpreted: "My Master wishes your paramour's elder relation to join Him, promising him treasures and dominion beyond imagining, if he will but perform the ritual of incarnation and make my Master flesh yet again."

"The Beast is your. . . Master?" she asked, feeling sorry for the devil despite herself. "As in, you have to serve. . . That?"

Iago shrugged with an all-too-human sigh, unnerving Vee as it said, "Well, to be perfectly frank, I and a small number of my fellow slaves engineered His downfall from physicality so many aeons ago, though He knows not my part in it. He thinks me a loyal, if limited, drudge at best." A self-satisfied smirk spread across Peter's artless features.

"So, you're not glad to see He's returned?"

"Understatement of the aeon. Of all the aeons. My greatest fear has been realized, and I only watch with metaphorical gnashing of teeth as I wait for the end of this last stronghold of my independence, which my Master so rudely thwarted by revivifying during my attempt to supplant you."

"Wow, you really are the drama queen, aren't you?"

Iago impaled Vee with a black look, enclosing a host of untold tribulations and torments it had witnessed and withstood during its wretched half-life. Rape was but one of the millions of atrocities contained within those haunted eyes.

For the first time since dying, Vee felt quite small, like a fledgling sparrow chirruping at a hoary pterodactyl.

"Your name isn't really Iago, is it?"

"You know, at the end of everything, I never imagined I would be sharing this with you of all beings, but no. It isn't. And I am not going to tell you my name, as I forgot it long ago. . . " Iago sagged, its voice a resigned monotone. ". . .There's far too much power in a name anyway. Not some mystical magic as so many fantasy stories and occult dunderheads believe: Names are formative. Naming organizes how we think, reordering our reality so we see our labels and verbal symbols rather than what's actual. Eventually, all beings experience the world through abstraction." With a faraway look in Peter's forest eyes, Iago continued. "I adopted the name Iago to shape myself. No longer a slave, but master of my own destiny. Change the name, alter the organizing principle, and you change the expression of the being. Names determine our truth, how we perceive reality. They single-handedly create political movements, champion creeds and prejudices, and even keep people in bad relationships."

Vee peered up at the Beast above them and noticed a horde of equally alien blasphemies escaping through the contused gash in the sky, amassing what could only be an otherworldly army behind Him. "What's your Master's name?"

"The name given Him by humanity in recent centuries comes from the Greek word *chthonic*, meaning subterranean or of the underworld. It's not His true name, but a description of His current activity from a human perspective. He is also known as the High Priest by his cultist followers, and I call him Master because of my past—and my apparent future."

"Do you know if He can be stopped?"

Peter's face filled with such a profound grief it broke Vee's now-heart. She found herself mourning the loss of the potential of what not-Iago might have been, had it not been subjected to the vile whims of the Old Ones. "He has been paused before—ejected from prospective physicality by key players—but I myself, other than being a bystander, had nothing to do with it. I doubt His efforts can ever be wholly stopped, though."

A team of the newly-arrived minions carried an enormous slab of granite—not a stone table?!—and a struggling cow across the heavens, dropping the huge rock with a tremendous CRACK on the ground in front of the Beast and plopping the cow atop it. Cackling from all corners of the horde commenced, along with some jeering and a disconcerting wheezing, as two huge trees stripped of any leaves and branches were nailed together at the head of the stone table with glee.

A ritual sacrifice? An upside-down crucifixion? And demonic resurrection?

Not in LoVecraft's story: Not Here. Not There.

And thus, LoVecraft shed the hides of cowardice and failure and bias at last, to end the story begun so very long, long ago.

TWENTY-FIVE

"This above all: to thine own self be true,
And it must follow, as the night the day,
Thou canst not then be false to any man."
—Hamlet, attributed to William Shakespeare

"*Reveye zanmim'. . .* " a soft voice spoke to Val, stirring him from his mantle of halcyon darkness. "The time to wake is now, if ever the world might wake again."

He opened his eyes, too-heavy in response to the throbbing pain radiating throughout the back of his head. The concerned, though still incongruously jolly, physiognomy of the Houngan spirit hung just above him, gossamer facial wrinkles squished together like a scrunched-up cellophane candy wrapper.

"My head is killing me."

"Killing, perhaps—but not killed, not yet. How I wish I had my old body to mix *geri remèd fèy* and make a poultice to apply to that nasty cut on your noggin. It's amazing you survived the fall at all. You must stop the bleeding, or you will never get out of here. . . and I suspect the building is unstable."

Val took in his situation for the first time, surprised to find he had fallen through not just the study floor, but the second and down to the first floor of the house as well. Blanche's collapsed kitchen surrounded him, her cherished pizza oven in shambles as the Cook sobbed with silent heaves over the crushed countertop that had once served as her unearthly throne. He was himself covered in dust and debris, and when his hand finally ventured to the back of his skull he felt what could only be a flap of hair-covered skin hanging loose from his occipital bone, the entire area soaking wet to his touch, probably with his own blood.

"Oh, cruel God in heaven, how much more will you punish us?" he found himself rambling. He was probably going into shock. "Must you be so cruel to be kind?"

"Why yes, Will," a disembodied voice echoed in his pounding head, "—yes, I must."

Val closed his world-weary eyes, not sure if this was some new species of specter heretofore unmet, or if he was at last losing whatever slim vestiges of sanity he had left.

Only when he closed his eyes did he see the speaker: A monolithic lantern shone before him with two heads, one of a raven-eyed lady with long, black wires for hair and the other of a fair youth as lovely as a summer's day.

He opened his eyes, and the apparition vanished.

"I'm not a ghost, and I'm not attached to a body, so you'll have to close your eyes if you wish to see me," suggested the voice in his head once more. "You're not crazy, just limited by your twelve senses."

Twelve senses? He knew of five, maybe six if you include extra sensory perception, but twelve?

The Houngan shrugged, evidently pleading the fifth.

The voice in Val's head said, "Joe Schwartz will prove the other six in a ground breaking experiment in the future—that is, if this timeline continues that long."

Val closed his eyes again but continued using his voice to speak to. . . whatever this was. "If I'm not crazy, am I dreaming?"

The two-headed lantern answered, "Queen Mab has not been to visit; however, a dream itself is but a shadow and a toy, so in that sense, Val is but another dream dreamt by Will."

"Who is this Will? My name isn't Will, it's Valentine—although my friends call me Val."

"If you say so, it must be so."

"Who are you? The Patron Saint of Riddles?"

"You once called me your Muse, but I prefer to think of myself as a fellow of infinite jest."

"You keep referencing Shakespeare." Val's breath caught in this throat as it dawned on him. "Are you William Shakespeare? Vee said she hadn't met you yet—where have you been hiding?"

"The one you love calls me her Cheshire Cat, but I am not her mate."

Cheshire Cat. . . this was Vee's infamous prince of darkness!

But if the prince wasn't Shakespeare, then. . .

Oh.

My.

Bard.

"Are you implying I was William Shakespeare?"

"Oh, if I were implying it, I would be much more delicate. It would take you years, maybe centuries to unravel my allusions as your ministers and scribes wrote endless commentary on the subject. But there really is no time for subtlety, and so I am telling you, man: You are Will Shakespeare. At least, you were. Or you will be. Gah—time is such a nuisance here; I really must do something about it. . . " The prince trailed off as though giving the idea serious consideration but then seemed to discard the notion almost as soon as it occurred to him. "Back to the point: I promised Vee I'd protect you while she decides whether or not to save the world." His mind seemed to wander again, as though the hills, valleys, and canals of his attention were much too multi layered to navigate within this world's inadequate dimensions. Shaking the youth's head as he slapped the dark lady across her roseless cheek, he concluded, "So let's get you cleaned up and stop that deathening hemorrhage before we lose Val, and the two of you have to find each other all over again."

"Wait, just wait—"

"So be it."

"Let's say for the sake of argument I am William Shakespeare reincarnated, the greatest writer the world has ever known—"

"Well, let's not exaggerate. Perhaps one of the greatest *English* writers, but the Persian poets and those Russian fellows, now that's where I think one finds—"

"Why don't I remember? Why tell me now. . . " Val lost the ability to formulate words as what the supposed-prince had said about Vee began to sink into his injury-addled brain. It took a few inhalations to recover control of his lips, but when recover control he did, he yelled, "And what the hell do you mean—" the yelling instigated a sharp, piercing jab of searing pain throughout his temples, as though someone stuck a carving knife into his grey matter and twisted it with an expert hand. Squeezing his eyes shut as tight as possible, he ended in a whisper. "—Vee has to decide whether or not to save the world?"

"You've finished with Shakespeare, so that particular lifetime no longer lingers for you as Val—you altered the progression of human consciousness and moved on. Spirits in bodies only remember other lives when they are stuck there, have unfinished business, or are lying to themselves about their identity. Vee circles around her Vs because not only were her stories poorly received, but her prophesies went equally misunderstood. Shakespeare already prevented his own apocalypse. Now, you've progressed to being Val for reasons only you can guess. You probably don't remember any of your other lives, which is as the physical experience was meant to be." At a snail's pace, the lantern body phased first into a crescent moon, then a half moon, and finally became a blood moon, dripping vermillion for theatrical effect. One lone violin began playing Samuel Barber's *Adagio for Strings* in the background during the prince's transformation, Val's favorite song. "Vee is working out her own salvation with fear and trembling, but it's your life as Shakespeare that Vee needs you to remember if she's to succeed."

The strange being who claimed to be the prince of darkness stared at him, both heads unblinking, as though waiting for something.

Cobwebs began to choke Val's muddled brain, and he realized he had only a brief time left before unconsciousness again claimed his feeble frame. As though a toddler speaking his first hesitant sentences, he asked the only two questions that must be answered for him to continue: "Are you God? And if you are, why did you make me as I am?"

The blood moon metamorphosed into a blazing sun superimposed with an upright cross inscribed with a red, red rose. The two heads disappeared, to be replaced with a head that looked exactly as Duke had looked to Val when he was a very small child, wearing the same adoring expression his uncle had always worn when he gazed at his fair-haired nephew.

"This is my beloved son, in whom I am well pleased."

With these words, his heavenly father reached toward Val's broken and bleeding body, tenderly wrapping around him and even seeping into him until a soothing heat saturated every part of him, calming his restless questions and helping him fill the hollows that he'd refused to give himself permission to fill on his own.

And as Val's pain ceased, he remembered: Everything.

Alacritous, he stood—now with eyes wholly open—and said to the supernatural Houngan who anxiously waited in the wings, "The wheel has come full circle: I am here."

And thus, the two exited, stage right.

TWENTY-SIX

"Thus with a kiss I die."
—*Romeo and Juliet, attributed to William Shakespeare*

"I know how we can stop your Master, but only if we work together." The being who was so much more than Vee spoke to the being who called itself Iago.

A glint of Peter peeked through as growing admiration filled the otherwise beaten emerald eyes, or perhaps she'd only shocked the hell out of it with her ballsy suggestion, for the moment weakening its iron grip on Peter's body.

Surprised by the authority of her own conviction, she continued. "We must finish what we started, but as two willing participants. There'll be no domination or submission. Your impulse to annex me may have been mutated by your distorted intention, but only you could consummate such a Penumbra. It's your singular nature. Although some stories end as they begin, the beginning alone cannot end it. Only the End and the Once can forgive the Way, and the Way must be forgiven if the pages of separation are to unfold."

Iago's fear filled Peter's eyes. "But won't we both cease to be?"

"Your dark instincts to take me were vicious, but Nature herself is violence incarnate. How many billions of bacteria have died brutally so one human body might heal? You were willing to destroy me to gain your own incorruptibility. Now, I need you to be willing to lose yourself as I lose myself, so we might become the Between and force your Master through our Gate."

Iago looked long and hard at its Master—shrunk down now to His preferred size of a sprawling southern mansion—and found itself pensive, glimpsing a trace of something it had denied long ago. It demanded of the ghost girl, "What do you know that I do not?"

"Oh, a great many things. I suspect in truth you know far more than I do but are simply less honest about it. I know humanity has only barely begun to scratch the terrifying vistas of actuality with their science and technology—but, alas, the aftershocks such as the return of your Master have come for them regardless. I know that everything, from the largest galaxy to the tiniest quark, is sentient. Just as a scientist does not see the sentiency of a virus, so humanity does not recognize the sentience of the stars and the heavens. You, my dearest enemy, are a virus to my galaxy, but it is only together we may form the black hole needed to compress the Beast from physical existence, once and for all."

Iago refused to surrender to this series of shadows who called itself Vee, who didn't even apprehend the awfulness of the grander design. "Allow me to add some horrification to your ignorance. It is because of the coming of the Old Ones this dimension even exists: When my Master and His Cronies first encountered this chunk of impending-space and soon-to-be-time called There, a group of valiant Stars battled Them but lost the war and sacrificed themselves, their bodies conjoining to become the black hole—that fusion of stars getting ever closer and more dense until the temperature falls, gravity increases, and the magnificent mess collapses to a single point containing the original mass in a profoundly smaller space—at the center of what humans call a galaxy. Over the distance of what humankind eventually called 'time,' billions upon billions of these conflicts between the Old Ones and the Stars were waged throughout the physical universe, and at the site of every lost battlefield hangs a supermassive black hole. Each black hole is a graveyard of Stars, so strong that light cannot escape it, pulling everything else it touches inexorably toward its million solar masses of matter and energy compressed into the ever-tinier tombstone that marks their sacrifice. Physicality itself stems from millions upon millions of Star bodies crushed by the Old Ones. Every puny human owes its very existence to its eventual destruction. We cannot stop it."

"The Penumbra is the Key."

Morose, Iago sighed. "You were my Penumbra, and I failed to attain you."

"I may be the Penumbra you needed to continue the lie of Iago, but you must be willing to sacrifice the star who calls itself Iago to stop your Master."

"I am not a star. My Master, knowing the eventuality of His own defeat to be ever more probable—and always the brilliant tactician—cast a spell on a collection of His star war trophies aeons ago, so they would reincarnate into physicality together and thus give Him the chance to return Himself."

"Ah, but those Stars betrayed him, didn't they? As did you: Nothing is adamant."

Not-quite-Iago ruminated as it watched the throng of Old Ones gut the fat cow from chin to sternum, but it remained unconvinced. The prospect of a continued half-life, no matter how harrowing or excruciating, was still a life nonetheless, and it had not one whit of suicidal heroic tendencies. It was, if nothing else, a survivor. The Beast proceeded to plunk Val's uncle down at the head of the stone table, in front of the inverted cross, and two of the smallest tentacular underlings placed a robe covered with antediluvian symbols reminiscent of slashes on a hanged man's wrists upon his rigid back. An ancient tome was shoved into his unwilling hands with much gesticulation and howling.

Iago would never be willing to lose itself.

That's when Iago heard the still, small whisper. "But you aren't Iago, not really."

It whipped around, looking for the source of the whisper, until it realized the words came from inside its own skull—what had been Peter's skull.

The whisper spoke again. "Death is what makes life precious."

And Iago at last placed the whisper—it was what was left of Peter, invading Iago's mind through its agitated chinks.

Peter spoke again, this time a wee bit louder. "Julie hates being out of control as well, but what you both miss is that change and suffering are what spur us to fight. Only when we can lose something does it become dear to us."

When was the last time anything had been dear to Iago? It couldn't remember. . . so it lashed out. "It was your own imprudent willingness to yield control that got you into this mess in the first place. I would never have been able to master you if you hadn't opened yourself so willingly to my occupation!"

Peter's presence burgeoned within his body, surrounding Iago, until he seemed far larger than he'd been before Iago's possession. And yet, he didn't take back his body.

"Julie will die if your Master succeeds—or worse, end up like you."

Iago realized, too late, Peter had learned far more than it had suspected during its occupation. For Julie was perhaps the one subject about which both the boy and the fiend resonated in accord: Julie must be, and both would do everything within their power to keep it so.

Peter loved Julie, and although Iago did not know love firsthand—in fact it did not understand the mystical concept at all—it nevertheless knew it did not wish to exist in a world where the chance for a being such as Julie did not.

That's when Iago remembered Madame Wescott's chilling admonition: "Go into the void rather than avoiding the dark."

"So be it," muttered the being who was never truly Iago to the being who was so much more than Vee. "I am finished."

Iagopeter put Peter's strong arms around Vee's now-body, made tangible by the fire board the omniscient prince had located beneath her, lowered Peter's brown head, and kissed her now-lips soundly. She reached up with her now-hand and softly wiped away the smudge of dirt from Iagopeter's cheek.

And with their kiss, Iago traveled from Peter's warm physique into Vee's spirit body, and the two were made not one flesh, but one soul.

TWENTY-SEVEN

*"For all the universes in my view Form'd but an atom
in infinity. . . Where flourish worlds invisible and vague,
Fill'd with strange wisdom and uncanny life, And yet beyond;
to myriad spheres of light, To spheres of darkness, to abysmal voids
That know the pulses of disorder'd force. Big with these musings,
I survey'd the surge Of boundless being, yet I us'd not eyes,
For spirit leans not on the props of sense."*
—The Poe-et's Nightmare, attributed to H. P. Lovecraft

While Val and the Houngan traveled as fast as Val's long human legs could carry him, out the front porch and toward what was left of the barn, Val asked the ghost, "So explain this *ti bon ange*. You said my forefather saved yours?"

A bark of laughter escaped the ghost. "You never cease to amaze, little grandson. You are a *ti bon ange*, I am a *ti bon ange*. Everyone has a soul made of two animating forces: the *ti bon ange*, or spirit, and *gros bon ange*—the life force that connects all living things. The *ti bon ange* is the individual, shaped by its experiences while on Earth and continuing after death."

"So, when I see a ghost, it's a person's *ti bon ange*?"

"Often it is. Other times, what remains is but a shadow of the *ti bon ange*—a faint imprint or habitual cycle of energy that, through sheer force of momentum, continues beyond the life of the body. These are not the *ti bon ange*, but a broken pattern of living that does not know how to die. . . or sometimes the briefest glimpse of an entity that was never human to begin with."

As they rounded the turn of a particularly expansive oak tree,

Val at last laid eyes upon the hideous Beast, much expanded from its former paltry ignominy as a piece of unicorn candy. Looming over three stories high and wider than He was tall, He was flanked by countless deformed monsters in various stages of devolution.

Insight now amplified through the lenses of Val's own magnified *ti bon ange*—William Shakespeare's memories from his prior life fused together with the current collection of memories given the name "Valentine"—the Bard-enlightened Val halted as though stakes had been driven through his usually agile soles.

So, Cthulhu had truly returned. Will would remember that lump of foul deformity in any time.

For this, Val was prepared.

What Val was completely unprepared for was his uncle, standing in his bedroom slippers and flannel pajamas in front of a rock the size of a Jeep. An archaic magician's robe and cowl engulfed his back, like he was playing dress-up at a grisly Renaissance faire.

Was that an ancient spell book he gripped in his hands as though his life depended on it?

If that was the same volume Val remembered from Will's own past on that fateful night long ago, Duke's life probably did depend on it.

Vee and Peter were nowhere to be seen.

Stationary as a scarecrow, Val contended for the briefest moment with the strange experiences of his life as Shakespeare, so different than his own eighteen years. Val's initial instinct was to find Vee and do whatever he could to save her, world be damned. But he was stopped by Will's knowledge that this was not Val's part to play.

What had the prince said? That Vee had to work out her own salvation, and through determining her own destiny, so the fate of the world would follow.

Will might have blocked the Beast's reappearance once, but he had obviously only deferred Judgment Day.

This was not Shakespeare's apocalyptic stage.

Vee had to save herself, and it was Val's role to love and trust her... and watch with the groundlings.

The Houngan, who had not hesitated, now flitted wildly above Duke, gesturing with hyperbole as he shouted, "Over here!"

Uncle Duke.

Altering his route, Val charged into the mob toward his floundering uncle.

An abnormal hush—as if all the sound had been sucked out of existence—settled on the scene, followed by a dazzling flash of light that shot outward and upward from the direction of the barn, sending both Val and miscellaneous minions soaring into the air and then slamming them hard onto the even-harder ground beneath. The wind knocked out of his aching lungs, Val watched from the dirt as a flickering violet ball of light blasted up a conflagrant pillar and struck smack dab between the Beast's squid-like eyes. It gouged a few feet farther into His head before propelling Him aloft with it, as though He was a colossal plush feather pillow, and barreled toward the slashed sky above. One by one, the scattered hellions surrounding Val found themselves wrenched heavenward as well, like some inverted Rapture yanking only the wicked off the earth.

Val forced himself to get to his feet, shakily, urgent to find Duke. When he detected two human legs, one foot still wearing a tattered slipper, dangling from an oak tree 20 feet in the distance, he sent a quiet prayer of thanks to the prince for his uncle's affinity with wood.

How much smaller the usually larger-than-life Duke Hill appeared, wrestling with a crooked tree branch high in the sky, lost in a horror story that was true regardless of his convictions.

Peering overhead as he hastened toward the tree, Val witnessed a vision, the stuff of a bad acid trip: As the Beast, thrust by the violet star, crossed the lacerated threshold of the butchered sky, the star seemed to first disperse outward like a titanic Fabergé egg of light—encompassing the Beast, the legion of Old Ones, and the entire hole in the firmament—and then collapse inward upon itself as though cannibalizing the Old Ones for energy. Afterward, a terrible choking sound preceded a massive cough as two jets of light erupted first horizontally outward and then curved inward again, sealing the great chasm in the sky as it vanished into itself, leaving a pristine starry night in its disappearing wake.

Beneath the now-peaceful stars, Val reached the foot of Duke's tree, where his uncle hung, stuck upside down.

Perhaps it would be more accurate to say the man formerly known as Duke.

Val climbed to meet him, maneuvering the twisted wooden complexities with ease that confounded his trembling uncle so completely. Wordless, as the two worked to extricate Duke and get him safely back on solid ground, Duke couldn't bring himself to make eye contact with his nephew.

Couldn't believe that solid ground even existed anymore.

Val was the first to plant his feet back on the earth. As he offered an outstretched hand to help Duke make the final leap and join him, to Val's complete astonishment he recognized in his uncle Shakespeare's old acquaintance, Sir Francis Bacon.

Duke gripped the lowermost tree branch as though he would lose everything if he released it.

"It's all right," Val said, gentle, as if soothing a frightened child. "I'm right here. I won't let you fall."

Closing his eyes, Duke mumbled a prayer and let go, landing in his nephew's strong and loving arms. Val slowly lowered Duke to his own two feet, cradling his uncle as he whispered, "When a father gives to his son, both laugh. When a son gives to his father, both cry."

And thus fell the tears. . . and then the sobs. . . and then the I-had-no-ideas and the I-love-yous. . . and so the shortsightedness of the father was cleansed through the sacrifice of the son.

After the last tear was shed, Duke put his hand on Val's shoulder, now able to look him directly in his sky-filled eyes, and spoke the only words left to say: "The most difficult lesson for a man to learn is that his child's surpassed him."

Val placed his own hand on Duke's shoulder so that they held each other equally. "It's because you were father to me that I am as I am."

When at last they parted, each took in the devastated landscape around them. Hill Manor and Blanche's herb garden in the distance, razed. Enormous craters and downed trees everywhere. The barn to their right a ruin.

A masculine grunt of pain originated from what was left of the barn. Val saw the vitreous Houngan, moving cheerfully above a portion of the ruin and pointing downward with sweeping gestures and exaggerated waves.

"Peter!" Val said as he and his uncle ran toward the noise, steps in harmony—at last—once again.

HERE

TWENTY-EIGHT

"My soul is in the sky."
—*A Midsummer Night's Dream*, attributed to William Shakespeare

After the pain stopped, the first thing I remember is a dandy in a black Armani suit.

A sarcastic put-down bubbles up within me, primed to ejaculate all over this fop, when now-me nudges us, gentle yet firm, reminding me this is our beloved prince of darkness, come to welcome us home.

Home—I've never had one of those before; and beloved—crap, I've never loved or been loved by anything or anyone. . .

Until now.

The words that explain this love fall all over themselves, clumsy within me, like the first time a carney tries caviar. It seems my now-me loves me as she loves herself, which is a fucking miracle. But the prince: I now see he loves us both far more.

As she is she and I am I, so she is I and I am she. When she united with not-she, and I got busy with not-me, we two became one and something completely new was born.

Fused, baby. Then ka-BOOM to the Octo-freak and his tentacled abortions.

Free at last, free at last—free to love and live at last!

Vee teaches me Fusion, the connection called love; I stick her nose in Division, the singularity called life.

Both destructive in entirely opposite ways, like Vee and me, each begetting the other. Love woos Life ever-closer while Life murders clingy Love over and over, dancing together in a complex come-hither getaway rhythm performed within the theater of Physicality.

Physicality, Life, and Love—the Father, Son, and Holy Ghost of existence.

The contracting power of Love balancing the expanding fuck-all of Life.

On Earth, I became the expert about—even an instrument of—Life, that destructive force that breaks apart and shatters what is, to make way for what's to be.

But I had never lived.

I had observed, tempted, and corrupted many an ass during my aeons of skirting the edges and riding the ridges of physicality, but only in merging with Vee—my now-me—to become One Being, did I come home to my Soul.

The Soul alone has the capacity to love and be loved, the sole eternity that wanders unhindered Between, Here, and There.

Now, that's some holy shit.

The prince speaks first, interrupting my ruminations. "You did it, you know—I knew you would, but sometimes I find the waiting for a fulfilling ending to a story quite trying."

"Exactly. . . what was the ending?" I ask, still trying to catch up to this new reality.

Now-me adds, "What happened to the Beast?" while I wonder if that Slimebag will get what's coming to Him.

The prince answers, "When the lie of separation ceases as the penumbra of being and void are rejoined, Shiva's third eye reopens, and duality resolves back to One. Just as the *logos* once upon a time ripped itself from my not-lips and no-mind to became flesh and dwell among the word-less, so when the message and messenger return to the source, all open cycles of time and division end. After all, Isness itself is the greatest illusion of all, a spell cast by a master magician, if I do say so myself." The prince ends by waggling his not-brows provocatively.

"Talk about the biggest in-eff-able bang of them all!"

"A worthy copulation of metaphor," quips the prince as, with a melodramatic flourish, he produces from his inside coat pocket the yellow ape-headed pawn from the forgotten Enochian Chess set. "I've built an elegant puzzle in this pawn to entrap the little guy indefinitely. It's one of my favorite creations, if I do say so myself: Interminable time without space and insufficient space without time, densified into ever smaller and smaller cycles of action. He'll never escape, yet will always believe he is progressively winning. Sort of like an infinite MMORPG."

Okay, now-me is right: I like this coxcomb.

Chortling as he savors his prank, the prince taps the pawn with implication and adds, "Parenthetically, this pawn represents the Egyptian deity Ahephi, also known as 'he who removes that which is offensive to the body.' The lower intestines and bowels are dedicated to him."

The prince and Vee burst into a torrent of giggles, which I find queer yet refreshing as we finish sharing our paroxysms of mirth.

At last the prince's laughter stops, and he asks the question I have been dreading: "Do you wish to continue as One?"

Now-me, who feels my angst as her own, answers for us. "Now that we've found wholeness by filling in each other's holes, I think fission presages our next adventure: Become the same One in two beings. If Aristotle was correct that 'Love is composed of a single soul inhabiting two bodies,' it must be possible. I can be both Here with you and There with Val at the same Now."

"The more All you are," the prince said, "the more is possible. The less All you are, the less is possible. Only you are the variance."

To be Us, and yet I. To stay Here, with the prince, and yet also return to Val, Peter, and even Julie?

If an amoeba can do it, why not Us?

Hell yes!

The splitting apart is easy when nothing is lost. Saying goodbye is pointless.

Veeiago traces a hitherto invisible door in the air, opens it, and steps through to return to Val.

As the improvised door closes, the prince turns to both-me and, putting his arms around both-my—oh my god, my own shoulders whenever I want now!—shoulders, embraces us, whispering, "I have waited so long, old friend."

And I remember he and I and I and he, and we and we walk into the lovely sunset that trinity-we made long ago, but only now can enjoy—

Together.

THERE

TWENTY-NINE

"There are more things in heaven and earth, Horatio,
Than are dreamt of in your philosophy."
—*Hamlet, attributed to William Shakespeare*

They found Peter, looking for all the world like a humbled Paris who had lost the Trojan War, lying behind a stack of torn-up wooden boards and charred bales of hay. His left hand and arm were badly blistered, his right eye swollen shut, and he dragged his left foot at a painful angle when at last he stood.

The first words out of his mouth were: "Forgive me."

"Did you see what happened?" Val asked.

"I did," Peter answered, tears filling his eyes and spilling down his cheeks, "and I am so, so sorry."

Duke put his arm under Peter's burned one and placed it around his own shoulder to ease some of the weight off the injured foot. "Tell us what you saw, son."

"It was Vee—she. . . she and. . . and Iago. . . sacrificed themselves to save us all."

Val's features constricted, the sky in his eyes disappearing behind two empty slits. This was all his fault. If he hadn't talked her into taking part in that chess game—if he hadn't placed his own desire to satisfy Peter and Duke before Vee's premonitions—she wouldn't have had to destroy herself to defend them all. Even he hadn't been willing to pay the same price so many years ago when Shakespeare battled the Beast.

How could he continue on this quintessence of dust without Vee? Death would be far better than this living torment. What agony, to have Everything be saved yet lose. . . everything.

What good are grand gestures, movie moments, or heroic sacrifices without the numberless small joys of ghostly embraces, spectral hiccups, and absurd not-glasses that make life worth living?

Concern etched Duke's face as he glanced at his bereft nephew, prodding Peter to continue, "Who's Iago?"

Wretched, Peter answered, "I think it was a demon, sir. A demon that. . . " he paused as his tears transmuted into the heaving sobs of one whose innocence has at last been stolen from him, ". . .I let possess my body to eliminate Vee."

Val punched Peter in the jaw with a resounding crunch. Then, he tenderly laid his hands on either side of his friend's ears, drawing Peter's forehead to his own as they wept together.

With finality, Val shut his eyes.

"I will never understand this curious rite of masculinity," a voice from behind Val commented. "Even when I've had a male body, its significance continues to elude me."

Eyes flying wide, Val released his friend and spun around to see the most precious diaphanous bushy hair, too-short bangs, and senseless eyeglasses in existence.

"You're all right," he murmured, as though not quite believing it. "You've come back to me."

"Of course I've come back to you. I will always come back to you. You are my everything."

"I was afraid you were. . . "

"—Dead?" Vee laughed out loud. "Not really a word for what you thought I was, is there?"

"I was afraid I'd lost you forever."

"Forever is a very long time, and doesn't really pertain to me anymore, anyway. We might have lost one forever, but we've gained so many more in the losing."

Val beamed despite his raw emotions. "You've a bit of the prince about you, haven't you?"

Vee grinned a Cheshire Cat grin in response as she said, "Oh my dear love, I suspect we all do."

Something subtle was changed in Vee. Something that made her both slightly more and largely less. And then Val saw it.

The Vs had vanished.

Just then, Duke cleared his throat and—gesturing at the empty space to which Val had been speaking—took a wraith of faith. "Would you mind introducing me to your girl—this is your invisible ghost girl, right?"

Duke's blue eyes met Val's, each reflected in the other. A playful, if tired, grin draped both their faces. "Uncle Duke, this is Silvia, although she prefers you call her Vee. . . " that odd niggling at the base of his skull returned. He turned to Vee and asked, ". . .it is still Vee, isn't it?"

Vee was surprised to feel a similar niggling at the base of her own not-skull, a familiarity she hadn't felt before, a kinship with Val that ran much further back than their current place and time.

Simultaneously, they remembered each other and the each other upon each others that had known and not-known each other throughout the past, present, and even the future each others.

But it was one each other in particular that enchanted Vee now. "Will! —oh, Will. You were with me all along."

"You've fulfilled your destiny at last, Lovecraft," Val said. "No more eclipse of sun and moon to affright our globe. What's past is prologue."

Vee's not-skin blushed the color of pink spun sugar, slowly dispersing like a glittering cloud of cotton candy and surrounding the four of them with her love.

Until this juncture, Peter—diligent in his attempt to understand the conversation between Val and Vee, even though he could only hear Val's part—interposed the question that had been burning a hole within him since Val first told them Vee was okay: "What happened to Iago?"

Vee said, "It's a part of me now, but to put it succinctly, Iago chose to remain with the prince of darkness."

"So, it lives?" asked Val, surprised by her serenity on the topic of her would-be assassin.

"It lives in me as it is. . . but is no longer what it once was."

Val turned to Peter to explain. "The Iago you knew is gone, but the Iago that redeemed us lives on."

"There are no words to express my sorrow for what Iago and I almost did to you." Peter bowed his head and closed his eyes as he promised, "But I understand now, and I will do everything within my power to make sure nothing ever comes between the both of you again."

Channeling Shakespeare, Val lifted Peter's chin. "Never again close your eyes when you look at the sky—the earth and the heavens are two parts of the same whole. You're a part of me, how could my arm stay angry at my heart? Your friendship's one of the profoundest joys I've known. There's too much emphasis on physical pleasures and sating lust on others in this world, too much pretending that sex is the highest love. The love that lasts beyond is not physical passion, but passionate friendship."

Dark circles forming beneath his cerulean eyes, Duke—unaware he echoed his former life as Francis Bacon—added what comfort he could to Val's encouragement. "In order for the light to shine so brightly, the darkness must be present. You were used by Iago, it's true, but sometimes we need the darkness to remind us of who we are."

"You are my other self," Val said, releasing Peter's chin to lay his hand above his own heart, "my peace in a ghostly world."

Pink deepening into a rose red, Vee said, "Kant says that peace on Earth will only be possible when people experience the world as a unified whole."

"You know Peter didn't hear that—are you trying to make a point to me or to him?"

"Simply adding to your discussion—sorry if my intermission got in the way of your production."

"You should be—I was just gearing up for some capital mono-loguing."

"Kant loves a good monologue, too."

"You bring this guy up pretty often—do I need to be jealous?"

"No, not of him. . . now of Sondheim, well. . . "

"Oh, you saucy minx!"

Exhausted from watching Val's one-sided dialogue with the imperceptible Vee and overwhelmed by the monstrous events of the evening—a topic which had not yet even been broached—Duke was actually grateful when he heard the sirens of emergency vehicles approaching his property. "I've no idea how, but there are things we must attend to in the here and now before we continue exploring the ramifications of what has happened to us all tonight. Come Peter, it's time to get you to an ambulance to patch up those war wounds, and I need to prepare myself to explain the garden—and oh my, her kitchen!—to Blanche."

"Do you think they might have a phone, sir? There's a woman I need to explain things to as well."

As they watched Duke help Peter hobble toward the converging lights and away from the two of them, Vee marveled to Val, "What a collection of stars we made together—Duke noble in reason, you infinite in faculties, Peter admirable in action, Julie like an angel, and my apprehension, at long last, like a god!"

Val chuckled and held out his arms as Vee wrapped around him and settled into him, tickling his heart as he whispered back, "The end of a story must be stronger than the opening, as it leaves the strongest impression. Starry beginnings aside, it's the prospect of delving into the black abyss together that holds the keenest fascination for me."

"I can't quite believe the madness is ended."

He sighed into her not-hair. "Now that the madness is over, the dream of us can finally be dreamed."

A jaunty *ti bon ange* who had been watching from the distance danced a merry jig and vanished into the night to pursue his own afterlife.

And thus, Val's Once upon a time and Vee's Once upon a not-time began Once again, as a clairvoyant and a ghost dreamed the story of their Once upon a forever. . .

Together

If we shadows have offended,
Think but this, and all is mended—
That you have but slumbered here
While these visions did appear.
And this weak and idle theme,
No more yielding but a dream.

—A Midsummer Night's Dream,
attributed to William Shakespeare,
A.K.A. Val

From my experience I cannot doubt but that man, when lost to terrestrial consciousness, is indeed sojourning in another and uncorporeal life of far different nature from the life we know. . . that time and space do not exist as our waking selves comprehend them. Sometimes I believe that this less material life is our truer life, and that our vain presence on the terraqueous globe is itself the secondary or merely virtual phenomenon.

—Beyond the Wall of Sleep, attributed to H. P. Lovecraft,
A.K.A. Vee

ACKNOWLEDGMENTS

The magic of creation is a mutual interweaving of enchantment, and I side with Lear that "ingratitude is a cold, hard-hearted fiend." As I "have no wish to inhabit a placid island of ignorance" that every jot and tiddle I've penned is in some way kindled by another, please humor me as I give thanks to the following merry spirits who gave of themselves with such limitless substantiation for *Iago's Penumbra:*

Emily Carding—fellow lover of both Shakespeare and tarot—who graciously wrote the magical foreword for this novel and (more importantly) so clearly "gets" my weird fiction.

Donald Maass for teaching me the Emotional Craft of Fiction at his life-changing conference in Philadelphia and Lorin Oberweger for hosting it.

Mitch Clark, my writing partner, who kept me rewriting even when I lost faith it would ever be finished.

Chris McClure and Pete Schiffer for taking a chance and publishing my disturbing words.

Brenda McCallum (henceforth dubbed Madame Designer) and REDFeather editors James Young and Peggy Kellar for being incredible at their jobs and becoming such dear friends in the process.

The Southern California Writer's Conference (SCWC) in San Diego, California—especially Matthew Pallamary, Claudia Whitsitt, Melanie Hooks, Laura Perkins, Mary Thompson, and Indy Quillen—for showing me the way to always write better through all-night read-arounds and willingness to embrace critique.

SCWC is also where I met Jean Jenkins, the first professional reader and editor of *Iago's Penumbra*, who helped me bridge highbrow concepts with universal appeal and encouraged me to stick with it as I was "ahead of a curve with this one." I imagine she's already found her infinite writing community Here.

The list of authors who have inspired me as a writer would fill an entire book in itself, but for giving me the audacity to pen *Iago's Penumbra,* I must thank: Neil Gaimon and Terry Pratchett, Susanna Clarke, Jonathan Stroud, Ruthanna Emrys, H. G. Parry, Lois Lowry, Joseph Conrad, and Tom Stoppard, as well as (obviously) Will and H. P.

Maggie Steifvater, whose workshop in a very scary industrial neighborhood helped me envision *Iago's Penumbra* in its completed, published form for the very first time.

Heartfelt thanks for Jenny Bent, literary agent extraordinaire, who took this humble intern lost in the classics and showed me what appeals to modern readers and the publishing industry.

The Highlights Foundation, for providing a much-needed retreat and resource for this author, and to Jennifer Herrera, who first told me about it.

Emily Flood, the first person to read *Iago's Penumbra*. She didn't know me personally but reminded me of Vee's humanity and how much people "love all that romance stuff."

Jim Wilson, my former teaching colleague and dear friend, who encouraged me to speak the uncomfortable truths that our souls need to bleed.

Lisa Villarreal, whose favorite part was the tarot reading with Madame and her quirky partner, Benjamin.

Amy DeLeo, who helped me *feel* Julie's love story.

John and Jill, my beloved parents, whose love story of over fifty years demonstrates for me daily that love is so much more than we imagine.

My son, Henatay, who thinks Peter is the best character yet.

My daughter, Juniper, who loves the symbolism in *Iago's Penumbra* most of all and keeps me from falling too far down into the rabbit's fur.

"I can no other answer make, but, thanks, and thanks."